MENDOCINO

and other stories

MENDOCINO

and other stories

ANN PACKER

CHRONICLE BOOKS

SAN FRANCISCO

For support during the writing of this book the author would like to thank the Iowa Writers' Workshop, the Wisconsin Institute for Creative Writing, and James Michener and the Copernicus Society of America.

Many thanks also to some willing readers and helpful critics: Jane Aaron, Fred Leebron, Kathryn Rhett, and especially Jon James.

Some of the stories in this collection originally appeared in the following publications, sometimes in slightly different form: The New Yorker, "Mendocino"; Ploughshares, "Nerves"; Indiana Review, "Babies"; The Cream City Review, "Hightops"; The Threepenny Review, "The Glass House"; Boulevard, "Lightening"; The Missouri Review, "Tillman and I"; The Gettysburg Review, "Ninety." "Mendocino" also appeared in Contemporary West Coast Stories. "Babies" also appeared in Prize Stories 1992: The O. Henry Awards.

Printed in the United States of America.

Library of Congress Cataloging-in-Publication Data

Packer, Ann, 1959–
Mendocino and other stories / Ann Packer.
p. cm.
ISBN 0-8118-0629-4
I. Title.
PS3566.A315M46   1994   93-36315
813'.54—dc20   CIP

Cover design: Gretchen Scoble
Book typography and composition: Not Your Type
Cover photograph: Thea Schrack

Distributed in Canada by Raincoast Books,
112 East Third Avenue, Vancouver, B.C. V5T 1C8

10 9 8 7 6 5 4 3 2 1

Chronicle Books
275 Fifth Street
San Francisco, CA
94103

To my mother

contents

Bliss is driving north on Highway 1, looking at the crashing Pacific. She would like to pull the car over and walk along the water's edge, but there is no beach here, only cliffs jutting out over the ocean. The mountains, the road, the water—it's so gorgeous it's getting monotonous. So she begins to make small promises to herself. If Gerald starts in on the beauty of the self-sufficient life, she will allow herself a solitary one-hour walk. If Marisa invites her to join in the baking of bread or the pickling of cucumbers or the gathering of fresh-laid eggs, she will invent a friend who lives nearby with whom she has promised to have a drink. These people—her younger brother, Gerald, and his girlfriend, Marisa (his R.F.L., as he calls her, his Reason For Living, and, really, this irks Bliss as much as anything else)—live in Mendocino County, two and a half hours north of San Francisco, a mile from the coast, in a small, isolated house of their own design. It is, Bliss remembers, a nice enough house, made tacky by a pair of stained glass windows that flank the front door—windows that Marisa made. She is, Gerald has said more than once, an *artisan*. Life for Marisa—and, now, for Gerald— is about using your hands whenever you can. Bliss has been tempted in the past to point out that your brain must contribute something to this equation, but she is determined to keep all snide remarks to herself on this visit. After all, it will be the first time she has seen them in over a year. And, too, today is the tenth anniversary of their father's suicide. She wants to be on her best behavior.

Bliss would like to think that this reunion was Gerald's idea— a peace offering of sorts—but she is sure that Marisa is behind it. Even the way Gerald asked her sounded like Marisa: didn't she think it would be nice if they could "be together" for a weekend. Until a couple of years ago—until Marisa—Gerald was a sensible man. Stodgy even, with his job working for a big accounting firm, with his careful haircuts and his fuel-efficient cars. They had a nice relationship; every four or five months Bliss would fly up from L. A. and Gerald would squire her around San Francisco, surprising her with tickets to chamber music concerts, with out-of-the-way Asian restaurants. They would exchange work stories, and, into a second bottle of wine, confide in each other the news of their most recent failures at love. It amazes Bliss that until this moment she never once realized it was because they were failures that they talked about them. Now Gerald has his success, and it is as if the two of them had never been anything but what they are now: wary, cordial.

As Bliss turns from the coastal highway onto the road to Gerald and Marisa's property, she realizes that she has come empty-handed: no bottle of wine, no flowers, nothing. It would be worse if this were her first visit—she has been here once before, a year ago June, when Gerald and Marisa threw a housewarming party and she flew up for the day with Jason—but still, she ought to have something. So she makes a U-turn on the narrow road and heads back to the little store she passed a few miles back.

She didn't get a very good look at the place when she drove by, and it's a disappointment. She was hoping for a little country fruit and vegetable stand; she could have bought a dozen dusty peaches and offered them as coals to Newcastle—Gerald, at least, would have gotten it. She'll be lucky if this place has a head of iceberg; it might as well be a 7-Eleven.

She walks up and down the aisles, looking for something halfway suitable. The only beer they have isn't expensive enough to give someone as a gift, and when she looks at the refrigerator section, thinking she might find some cheese, there's next to nothing there, either— just Velveeta and the kind of cream cheese that's whipped and has things added to it. She is drifting through the store, ordering herself to buy *something*, when she comes to the packaged cookies. She puts her hand out to a package, retracts it, then reaches again and picks the cookies up. They are Ideal bars—Gerald's favorite cookies when they were children. She's surprised they still make them; she hasn't seen or thought of them in years. The packaging hasn't changed a bit, though, and now she remembers Gerald hoarding whole packages of them in his room, eating them in bed at night. Their rooms shared a wall, and sometimes when she'd turned off her light and was lying wide awake in bed she could hear the cellophane crinkling.

She buys six packages. It seems a ridiculous number, as she tosses them onto the seat of the car and heads back up the road. One, maybe, or two, but six? She doesn't want to think of what Marisa will say.

It is almost dusk when Bliss turns down the long driveway leading to their house. She left L.A. at six this morning, and her shoulders ache. She should have flown and rented a car at the airport, as she and Jason did last summer, but she'd convinced herself it would be fun to drive. She thinks now that the real reason she drove was to put off this moment for as long as she could.

She gets out of the car and stretches her arms over her head, bending from side to side; she hopes they have a decent bed. Then the front door opens and there is Gerald, in shorts and hiking boots and with—she can't believe it—a beard.

"The weary traveller," he says, coming down the walk to her car. "Are you dead?"

"Yes," she says. "I'm dead and I've gone to heaven and met this man who looks so familiar to me." She reaches up and touches his beard. "This is new," she says.

"Like it?"

He is darker than she, and with the beard his face has a slightly menacing look. "It makes you look older," she says.

"Than who?"

She is about to answer with some kind joke ("Than me, the aging spinster") when she realizes that he isn't really paying attention—he's looking back at the house.

Marisa appears, and Bliss has to admit it: she's beautiful. She is one of those tall, earthy women with frizzy hair—brown, in this case —but her size and strength are very feminine. She wears a flowered skirt and a man's sleeveless undershirt, and her arms and legs are lean, golden. Bliss can understand why Gerald is attracted to her— and attracted he is. When she joins them at Bliss's car, he puts an arm around her waist and squeezes her, as if she were the one who had just arrived.

"How are you?" Marisa asks. It sounds to Bliss like an invitation to make a long confession.

"OK," Bliss says. "You look great. Both of you—you look so healthy and fit."

"We are," says Marisa, and Bliss thinks, Well, the battle lines are drawn.

They go into the house, Gerald carrying her suitcase and Bliss holding the brown bag that contains the cookies. Gerald leads her to the guest room, which is in the back of the house, next to the kitchen. He sets the suitcase down and turns to her. For a moment she thinks he is going to tell her something—a secret, something he hasn't told Marisa, even something *about* Marisa—but all he says is "The bathroom's through there if you want to wash up. Come on into the kitchen whenever you're ready."

He leaves, and she realizes she's been hugging the cookies to her chest; and this would have been the perfect time to give them to him. She sits on the bed, and when she finds that it's nice and firm, her relief is so great she's surprised. She goes into the bathroom to splash some water on her face.

In the kitchen Marisa is chopping vegetables; Gerald is uncorking a bottle of wine. The windowsills are lined with jars of things, Bliss can't tell what—they are murky and either red or purple or green. Marisa sees her looking at them and says, "I'm so far behind on my canning."

"Don't listen to her," Gerald says. "You should see the cellar." He offers Bliss a glass of wine and she takes it, warning herself to be careful—the last thing she wants is to have to get through tomorrow with a hangover.

"Why don't you show Bliss around while I get dinner ready?" Marisa says. "Before it gets too dark." It seems to Bliss that Marisa has this—has everything—all planned out.

"Blister?" Gerald says, and she blushes with pleasure; he hasn't called her that in years.

"I'd love it."

"Bring your wine." He heads for the doorway, then turns back and looks at her feet. "Actually, do you have any other shoes? It's a bit muddy in places."

She does, but they're no more suitable for mud than these. She's suddenly very embarrassed—as if they could know what's in her suitcase, or in her closet at home: nothing rugged. "Think I'm a prima donna, do you?" she says. "What's a little mud?"

Gerald shrugs, but Marisa says, "You can't go out in those, you'll ruin them. We've had rain almost every day for the last two weeks." She goes to a closet and pulls out some rubber boots that remind Bliss of a pair she had in elementary school. "Here," Marisa says, "try these."

They're huge, probably three or four sizes too big, but Bliss slips off her sandals and steps into the boots. "OK," she says. "Great. Thanks."

"They're too big, aren't they?" Marisa says. "Wait, I'll get you some socks."

"Jesus, Mare, we're only going to be gone for ten minutes," Gerald says, but this doesn't seem to have any effect on Marisa; she disappears, then returns with two pairs of heavy socks for Bliss.

By the time they get outside, the light has nearly faded. Everything is a deep violet—the sky, the field behind the house, even Gerald's face. Bliss wishes she could tell what his expression is; is he irritated at Marisa?

"This way," he says, setting off around the house. "We've done a lot since you were here."

First he shows her the herb garden, a fenced-off square with neat little rows of more herbs than Bliss can imagine anyone wanting. He points them out, one by one, and Bliss tries to make admiring sounds. Then he launches into an explanation of how great it is to grow your own herbs, how they're useful for much more than just cooking. He bends and picks something, then holds it up to her nose. "Smell good?" he says.

It does, but she doesn't know what it is. "Mmm."

"It's rosemary," he says.

"Nice."

He looks down at the plants and scuffs at the earth with the toe of his boot. "We've been thinking," he says, but he doesn't go on.

"I wouldn't worry about it too much," Bliss says. "I do it, too, sometimes." Immediately she's sorry.

"Should I tell you this?" Gerald says. "Oh, why not. We've been thinking of having a baby."

Bliss is stunned. Not that it's so hard to imagine Gerald as a father —she's always thought he should have children. And Marisa was obviously born to have babies, the ultimate show of capability. But she realizes that in the back of her mind she's been waiting for him to go back to San Francisco, to being who he was.

"Are you?" she says finally. "Wow."

He waves the rosemary in her face. "Marisa wants to have a girl and name her Rosemary."

"Nice," Bliss says. And if it's a boy, Oregano?

They stand still in the herb garden for a little while longer, then Gerald says, "Come see the chicken coop. I built it myself."

When Gerald's tour is over it is truly dark, the kind of clear, chilly night that's rare in Bliss's part of the state. There are so many stars out it looks like there's barely enough room for them all in the sky. She wonders whether Gerald can still identify the constellations; one winter when they were children, their father set up a telescope on the back porch, and after dinner on clear nights he'd tell them to put on their coats and they'd troop outside to look at the sky. Bliss remembers how impatient her father was with her: No, Bliss, he'd say, *that's* Taurus; I've told you before. You're not using your head. She'd look over and see her mother silhouetted in the doorway, and although she knew her mother would welcome her back inside—Let Gerald do it, her mother would say, then your father will be satisfied—Bliss would stay outside, fingers getting numb, and try to remember.

When they reach the front door, Gerald stops and says, "I hope you don't mind vegetarian."

"Not at all," Bliss says. "It'll do me good to be so wholesome."

Gerald bites his lip, and she sees that this time she has offended him. "Seed to table," he says. "I know you think it's dumb or pretentious or something, but it's really important to me. It makes me feel like I'm in control of my life. Or at least part of it."

He turns to open the door. To stop him she says, "I don't think it's dumb at all," and she's surprised to find that this is true. It's the way she sometimes feels about the bookstore: she and her partner order books and the books arrive and they put them on the shelves and people buy them. "It's like the bookstore," she says.

"I'm not sure I get the connection," Gerald says. "But thanks. It matters to me that you don't condemn my life."

The directness of this unsettles her; it has always unsettled her that he can say something so revealing, so personal, and not have the saying of it undo him. It's the kind of confession that would choke her up. He stares at her for a moment, but the only reply she can think of is "Don't you ever miss eating meat?"

He laughs. "Not much. And when I do I get in the truck and drive over to Santa Rosa to a place that makes a great meatball sub." He grins and opens the door, motioning her to go in ahead of him. Once they're inside, he heads for the kitchen, but she stops to take off the muddy boots. It's silly, really, but as she peels the socks down over her feet she's filled with the strangest feeling of satisfaction: Marisa may not like it—she may not even know it—but when he wants to he still eats meat.

There's a delicious, spicy smell coming from the kitchen as Bliss heads down the hall. When she gets there, though, she stops in the doorway: Gerald and Marisa are standing at the sink, talking in low tones. Marisa has pulled her hair into some kind of bun, and Gerald is running his finger up and down her neck.

"Hi," Bliss says.

They pull apart and turn to face her. "Hi," says Marisa.

"Hungry?" Gerald asks. "I'm starved."

Marisa pats his shoulder. "Lucky you," she says. "Dinner's almost ready." She smiles at Bliss.

"Almost?" he says in mock outrage.

She laughs. "It will be as soon as you get the salad out."

Bliss stands in a corner and watches as they move around the kitchen, taking things from the refrigerator and stovetop and oven and putting them on the table. They don't look at each other or touch, but they're *connected* somehow—it's as if they were performing some kind of dance they'd been rehearsing for months.

They all sit, and Marisa serves their plates with rice and some kind of vegetable mixture—ratatouille, Bliss decides. They talk for a while about the things Gerald showed her—the chickens, the last of the tomatoes, the woodshop—and then Gerald asks about the bookstore. Bliss tells a story about a guy, Walter, whom she hired a few weeks ago to be a cashier. He seemed perfect—he lived around the corner, said he could work extra hours whenever she wanted, even volunteered to open the store for her one morning when she had to go to the dentist. Then one night she was on her way home from having dinner with a friend and decided to stop at the store for a book. When she got there she found Walter and three of his friends sitting on the floor eating take-out pizza, passing around a fifth of vodka, and paging through bookstore books with their greasy fingers. "The thing that really got me," Bliss says, "is that when I told them to get out, they just walked off and left the pizza lying in the middle of the floor."

"That is terrible," Marisa says. Her forearms are resting on the edge of the table and she has tightened her hands into fists. When Bliss looks at her face, she thinks she sees tears in her eyes. "People like that have no consideration."

This seems self-evident to Bliss—obviously Walter is a jerk; that's the point.

But Marisa goes on. "He'll probably never learn, either. You know? He'll probably go through life trespassing on people's decency, never doing a single thing for anybody. Someday he'll marry some poor woman and ruin her life. God, that kind of thing makes me sick!"

Bliss is embarrassed. She looks away from Marisa's red face at Gerald; he's got such a worried look on his face that she wishes she could reach across the table and touch his arm. He looks the way he used to at the dinner table at home, toward the end, when her father was always angry at her mother. Is it not true, her father would say to her mother, that you told me you were going to finish that typing by dinner? Gerald, her father would say, what do you suppose could have happened? Do you suppose it just slipped your mother's mind that she had twenty pages to type for me today? Or do you suppose she was too God-damned busy talking to her friends at the grocery store to think of anything else? Well? Well, Gerald? Well?

Gerald looks up at Bliss, and she can see that his mind is whirling. She smiles at him—she will say the first thing that she can think of. But he beats her to it. "What kind of pizza was it?" he asks.

Then he gets up and goes around behind Marisa's chair and leans down low, and when his arms reach around her, tears begin to stream from her eyes. Bliss looks down at her plate and pokes at the remains of her dinner with her fork. If this doesn't stop soon, she'll have to leave the room. When she looks up again, Gerald is staring at her, his face hard and challenging.

Finally Marisa reaches for her napkin and dabs at her face. She looks up at Bliss and says, "Sorry."

Bliss smiles and shrugs.

Gerald gives Marisa's shoulder a final pat and straightens up. Then Marisa pushes her chair back and stands, too. "Well," she says, as if nothing had happened, "are we done? I'll get going on the dishes. Why don't you two make a fire in the other room?" She carries a few things to the sink and begins to run the water. She turns back to Bliss. "I'm sorry we don't have any dessert," she says.

"We've got fruit," says Gerald. "Want a plum?"

"I'm fine," says Bliss. "It was delicious." She takes her plate to the sink and sets it down. This is not the right moment for the cookies.

The living room is sparsely furnished—just two armchairs and several large pillows on the floor.

"Sit," Gerald says, coming up behind her. He pats one of the chairs.

"Don't you guys want the chairs?" Bliss says. "I'll sit on one of those."

"Nonsense," he says.

So she sits in one of the chairs and watches him build the fire. Marisa's scene has disturbed her—does she do this kind of thing a lot?—but curious as Bliss is, she hopes Gerald won't bring it up. She doesn't really want to talk about it.

"That was a good dinner," she says.

"Thanks," he says, without turning around. He lights a match and touches the flame to some newspaper, then sits looking into the fireplace. Finally he turns to face her. "Listen," he says, "let's just drop what happened in the kitchen, OK?"

"Of course," Bliss says. "I wasn't going to—"

"She's just a little on edge is all," Gerald says. "Having a visitor."

Bliss blushes. It wasn't *her* idea to come up here.

"I don't mean it like that," Gerald says. "She just wants you to like her."

He doesn't seem to expect a response; he turns back to the fireplace and pokes at the logs with a piece of kindling. She should say, "Oh, I do like her," but it would sound so forced; her mother used to sit on the edge of her bed at night and say, "I love you, baby," and then, after the slightest pause, "Do you love me?"

"That should catch," Gerald says, standing up. He claps his hands together to get rid of the wood dust, then sits in the other chair. "We were thrilled when it started getting cooler again. There's a guy up the road who lets me chop firewood for free."

"Just like that?"

"Well, I give him a hand when he needs it. I helped him build a new kitchen."

"How'd you learn how to do all this stuff, anyway?"

"I must have a natural aptitude," Gerald says. They both laugh; he was the kind of child who, in art class, used his Popsicle sticks for abstract sculpture when everyone else was making a birdhouse.

"No, really," Bliss says.

"I wanted to," Gerald says. "That's really all it takes."

Marisa comes in from the kitchen carrying a tray. "I made some tea," she says. She offers the tray to Bliss, and Bliss thanks her and takes a mug. It smells strange, and she decides that it's some kind of herbal tea, made from their herbs. She would give anything for a cup of coffee right now.

Gerald takes a mug, and Marisa sets the tray on the floor at Gerald's feet. She pulls a pillow over and sits on it, leaning against his legs. No one says anything.

Bliss sips her tea, which tastes a little like almonds, and looks around the room for something to remark on. The walls are bare except for bunches of dried leaves—more herbs?—hanging in great clumps. There's a little stained glass something-or-other in one of the windows, and Bliss thinks, OK, that'll do; she's about to ask Marisa if she made it when Gerald clears his throat.

"So," he says, "ten years."

Bliss looks into her tea. It has been in the back of her mind that he might bring it up; she just hoped he wouldn't. She always thought they had a tacit agreement not to discuss it. She looks up and sees that Marisa has straightened a little, and she feels a flash of anger at her, as if she put the words into Gerald's mouth. They're both waiting for her to reply. "Yeah," she says.

"I think it was even a Friday," Gerald says.

"No," Bliss says, "it was a Wednesday." She remembers this distinctly. She was at home from college for the weekend and she'd driven back to school early on the Monday morning; then late that night her mother had called and said that her father hadn't come home, and she called again Tuesday afternoon to say he still wasn't home so Bliss drove back; and on Wednesday morning the phone call came from the police: a chambermaid at a motel a hundred miles away had found his body. "I'm positive it was a Wednesday," Bliss says.

They are silent again. Bliss remembers driving over to the high school and waiting in the office while someone was sent to get Gerald from his class. Her old French teacher had come walking in, and her face lit up at the sight of Bliss. "What a wonderful surprise," she said. "How's school going? How are you?" Then Gerald appeared on the other side of the glass door, and for a moment, while Mlle. Barlow was still talking, Bliss looked through the glass at Gerald and realized from his expression that he had guessed why she was there.

She looks at Gerald now. She can tell that he's struggling with something—is he trying to get himself to say something more, or to keep quiet?

"Remember how I wanted to go back to school the next day?" he says. "What a jerk."

"No," Bliss says, "I completely understood how you felt. I had a paper due that Friday and I kept thinking, My paper, my paper, like someone was going to be mad at me if I didn't get it done."

"And who do you suppose that someone was?" Gerald says.

"No kidding."

"It was different, though," Gerald says. "I just wanted to get out of the house."

Bliss nods. It was different and it was the same. Who didn't want to get out of the house? Even her mother kept saying she had to get to the store so she could make dinner, when all afternoon people were coming over with casseroles and stews, more food than they could eat in a week.

"Why do you think he did it?" Marisa says, and Bliss closes her eyes.

Why did he do it? This is the central question of Bliss's life. It's so central that it's no longer really a question at all, so much as a state of mind. She has made her accommodation to it: it's as much who she is as anything else—her name, her face in the mirror. She has always thought Gerald felt the same way, that there was no real answer. Now she can't help thinking that Marisa has asked this question for him, that he asked her to ask it, and the idea of the two of them going over it all—late at night, in the dark—makes Bliss want to get up and run. Leave it alone, she wants to say. Leave it *alone*. But then she opens her eyes and wonders whether she's wrong: Gerald seems surprised, almost fearful. Is he as reluctant to say anything as she is? She looks at Marisa and realizes that she's *curious*—she asked because she really wants to know.

For every answer, there's another question. *What* was he so angry about? *How* did that turn into despair? *Why* did he finally give up? Out of nowhere Bliss remembers a time when she was thirteen or fourteen and so awkward and shy about going to school dances that she wouldn't tell her mother about them until the last minute, when it was too late to buy a new dress; she'd pretend to be disappointed that she couldn't go because she didn't have anything to wear. Her father got wind of it somehow, and at five o'clock on the afternoon of the Christmas dance he offered to drive her to the shopping center;

he took her from store to store, waiting patiently until she found something she liked. He was so *nice* about it—it was a dark green velvet dress and he told her it was perfect because it matched her eyes and made her skin look luminous. He actually said that—"luminous." How does this fit in?

"I guess," Bliss says, "he didn't want to go on living," and although this is so much *not* an answer, Marisa nods, as if she's satisfied.

Gerald puts his hand on Marisa's shoulder and she nestles between his legs and rests her head on his knee. He starts playing with the hair that's come out of her bun, twisting it around his finger, and it comes to Bliss all at once: her brother loves this woman. The business with the boots, his confession about the meatball sub, her outburst in the kitchen—they don't mean anything; they're the tiniest of truths about these people. He loves her.

Bliss sinks back into her chair and sips her tea, which has grown cold. She looks at the fire. It's a perfect fire, really: the flames are spread evenly across the logs and leap to a dramatic peak in the center of the fireplace. She's not sure she even knows how to make a fire; isn't there some special way you have to place the logs so there's just the right amount of space between them?

"Are you tired?" Gerald says. He's smiling at her, a sad kind of smile, and although she's not tired—she feels absolutely wide awake —she nods and yawns and stands up.

"It was a long drive," she says.

Marisa moves as if to stand, and Bliss says, "No, don't." She walks over and kisses Gerald on the cheek, hesitates for a moment, then leans down and kisses Marisa, too. "Good night," she says.

She lies on the bed in her room without undressing. She keeps seeing the morning with Jason when she first knew how it was going to be. They were at her apartment and they'd finished their coffee and were standing in the kitchen. She was waiting for him to suggest that they spend the day together, thinking, Say something, say something, until it was like an incantation in her mind. When he finally spoke, though, and said, "Bye, I'll call you," instead of disappointment she had felt an enormous rush of relief—a feeling, she thinks now, of things falling back into place. She doesn't know what her reason for living is, but it could never have been him. He was never her reason for anything except wearing more makeup than she felt comfortable in and pretending, for a few months, that she was part of something serious.

She changes into her nightgown and goes into the bathroom to brush her teeth. Lying on the counter, still in its wrapper, is a brand-new bar of scented soap. She's sure it wasn't there before. She picks it up and brings it to her face; through the blue paper she can smell the rich aroma of sandalwood. Marisa must have brought it in while she and Gerald were outside. It's an expensive soap, and she has a hard time imagining Marisa in one of those drugstores that call themselves pharmacies and sell imported brushes and combs one aisle over from the Maalox. She can't help feeling flattered—did Marisa buy this soap expressly for her?

She unwraps the soap and washes her face; it makes her skin feel clean and tight. Then she brushes her teeth, turns off the bathroom light, and gets into bed. Tomorrow she will give them the cookies. If Gerald's pleased by them, Marisa will be, too.

Lying in bed, still wide awake, she finds herself thinking of the last time she and Gerald had dinner alone together in San Francisco. He took her to a little Burmese place out by the park, and they pored over the menu, dismayed to find that everything sounded exactly like the Chinese food they'd had the night before. Then Bliss found a section of salads and they thought, Aha! something new! They agreed on a dish called Lap Dap Dok; it was described as a spicy salad made of tea leaves. It arrived at their table on a wide, shallow plate, and the waitress held it up for them to see. It was like a pinwheel: six different ingredients barely touching each other. Bliss had identified sliced chili peppers and peanuts and something that looked vaguely like chopped parsley when the waitress took a pair of spoons and mixed the whole thing together into a dark paste. Bliss helped herself to a large spoonful, then took a little bit between her chopsticks and put it in her mouth. Immediately she was horrified: it was bitter and sour and rotten-tasting all at the same time—easily the worst thing she'd ever eaten. She started to giggle, waiting for Gerald to taste it, and when he did his expression made her laugh even harder. "I wonder if this is what dung tastes like," he said, then he turned red and started to laugh, too. Soon they were both laughing so hard that people began to look at them. She remembers now how familiar that laughter felt to her—the sick, giggly, helpless laughter of two children in a world of their own.

How could a grown man with any self-respect sit in the Ghirardelli
Chocolate Factory at eleven o'clock in the morning and eat a hot
fudge sundae with mint chip ice cream, hold the nuts? It was
Charlie's own question; his answer was that he wasn't a grown man,
he was a grown boy, or maybe an ungrown man, pre-grown, never-
to-be grown. He was in the process of honing his self-pity into a
kind of artifact, an arrowhead he could keep in his pocket, its point
ever ready. He spooned pure hot fudge into his mouth and told
himself it was Linda's fault he was doing this—if he'd had someone
to account to he'd never have indulged himself in this way—but it
gave him no satisfaction to blame her. Linda was his wife, and fifteen
days earlier she'd taken a suitcase full of clothes and gone to stay
with her friend Cynthia "for a little while," leaving Charlie lower
than a dead man, as she would say. Maybe *that* was what had gone
wrong: she no longer said things like "lower than a dead man" or
"Nice play, Shakespeare." Where was that girl? Not, Charlie felt
sure, in San Francisco, this meanly cold, this coldly mean city to
which they'd moved five months before, from his beloved New York,
at her request. Whereupon she'd left him.

Charlie looked at his watch. It was now twelve minutes past
eleven, and although that left him thirty-three minutes to walk the
ten blocks to his doctor's appointment, he was stricken by a fear of
being late—a lifelong fear, one of his many crippling lifelong fears.
He forced down the last of his sundae as quickly as he could and
stood up. He put on his jacket, but as he was wrapping his scarf
around his neck he felt a sharp pain scorch the surface of his upper
arm, and he groaned and sat down again. He rubbed at the sore spot
with his other hand, a futile gesture, he knew: the pain was too fast
for him, disappearing so quickly he sometimes wondered whether it

existed at all. It was the other pain, the one in his elbow, that he
could count on. More of a dull ache, he would say to the doctor, a
consistent dull ache. He stood up again, and as he headed out of the
Chocolate Factory he patted his back pocket to make sure his note-
book was still there—it contained a list of all the symptoms he'd had,
back to the first radiating heat from his armpit to his fingers in June
of 1988. A few months ago Linda had joked that he had a sore arm
the way other people had a hobby. Sore? he'd wanted to say. I'm in
pain. He knew it was a bad sign that he no longer saw any humor in
his situation.

Walking along Beach Street toward the Cannery he saw a cable car
filling with tourists. Last to board was an elderly couple, and Charlie
watched as the conductor gently helped them up. The conductor
wore a dark uniform and a peaked cap, and for a moment Charlie
thought, What a great job! Then he thought, a conductor? He was
regressing—first the sundae and now this. And what do you want to
be when you grow up, little boy? Charlie worked thirty hours a week
at a frame shop on Chestnut, a few blocks from the apartment, and
he liked it—he got a discount on framing materials. Linda said she
knew it was a good *job*; she wanted him to have a career, but Charlie
put careers in a group with pets and lawns—people were always talking about them and tending to them, but they just weren't that in-
teresting.

In his search to discover what, after all, was wrong with his arm,
Charlie had been in many New York waiting rooms during the past
couple of years, but this was the first in California and he didn't
know what to make of it: it was empty. He was accustomed to a
two-hour waiting room wait followed by a forty-five minute exam-
ining room wait, sitting there in a paper nightgown. And the New
York doctors, who'd never think to apologize for keeping you—
Charlie had liked them: their clean, meaty hands, their arrogance.

A tall, red-haired woman in a white coat opened a door and said

Charlie's name. He followed her into the doctor's office, and when she circled the desk, sat down, and said, "So, your arm hurts," he blushed and buried his face in his hands. Dr. *Lee* Price. He'd gotten the name from Linda, who'd gotten it from someone in her office, and he hadn't thought—he just hadn't thought.

"Let me guess," she said. "You thought I was the nurse. You assumed Lee Price would be a man. You feel like an idiot—you're really not like this." She smiled at him. "Does that sum it up?"

"You forgot the part about how I'm much more of a feminist than a lot of women I know."

"So I did," she said. "So I did." She unfolded a pair of glasses and slid them on, and her eyes seemed to open up, a delicate pale green. "It's really Leonora," she said. "Big secret. Now tell me about your arm."

She didn't comment as he talked, but every few minutes she held up a finger for him to pause and scribbled something on an unlined sheet of paper. With her head angled toward the page he was free to stare at her, and he took in her softly curling auburn hair, her clear, creamy skin, her narrow body. Lovely, he thought, and then, *lovely?* It wasn't in his working vocabulary.

"Any headaches?" she asked, still bent over her notes.

"No more than two or three a day."

She looked up and narrowed her eyes. "And Tylenol does the trick, or no?"

"Tylenol or a nap. I've always had a lot of headaches."

She nodded and wrote something. "Do you sleep well?"

"I was all-state in high school. I only wish it were an Olympic event."

"A wise guy," she said, laughing. "Are you married?"

"I—" he said. "My—" There was an answer to this question—it began "Yes, but . . . ."

"I ask because sometimes people can have small seizures in their sleep without knowing it. If you were married your wife might have noticed if your sleep were disturbed at all."

"I'm married," he said. "But I'm pretty sure nothing like that's been going on."

"OK," she said. "Through that door and I'll take a look."

It was the usual neurological thing: she asked him to turn his neck in every conceivable way; she produced a small hammer and tested his reflexes; she took a set of keys from her pocket and ran them along the soles of his feet. Holding his eyelids open with her fingers, she looked into his eyes with a tiny light. Listen, Charlie wanted to say, I've been through all of this.

"Any weakness?" she asked, pocketing the little flashlight.

"I have a little trouble doing this." Charlie held up his forefinger and with his other hand bent the tip forward. "Bending it at the first joint—not exactly life-threatening."

She held her finger up against his. "Push," she said.

He tried to bend his fingertip onto hers, but nothing happened. "I noticed it on my camera, about six weeks ago. I had to use my middle finger to hit the shutter."

"It's odd, but I don't find anything unusual otherwise. When was your last neck x-ray?"

"About eight months ago." They had found something called "change" in his neck, but evidently it had been a red herring.

"EMG?"

"Excuse me?"

"You've never had an EMG?"

"Not to my knowledge," Charlie said.

"You'd know it. Let's see if we can get you in later this week. You have insurance, right?"

"I'm covered by my wife's group policy at work." In his jacket pocket was a claim form that Linda had messengered to him from the office—better than actually having to see him!

Dr. Price nodded and set down her clipboard. "What does she do, your wife?"

"She's an architect."

"And you stay home with the kids?"

Charlie put a finger to his chest. "The kid," he said.

Charlie had met Linda on the first day of their first year of college. They were at freshman orientation week: their college rented a camp an hour's drive from campus, and you stayed in cabins with triple level bunk beds and met during the day with upper classmen to discuss College Life. This was in the seventies, and everyone wanted to *talk*. On the first night each freshman was given a partner to interview for ten minutes and then introduce to a group of twenty. Charlie and his partner sat at a picnic table and she launched into her background with such zeal that Charlie didn't have to ask any questions. He sat there staring at her—this blond-haired, blue-eyed girl from Minnesota, who seemed to have had the kind of childhood his parents referred to as "TV mythology"—and he hoped this initial pairing wasn't going to last the whole week. His older brother had told him that the people you hung around with during your first few weeks at college ended up being your friends whether you liked them or not. Charlie had visions of himself saddled with this girl for the next four years, and he wanted to lean across the table and say, "Neat is the opposite of messy, damn it!"

The girl was Linda. Later that night, after the awkward introductions (she told the group, "This is Charlie from outside of Boston—he likes to read"), Charlie overheard her telling another girl that he had eyes you could drown in. He liked that, and for months, long after the word "saddled" was the last he'd have chosen to describe his feelings about her, he tried to get her to say it to him—eyes you could drown in. Then he woke up in the middle of the night one night late in the spring of their freshman year, and looked at her, and he realized it was he who had fallen into her, so deeply into her that he couldn't feel any boundaries. He was the doubter—he hated himself for it, but he tested her in mean, small ways, flirting with other girls, disappearing into silence for days at a time—but he never found the edge of what he was to her; he was contained by her in a way that frightened and exalted him.

Now, fourteen years later, she was gone, and it wasn't so much that he was angry or depressed or even scared: he was adrift.

During hard times Charlie found it helpful to formulate a philosophy of life, and the past fifteen days had yielded him a particularly effective one: Bob Dylan. What he perhaps liked best about it was that Dylan had so little appeal to women, meaning Linda. He was an anti sex symbol, or maybe an anti-sex symbol. That beard, she would say, shuddering. *That thumbnail.*

When he got home from Dr. Price's, Charlie put "Tangled Up In Blue" on the stereo, turned the volume high, and lay down on the living room rug. Dr. Price had prescribed yet another anti-inflammatory drug, and Charlie had taken his dose, along with some codeine, and now waited for the customary queasy grogginess to overcome him. He knew that the new drug would help for a while, but that a few weeks after he stopped it the pain would balloon into his elbow again. The reason he had waited so long to find a doctor in San Francisco was that he was terrified of becoming addicted. Addicted to Dolobid—not a very hip way to go.

The phone rang, and he turned off the stereo and answered it. It was Linda, her voice, and it made him ache.

"How'd it go?" she said. "What'd he say?"

She, Charlie thought. "I have to go back on Friday morning," he said. "For an EMG."

"A what?"

"Electro-something." He paused; this was sure to displease her. "I'm not exactly sure what it is. I forgot to ask."

"You're so funny," she said stiffly.

"A real laughingstock."

"I'm sorry—I just don't see how you could forget to ask something like that."

"My arm hurt."

Linda was silent, and he tried to think of a way to save the conversation. "Sorry," he said finally. "I'm all drugged up."

"Well, guess what? Kiro asked me to work on the clinic in Walnut Creek."

"Lin," Charlie said, "that's great. We should celebrate. Or you should. Congratulations."

She was silent again, and then she said, in a bright, public voice, "I should get going but I'll talk to you soon, OK?"

"OK," Charlie said. "Okey dokey. Till then."

He said goodbye, hung up the phone, and turned the stereo back on. "Oh, shut up," he said to Dylan, and switched the receiver to the radio. He lay back on the rug. Something baroque was playing, and as the violins climbed higher and higher, winding around each other in ever tighter circles, Charlie thought of a string pulled taut, a single translucent nerve stretched end to end, fingertip to brain.

An EMG, it turned out, was really two tests. Charlie lay on a padded table, his arm on a pillow at his side, and looked at the pair of imposing machines that would measure the velocity of his nerves and the electric activity in his muscles. He felt queasy.

Dr. Price smiled at him. "We'll do the nerve velocity test first," she said. "It may be a little uncomfortable."

"I've heard that line before."

Again she smiled at him. She adjusted the position of his forearm, then carefully taped a wire to it. "Ready?"

"Wait," Charlie said. "Is it a high voltage?" He tried to look as if he were kidding. "Could you accidentally give me too much?" Yuk, yuk.

"Don't be scared," she said. She was so close he could feel her breath on the bare skin of his upper arm. "The strongest shock you could get from this thing wouldn't feel much worse than a sharp kick." She held a two-pronged fork to his neck. "We'll start with the worst so you'll know there's nothing to worry about."

The current slammed into his neck, and then it was over. "That wasn't so bad," Charlie said, laughing a little. "That was nothing."

She made a note, then continued down his arm, shocking him here, then there. The worst of it was how she pulled the hairs on his arm when she lifted the tape off.

"What a guy," she said. "Next time I give a demonstration can I call you?"

She set the wires and the fork on the table behind her. She held up a thin cord, on the end of which was a sliver of a needle, an inch and a half long. "Some people think this is worse," she said, "but it shouldn't give you any trouble. Ready?"

She slid the needle into a muscle in his forearm, and Charlie felt tears pricking at his eyes. "Ah," he said, and then, because it had sounded embarrassingly sexual, "Ow."

"OK," she said, "now make a fist."

Such a small, thin needle for such a great, big pain. Charlie's entire arm hurt, not just where the needle jutted out, but in his hand and wrist, too. She moved the needle around and he thought he might actually cry. He was aware of a strange crackling sound, like a staticky TV, and he realized it was coming from the monitor.

"There," Dr. Price said, "that wasn't so bad, was it?" She pulled the needle out of his arm, leaving him feeling bruised and exhausted. "Just a few more of these."

Half an hour later, the test over, they sat in her office. Charlie rubbed his hand up and down his arm. He was giddy with relief, eager to be terribly funny or audacious.

He looked at Dr. Price—Lee, Leonora, not such a bad name, really —and he willed himself into a crush on her. That red hair, those green eyes, the fetching white coat: he wanted her, or perhaps he only wanted to want her. Did the fact that it was only eleven o'clock in the morning mean he couldn't suggest they go for a drink? He longed to say "Let's ditch this hotdog stand"—it was a Linda line, but he felt he could use it with aplomb, without the least pang of sentimentality. They could have a drink and then a quick wedding, two or three red-haired kids, and a ranch-style house in the suburbs to which he would repair each evening, loosening the knot in his tie, eager for the martini she would have waiting for him. He only had joke ties now—a tie that looked like fish scales, a vintage tie a full five inches wide, even a tie made of wood—but he could buy one with little white dots, and he would, he would.

". . . very useful," she was saying. "At least we've ruled out any denervation."

"What?" Charlie said.

"You passed the test, Mr. Goldman."

"I did?"

"Don't look so morose. Go, take pictures with your middle finger, be happy."

"But my arm," Charlie said. "My arm hurts."

"Take the Dolobid," she said, standing up. "You said you'd worn a cervical collar for a while—do you still have it?" He nodded. "Wear it for a month or two. Sleep in it." She smiled. "You can call me if the pain gets worse."

Back in his own neighborhood Charlie wandered toward the frame shop, his arm twinging occasionally in memory of the assault it had suffered, and he decided to ask for the afternoon off. He passed in front of a men's clothing store, and after a moment back-tracked and stood looking in its window. Men at Work, the store was called —the other kind of work. It was a store Linda liked; when they'd first arrived in San Francisco they'd gone out walking almost every evening, and she'd steered them into this shop several times: she'd held up combinations of shirts and ties for his appraisal, saying he'd look great in this blue or that brown. Charlie was a jeans man, but he hadn't minded—he'd even tried on the odd suit to please her. He understood: he liked watching her try on clothes, too. It was a way of interpolating his love for her: Linda in the silk dress, Linda in the leather jacket, Linda in the slender grey suit—he loved them all. He thought of going in and buying a tie to wear as a surprise for her the next time he saw her—not one with little white dots, but one he actually liked—but then he thought that it would be much better to ask her to come with him, to help him choose one. It was really a pretty good idea—maybe he'd even let her talk him into a suit. Was it so hard, after all, to imagine himself dressed in a suit and tie, taking the bus downtown every morning? He could see himself carrying a briefcase, could even picture himself passing through a revolving door and standing at a bank of elevators avoiding eye contact with the other people who were standing there. He could see himself stepping into the elevator, facing the doors, could picture the elevator rising smoothly and speedily to, say, the twenty-third floor—but then what? What did people do in those towers all day long? What was *in* the briefcase—a tuna sandwich and an apple? Charlie couldn't get himself out of the elevator.

At the frame shop he found Kendra, the nicer of the two owners, in the back room, cutting some mats. Cutting mats—now there was work that made sense. He was almost tempted to work his shift, but not quite.

"Poor you," Kendra said when he'd explained about the EMG. "I don't trust doctors at all anymore. Do you know, my gynecologist told me I should have a hysterectomy just because I'm forty-five and I have a little trouble now and then? 'We'll just take it out,' he said. Can you believe it?"

Charlie shook his head.

"If I were you I would go next door and have a nice cup of herbal tea, and then go for a good long walk. You probably just pulled a muscle! An EKG, for goodness sakes. You can't trust them."

He thanked her and left the shop. E*M*G, he thought. He raised his arm quickly and the pain drilled at him: still there. It was comforting, in a way.

At home Charlie sat down next to the phone. He missed New

York, missed his friends—they'd never think to mention herbal tea without irony. And as for a good long walk, if he'd been in New York he'd have been instructed to get into a cab and go straight home to bed—much sounder advice. He longed to call one of his friends in New York, but whom could he call without having to tell about Linda? Instead he called his brother's office in Boston.

"Chuck!" Richard's voice boomed through the phone. "What's the good word?"

Was there one? Richard seemed to be in one of his increasingly frequent Hail-Fellow-Well-Met moods. "Nothing," Charlie said. "I was at this doctor's—she gave me this test."

"She?"

"Yeah—red hair, green eyes, white coat."

"Uh oh," Richard said. "Lust alert."

Who was this person? This was not the kind of thing Charlie needed to hear.

"I take it," Richard said, "that Linda is still among the missing?"

"You take it right."

"She'll be back, kid. She will."

"Yeah," Charlie said. "She just needed some space." She'd actually used that word, which had made the whole thing all the worse. "Space." It wasn't how she talked– wasn't, Charlie told himself, how *they* talked.

"What'd you go to a doctor for, anyway?" Richard said. Charlie could hear him moving papers around. "Your arm?"

"Yeah."

"Hmm. You know, I have a theory about your arm. Would you like to hear it?"

"Not really."

"It's nerves, your arm. Ever think of that? Nerves, pure and simple."

Charlie waited in vain for Richard's dumb pun laugh. "It might be a nerve," he said finally. "Like I was trying to tell you, I had this test."

"And it was negative, right? Or positive, or whatever, but it didn't show anything, tell me I'm wrong. Have you never wondered why none of these tests shows anything?"

It was true: he'd had x-rays and blood tests and even a CAT scan. Would Richard have been happier if there were something terrible wrong? And there *was something* wrong. "I'm glad we had this chance to talk," Charlie said. "Give my love to Kathy and the kids."

"Charlie, Charlie, I'm sorry. I know it's a drag having your arm hurt, I do. But at least you have your legs, young friend!"

Charlie laughed: it was something their mother had said to Richard once.

"Charlie?" Richard said. "She will be back. You two are perfect together. You know what Kathy said a couple months ago? I shouldn't tell you this. She said she wished you and Linda were around more so the kids could see what a good marriage was all about. So there."

"Well," Charlie said. "I guess we showed her." He attempted a laugh. "Is everything OK?"

"Yeah, yeah. You know how it is. It's one day, then it's the next day. What can you do? You just go on."

This struck Charlie as immeasurably sad, and as soon as he could he made an excuse and got off the phone. You just go on and on and on.

He went into the bedroom and pulled open the bottom drawer of his dresser. There, wrapped in a dingy old plastic bag, was his cervical collar. He put it on and looked in the mirror: the man in the big white doughnut. To hell with neckties—he was taking the idea of the turtleneck to new limits. He felt like calling Dr. Price, but what could he say? Excuse me, but are there any tests to determine whether someone's really in pain? Excuse me, but are you busy tonight? He took a Dolobid and two codeine tablets and got into bed.

Peeling shrimp, Linda had said once, was like giving birth—no one ever told you how horrifying it was, you had to see for yourself.

Charlie was peeling a pound of jumbo and not minding it at all:
she had invited herself for dinner. As he worked he sang along to
"Just Like a Woman" and allowed himself to hope that she, that
tonight.... But she'd taken her diaphragm with her, he'd checked—
she'd probably taken it because she'd known he would check—and
while Charlie felt in his heart of hearts that a baby was just what
they needed, Linda was unlikely to see it that way.

For that matter, sex wasn't really the issue.

What was the issue?

By seven o'clock everything was set. The shrimp were ready for
sautéing, the snowpeas and carrots were ready for boiling, the shock-
ingly expensive raspberry tart was hidden in a cabinet, and the wine,
on which Charlie had spent most of an afternoon's pay, was icy cold.

By seven thirty, everything looked a little wilted.

At eight Charlie put on his cervical collar and sat on the edge of
the bed. He thought of Dr. Price saying, *Go, take pictures with your
middle finger, be happy*, and he hoped that she would remember what
she'd said to him and be stricken by remorse—preferably tonight.
And she'd call him and say, Charlie, I didn't mean it, I want to help
you. When the phone rang at eight thirty, though, it was Linda.

"Charlie?" she said.

He held the receiver away from his ear while she recited her apologies—something about work, something about Kiro. After a while he
broke in. "Let me guess: you'll call me soon. Goodbye." He hung up,
and when she didn't call back he returned to the kitchen and threw
away the shrimp and the snowpeas and the carrots, forced them into
the disposal with a wooden spoon. He took the tart from its hiding
place and carefully lifted it out of its box. Holding it with both hands,
he leaned over the sink and quickly ate half of it. He was about to
have another bite but instead said, "That's disgusting," and let what
was left fall from his hands. He could feel the glaze on his cheeks. He
started out of the kitchen but immediately turned back and shook
pepper over the remains, just in case he changed his mind.

In his dream Linda was about twenty-three, in blue jeans but neat in blue jeans—blue jeans that she'd ironed. They were new in New York, living in an apartment that was like one they'd lived in but smaller and darker and dirtier, and she was stacking things: stacks of dishes, stacks of books arranged by subject, stacks of his socks and underwear. He was lying on the naked mattress watching her, and she was babbling, threatening to alphabetize the spices while at the same time relating to him a story about her aunt Marge, the "funny" one—and they were happy, happy.

And when he woke she *was* there, but not in blue jeans. She was sitting upright on a chair by the door, her purse in her lap, wearing a pair of what she called "slacks" and a blouse and blazer—looking, Charlie thought, like a woman waiting to be interviewed for a job. He propped himself up on his elbows to get a better look, then sank back onto the bed. "Thanks for knocking," he said.

"I did," she said eagerly, seeing that he was awake. "Several times. *And* I rang the doorbell. I guess you're still a heavy sleeper."

"You were expecting major changes? It's only been three weeks."

She came over and sat on the edge of the bed. "I'm really sorry," she said. "Really, really sorry." She touched the cervical collar. "Poor thing."

He ripped open the Velcro fastening and tossed the collar to the floor.

"Please," she said. "Please forgive me."

"OK," Charlie said. "I forgive you."

She bent down and kissed him quickly, awkwardly, on the jaw. "I'll make us some breakfast, OK?"

When he had dressed he found her stretched out on the living room rug, balancing in her lap an old accordion file she kept in a small wooden trunk they used as an end table. She was sipping from a cup of coffee, and it was such a familiar sight that Charlie was moderately cheered: perhaps this was simply another phase of their life together. He got coffee for himself and stretched out next to her.

"Actually, you do look awfully thin," she said. "Have you been eating?"

"Mostly sugar in various forms. It gives me a certain clear-headedness."

"And so good for you." She sipped her coffee. "Did you pour pepper on a tart?"

They laughed, and she leaned over and kissed him again, easily; then she began looking through the file.

"What are you after in there, anyway?" Charlie said.

"My old address book—Kiro wants me to get in touch with Mackenzie about something."

"Oh." Mackenzie was an old professor of hers—it seemed to Charlie that he wasn't supposed to ask about what.

"Oh, look." Linda pulled a postcard from the file. "I can't believe it—remember this?" She held the card up for him to see: it showed a row of tiny cabins and a big sign that grandly proclaimed, KENABSCON-SETT INN—LODGE, CABINETTES. "Remember our cabinette?"

"You mean cabinet?" Charlie said. He remembered: a dank little bathroom, fringed chenille curtains, a bed like a topographical map. Somewhere in Maine. It had poured rain the entire time they were there, and they'd gone to the "lodge"—a little matchbox of an office with an easy chair crammed next to a fireplace—and bought fifty-two copies of this postcard so he could make them a deck of cards.

Linda turned the card over. "King of clubs," she said. "Remember?"

Charlie took the card. The king of clubs had been the best one: he'd drawn a cave man wearing an animal skin, a long-armed club over his shoulder. He hadn't known she'd saved it. He looked at her, and it seemed to him that she wasn't remembering as much as he was. It hadn't been just any weekend away but one organized around a particular date, September 25, 1981, and a particular purpose: the celebration? commemoration? of the fifth anniversary of the first time they'd slept together, their annual marker back in the days before they had a wedding anniversary to observe.

"Remember the lobster rolls?" she said.

He handed her the card and took his coffee cup into the kitchen. He saw the raspberry tart still lying in the sink, and he folded it into the drain. When he looked up Linda was standing in the doorway, watching him. "Are you OK?" she said.

"I'm great. I'd have to say I'm really just thriving."

"Charlie."

He shrugged and turned back to the sink to wash his coffee cup. There was a rule he seemed to be living by: do everything you can to make her want to stay away for good.

"Listen," she said. "Do you want to drive over to Walnut Creek with me today? I was going to go look at the site, maybe do some sketches. Kiro was there yesterday afternoon and I think he wanted me to go this weekend."

"I guess," Charlie said. Kiro, Kiro, Kiro. "What do you mean you *think* he wanted you to go? Did he ask you?"

"Kiro is amazing," she said, shaking her head slowly. "He doesn't have to ask for things. People just know what he needs, and they want to give it to him, whatever it is."

"Great management technique," Charlie said.

The fog was lifting in the East Bay; by the time they got to Walnut Creek the sky was clear, the air warm. In New York it would have been a treasure of a day, a tantalizing hint of spring, an occasion for buying bunches of tulips for your wife—but at least he was with his wife. "God," he said, "you forget you live in a state where it can be seventy degrees in November. It's always so damp and cold in the city."

"It's bracing," Linda said. "I like it."

She led him up a small rise, to a clearing backed by grey-brown hills. "Brilliant," she breathed. She turned to Charlie. "He thinks we should design a kind of medical village, which I think is *genius* now that I've seen this place, don't you? A sort of main house for the information desk and all the administrative offices, and then behind it, conforming to the line of the hills, an S of cottages attached by covered walkways. And everything connected underground, where the labs would be." She touched his arm. "What do you think?"

Charlie shrugged. "Kiro knows best."

Linda took a sketch pad from her shoulder bag, and he crossed the clearing and began to climb the hill behind it, through low scrub and rocks. When he got to the top he was winded and sweating lightly; his elbow ached. He sat on a boulder and looked down at the clearing. Linda looked tiny and serious—she looked as if she had nothing to do with him. Look up, he commanded her. But she was absorbed in her sketching.

Charlie lowered himself from the boulder onto the ground and lay back. The thing was, he didn't know *how* to think of their marriage as troubled; it had always seemed to him that they got along very well—no fights. He wondered if he could possibly unravel their lives back to the beginning of the trouble, and as he was wondering this another date from their shared past came to him: Halloween, 1983.

They were living uptown then, on 113th Street, in one of the nicest apartments they ever had; Linda was getting her master's in architecture at Columbia. Charlie worked at a camera store on 96th Street, and on his way home each evening he'd go up to Avery Hall to see if she was ready for a dinner break.

Remembering a jack-o'-lantern they'd carved one Halloween in college, Charlie picked up a pumpkin on his way to look for her that afternoon. She wasn't in any of her usual places, though, and none of her friends had seen her all day. He walked back down Broadway under a heavy grey sky and decided that he wouldn't start to worry until he got home and she wasn't there. But she was: the apartment had an unusually large kitchen with a view south, and Linda was standing at the sink washing dishes. She barely looked at him when he said hello. He put the pumpkin on a chair and took off his coat, and when he turned around he realized why it all seemed so strange. The table and the counters were covered with dishes; every dish they owned seemed to be out. He couldn't tell whether she had already washed them or was about to. "What are you doing?" he said.

She turned from the sink, her hands gloved with suds, and began to sob. "You don't care if things are clean," she cried. "It's totally up to me. Do you realize we've never washed our wedding china?" She waved at a stack of the formal, flowery plates; he didn't point out that they'd also never used them. "I don't mind," she said. "I like things to be clean. But you just ought to realize..." Her voice trailed off and she turned back to the sink, plunged her hands into the water, and began to sob harder.

And here was his mistake. He'd said, "Realize what?" He'd stood behind her without touching her and said, "Realize what?" And that evening he asked her again and again, until she finally told him to stop asking, she was fine. *That* was where they'd taken their wrong turn: into a place where you couldn't tell the difference between polite and happy, to this point, this dry hillside, this separation. When it was so simple, what he should have done: taken her in his arms and said, Darling, darling, please don't, please forgive me for whatever it is I've done to upset you, please, you're my beautiful girl—*my dahling, lovely gehl,* like a character in an old movie—and they'd be wonderful now; they'd be fine.

He found her back at the car, looking over her exquisite sketches—he loved her sketches, had always loved them. "You're very good at what you do," he said.

Once she would have said, happily, "Really?" Now she laughed a little dismissively and said, "So are you"—and he wondered what it was she thought he was good at.

"Charlie?" she said. "It's getting a little crowded at Cynthia's."

Cautiously, hopefully, he nodded.

"She hasn't said so, but I think she'd like her privacy back."

"It's a small apartment."

"Here's the thing—Kiro's offered me his carriage house for a few months." She looked at him, then quickly looked away.

"Kiro?" Charlie said. "This is all about Kiro? Jesus, Linda—too bad I'm not some fastidious little Japanese architect, is that it? He probably doesn't even have any hair on his chest." He slammed his fist against the car. "I can't believe you."

Charlie had met Kiro once; he remembered him as a small man in a double-breasted suit—a tiny man, really, who smoked tiny black cigarettes and drank a vile drink called a negroni: gin and sweet vermouth and Campari or something. Kiro's philosophy of life was probably cryptic and pretentious, his carriage house full of smooth black stones and thousand-dollar orchids, no furniture. She could sleep on the stones and eat the orchids, and then they'd see.

"Charlie, listen," Linda said. "This isn't about sex, I promise. Kiro is just my friend, my very—my very kind friend. He's not the issue."

"What's the issue, Linda?"

"I just"—she hesitated—"need some space right now."

That word again. He turned away from her, and because there was nothing else to do he got in the car. He watched her standing there, pretending to be looking at her sketches, her beautiful sketches. His *wife*.

She gathered her things together and got in next to him.

"Would it help," he said. "Would it help if I got an office job? You know, where I had to wear a suit and tie every day?"

"Charlie, God. Dress up and play a part? That's not how it works." She sighed and leaned against the door. "You're wasting yourself."

He started the car. She had never actually said it before, and while a sour little voice in him was saying, "No, I'm not; I'm *saving* myself," the rest of him had risen to a strange plateau where he felt oddly empowered—he was back on the hill, watching her from a great height.

How could a grown man with any self-respect sit in the emergency room waiting area of a major city hospital and cry? If he hadn't been in so much pain Charlie might have asked himself any number of questions, but as it was he was concentrating on staying as still as possible. He wasn't actually crying so much as tearing up at each involuntary movement of his neck and shoulders, which caused him more anguish than he'd ever known. *At least you have your legs, young friend.* It was true: if it hadn't been for them, he'd probably still be at home in bed, destined to a slow and painful death.

He'd woken up in agony that morning—the day after helping Linda move her stuff to Kiro's, so at first he'd been a bit skeptical: *nerves, pure and simple.* But he couldn't turn his head, couldn't move his arms without unbearable pain; the only way he'd finally been able to get out of bed was to swing his legs up and then use them as a lever to bring his body upright. Picking up the receiver and dialing were excruciating, but he'd finally reached Dr. Price at the hospital, and she'd agreed to see him there, and now it turned out that he had something new wrong: a winging scapula. It sounded like a kind of sailboat, but it was his shoulder blade, unleashed from its mooring.

"That would definitely be uncomfortable," Dr. Price had said.

A winging scapula was also unusual, and while it was probably a fluke (a coincidence that half his upper body was malfunctioning!), some possibilities had to be ruled out. In a little while he was going to go to Radiology for an MRI, and then later he was going to go somewhere else for an EEG. He was making his way through the alphabet.

Dr. Price reappeared and sat on the chair next to his. "Radiology is going to squeeze you in in just a few more minutes," she said.

"That sounds painful."

She laughed. "After that I've arranged to have you admitted—just for one night. When you're done there just come back down to Admitting and they'll have a bed for you, OK?"

"I guess so," Charlie said. At least maybe they would give him some morphine; he'd taken some codeine about an hour before, but it didn't seem to be helping much.

"We'll wait and do the EEG tomorrow," she said. "You'll be feeling a lot better by then."

"What exactly are we looking for?" The word in Charlie's mind was "tumor."

Dr. Price was silent for a moment. "Nothing we're going to find," she said, "how's that? I really think it was just moving that new dresser in."

"Right," Charlie said. "The dresser." He hadn't wanted to tell her what he'd really been doing yesterday: carrying twelve boxes of art books down three flights of stairs. He'd strapped together two at a time and carried them over his shoulder, the way the movers had done in New York. "Still," he said, "it's hard to believe this has nothing to do with my arm. What's really wrong with my arm?"

"It hurts," she said.

Thanks a lot, he thought, but then he turned, painfully, to look at her—pretty Dr. Price, whose job it was to know when to say "Don't worry"—and he thought: Well, yes.

She glanced at her watch and stood up. "Listen," she said. "You know who get winging scapulae? Soldiers, from carrying their guns. So you're in good company, huh?" Charlie watched her hurry away, toward people with problems way beyond unusual. Good company? he thought. He'd rather be alone.

Slowly, carefully, he got to his feet. He had a quarter in his pocket —he'd had the foresight to make sure of this before he left home— and now, walking gingerly to minimize the pain of each step, he started toward a cluster of pay phones. He told himself that what he was about to do wasn't so much calling for help as giving information: she would want to know, she had a right to know—she was his wife. And this time, Charlie had some hard information: he'd already known what an EEG was, and he'd asked and discovered exactly what an MRI was. It was Magnetic Resonance Imaging —formerly, Dr. Price had confided, Nuclear Magnetic Resonance, NMR, but they'd changed the name because people hadn't liked the word "nuclear." It was like a CAT scan, that big washing machine, except they could look at any part of you, and it wasn't invasive. Charlie was all for non-invasive.

He reached the phones. She would say: "Charlie, oh my God, no." Or maybe: "Oh, Charlie, no." She would be there waiting for him after the MRI, with flowers and magazines because she was a great believer in brightening a sick room. A "sick room"—that was another of those terms of hers. It used to be that if he had so much as a cold she'd turn into Cherry Ames, girl nurse—bringing him milk shakes and toast, because that's what her mother had brought her when she was sick. Chocolate milk shakes, so thick you had to eat them with a spoon.

Charlie inched his hand into his pocket, and a shiver of pain raced through his neck and shoulder. He knew that lifting his arm to dial would be even worse. And for what? An hour or two. Maybe a day or two. He pulled his empty hand from his pocket. What was that old joke? "Doctor, doctor, it hurts to dial the phone." "So don't dial it!"

If a CAT scanner was like a washing machine, an MRI machine was more like a delivery truck. Charlie had taken off "everything," including his wedding ring, and was standing in a paper gown watching the technician prepare the little stretcher he would lie on. And then the stretcher would slide into the machine . . . .

"Got all your jewelry off?" the technician said.

"Yeah," Charlie said, "I left my diamonds in my jeans pocket."

The technician was about Charlie's age, friendly. He laughed. "Metal's the problem," he said. "You know those covered elastic bands women wear in their hair? With a little piece of metal at the joint? I had a woman wearing one of those and when she came out her ponytail was on the other side of her head."

"I guess it's a good thing I don't have any metal staples in my body," Charlie said.

"Good in any case," said the technician. "Ready?"

It hurt to lie down, but once he was in position he actually felt better. The technician put a wedge under Charlie's knees and then enclosed his head in what Charlie could only think of as a cage.

"The idea," the technician said, "is not to move. It'll take about half an hour. I can take you out at any time, but then we'll have to start over. It'll sound like this." He moved out of Charlie's line of vision and knocked on the side of the machine.

"But what will I feel?" Charlie said.

"Nothing," the technician said. "You'll feel nothing."

He slid Charlie in, and Charlie thought it was a good thing he wasn't claustrophobic: he was lying in a dark tube just wide enough to contain him, his head in a cage, forbidden to move.

"Everything OK?" the technician asked. There was a little light down past Charlie's feet, and the technician was in that light.

"Yes," Charlie said. "I guess."

"I'll be going into the control room now," the technician said, "but I'll be able to hear you in there, OK?"

Charlie swallowed. Maybe he *was* claustrophobic. There was no reason for this to be any different from lying in bed, but it was. He tried closing his eyes, but he started to spin and had to open them again. Relax, he told himself. If only he had a mantra. He could choose one right now—"field," maybe, or "stream," those were peaceful words—but how relaxing could it be to say "field" over and over again, field, field, he feeled really silly with a mantra!

It was cold in the machine, but he could feel sweat trickling down his sides, collecting on his forehead, his upper lip. If he had a tumor it would appear as a blotch on the technician's monitor—a purple blotch, probably. If he had a tumor ...

But he knew he didn't. If he did he'd be having dizzy spells, vomiting: he'd be sick. He would have to put his affairs in order and he didn't have affairs, he had—a sore arm. *The way other people had a hobby.* Or a career. Or a marriage.

The noise started. From inside the machine it sounded sort of like the clanking of a radiator, but more, Charlie decided, like someone hitting the lid of a garbage can with a hammer, over and over again, arrhythmically. It was actually kind of soothing, in the way bad avant-garde music could sometimes be soothing, and it made Charlie think of his and Linda's last night in New York. They'd been taken out for drinks by their friends Ira and Jeannine, music-lovers who chose a little place in TriBeCa where a group called Eponymous was playing: three white guys with dreadlocks and sunglasses, one with a synthesizer, one with drums, and one with a whole battery of weapons including a hammer and a washboard. Linda was so tense that night—she kept looking at her watch, and kicking Charlie under the table every time Ira ordered another round of drinks—but Charlie had liked it, all of it, even the terrible band. Eponymous—where but in New York could you find a band like Eponymous, a band *called* Eponymous? He wondered what had become of them. He thought that as soon as he got out of here—this tube, this hospital—he would call Ira; Ira would know. He hadn't talked to Ira in almost two months, probably the longest they'd ever gone without talking since they first met. And Charlie *liked* Ira—loved him. And Jeannine, too, and their apartment with all of that overstuffed plush furniture from Ira's grandmother's place. Maybe he *wouldn't* call, he'd just show up at their door with a six of beer and some weird record he'd buy at Tower on his way down Broadway, and they wouldn't ask him any questions, they weren't like that, but they'd know, just as Charlie did, what the issue was: it was I-don't-love-you-anymore, and Charlie knew he'd known that for a long time.

Saving himself? Why talk of saving himself when he could spend himself? All in one place.

Several women in my office are pregnant. Jennifer, my creative director, a contradiction in terms if ever there was one, is pregnant. So is
Samantha, another copywriter and my one real friend here. And the
receptionist, Karen, is pregnant, too. Samantha's is due first: March
25th. Then Jennifer's on April 2nd, then Karen's on May 6th. There
has been talk of a betting pool. Which of them will deliver closest to
her due date? My money will be on Karen: she is just twenty-two,
too young to realize the possibilities for drama inherent in being
early or late.

They are flushed and slightly awkward, these women, and I wish
them all good fortune. To each of them I wish a big bouncing baby
with a fine set of lungs, to each of them the kind of birth that makes
the doctor and nurses beam with good will and self-congratulation.
Now there is a profession that must give incredible pleasure. Who
else gets to witness the most private joys of life?

I am a copywriter at Fitch Brown Llewellen, an advertising agency.
Ours is the Sears, Roebuck of advertising agencies. Not that we are
so large; not at all. But we are definitely derivative. Remember those
big shirts everyone was wearing a couple of years ago? With long,
wrinkled shirt-tails hanging out and small awkward collars? They
were worn over tight black pants or narrow mid-calf skirts. Well,
look around and then go to Sears, and you'll find that that's where
those shirts are now. You won't have to look hard; they'll be hanging
under a huge sign that says BIGSHIRTS.

Sears, Roebuck gets its ideas about style from the greater fashion
world and then appropriates not only the idea but also, as in that huge
sign, the credit for the idea. So it goes with Fitch Brown Llewellen.
The big one right now is our religious adherence to a type of ad first

used, brilliantly I might add, for Molson beer and the American Express card, not a few years ago. Upstairs, in the executive offices of FBL, this adherence is referred to as "buying into a principle." Down here, where the rest of us sit under buzzing fluorescent lights, we call it imitation.

I worry sometimes about those fluorescent lights. What is the effect on an unborn baby? Does an expectant mother have the right to ask such questions of 1) her doctor? 2) her boss? 3) her mother?

It is nine thirty in the morning, and Samantha is late for work. The apartment she shares with her husband, Josh, is only twenty blocks away, but she rarely arrives on time. She has taken to walking very slowly. She wears heavy, rubber-soled boots, rain or shine. She is thirty-eight, and has had two miscarriages.

My phone buzzes and I put down the newspaper and pick up the receiver.

"You'll never believe what I ate for dinner last night." It's Sam. Her office is two down from mine, but we do most of our talking on the phone.

"A hot fudge sundae with dill pickles," I say.

"What a cliché," she says. "I'm disappointed in you, Virginia."

"What did you have?" I picture her transformed, a wonderful mommy cook making herself hot cereal while Josh looks on, askance, from behind his reheated pizza.

"It's disgusting," she says.

"Well?"

"Saltines spread with mayonnaise, and I mean *numerous* saltines, twenty or more."

"That is disgusting, Sam," I say, but I feel a rush of warmth for her. I want to tell her that I read somewhere that you can't do better for your baby than to eat as many saltines as possible, every day.

"I know," she says, laughing. *"Oy gevalt."*

Since they got pregnant, Josh has been teaching her bits of his grandparents' Yiddish, a word or two a day, so the baby can start to feel a little Jewish.

I am working on a dog food campaign. Getting this assignment was the realization of my worst nightmare about advertising. My brother, the perennial student, warned me. He said, "You think it will be handsome couples drinking champagne or giving each other important diamonds. But Virginia, it may well be dog food."

The joke was on me. Kanine Krunch, it's called. At least it's the dry kind of dog food, the kind that comes in gigantic paper bags. At least it's not the wet, canned kind. That is some consolation.

On my lunch hour I have begun to look for baby presents. It's too early to buy, but I want to know what's out there. There's a wonderful mobile at Babes in Arms, a little store around the corner. It's got little pastel animals hanging off curved strips of wood. Pink kittens. Blue puppies. Purple giraffes. I don't know if Sam and Josh are going to go for the bright, primary color decorating schemes plugged by the baby magazines these days, or whether they'll choose soft and cuddly instead. But I'd like to think of them standing at the edge of the crib and touching the little animals so that they sway, gently, over the baby's head. I've got a few more weeks to decide.

For Karen, it will have to be something more practical. She and her husband, Donald, got married just a month ago, and on his postal clerk's salary they'll be struggling once she stops working. A little terry cloth sleeper, maybe. A soft little sweater with a matching cap. A year's supply of Pampers.

I don't know what I'll get Jennifer.

Kanine Krunch has one distinction: only one. It is very cheap. It is the dog food you would buy if your boyfriend arrived at your house with two large black labradors and asked you to "watch" them for a week or two while he went to Florida to see about buying a boat.

My assignment is to think of—no, to make up—another distinction. And then to "pop it" into an ad in which two extraordinarily attractive yet wonderfully mellow people have a desultory, non-aggressive (this is not a hard-sell) conversation about their pooches. The idea, of course, is that if you, the consumer, would only switch to Kanine Krunch, you would become extraordinarily attractive yet wonderfully mellow, too. What you're not supposed to notice is that this image of the good life comes straight from those Molson beer and American Express card ads. Therefore, in an attempt to claim originality, I will be asked to attach to this ad a line similar to "For the easy times in your life." Similar to, but different. That's the line Samantha used for the flip-top canned puddings.

Three months ago Jennifer called me into her office, all seriousness, to announce her pregnancy. She told me first, alone, because I was the one who would be handling her work while she was gone. She trusted me, she said, to keep the place calm while she was off having the baby.

"Six weeks, Virginia," she said. "Two before and four after. That means you'll have to go to Indiana."

"Right," I said. Indiana is where the client's main offices are. I've met the client once, here in town, but Jennifer was talking about the big meeting where we would show story boards and chew our fingernails. The client, of course, isn't a single person at all, but a group of nearly indistinguishable men of about forty who wear suits of a slightly too-light shade of grey.

"Actually," said Jennifer, "it'll be a great opportunity for you."

Up the ladder.

"It'll give upper management a chance to see how dedicated you are." She stood up, a signal that our talk was over. "In fact," she said, "you should thank me for getting pregnant."

I smiled, but resisted her suggestion. It didn't seem like a requirement of office protocol. I stood up and headed for the door.

"Virginia," she said.

I turned.

"Aren't you going to congratulate me?"

Her real face came through and for a moment she looked softer, almost vulnerable. I felt like going around to where she was standing behind her big teak desk and hugging her, but I didn't know how she'd take it. "Congratulations," I said. "It's wonderful."

"I'm really happy," said Jennifer. And then, as if she'd just remembered that business, after all, was business, she laughed and added, "John and I decided it was time to test market a new aspect of our relationship."

I pass by Karen's desk countless times a day—on my way to the bathroom, the supply closet, the elevators. Her job as receptionist allows her quite a bit of free time, and she has taken to knitting. She holds the baby-soft yarn low in her lap, ready to drop it into the open shopping bag between her feet. The executives wouldn't like it, if they knew. They would say it was unprofessional, and of course it is. It is an entirely domestic act, a miraculous thing, really. A pair of smooth sticks, mysterious turns of the wrist, and a little garment begins to appear.

She is making a christening gown.

"Sam," I moan into the phone, "I want to be pregnant." I am kidding, half. I am thirty-four and I am not married, nor, I suspect, was meant to be. Could I ever have a baby alone? Would I?

"No, you don't," says Sam. "Your face would turn fat and your ankles would swell and you'd have heartburn on a daily basis. Believe me."

"But I want a baby," I say. "A little bundle of joy."

"Virginia, you live in one room."

"I could partition."

She laughs. "Oh, Virginia," she says.

"Do you feel like a different person now?"

She's silent for a moment. "It's not really like that," she says. "I feel like something new is starting, like I'm going to be different, but I'm not yet."

"It's so incredible, when you think about it."

"I know," she says. "At the beginning, when all I felt was nauseated, it hardly seemed like what I was going through had anything to do with having an actual baby."

"But now it does?"

"Now it does."

A kind of hollow feeling comes over me. "Oh, God," I say.

Sam doesn't speak, but I can hear her breathing, slow and soft. "Listen," she says finally, "think of your freedom. What about men, what about relationships?"

"What about them?"

"Virginia," she says, teasing, "you're the queen of relationships. You couldn't stand not having at least five intrigues a year."

I am not the queen of relationships. I am more like the court jester. I'm the one who can comment, wittily, on them all. On the guys who, sliding a hand up your sweater, insist that they just want to be friends. On the men, the young and serious ones, who ask if it will make you feel claustrophobic if they leave a toothbrush in your bathroom (it will). On the fellows who sweep you off your feet for three weeks, then inform you sheepishly that the wife and kids will return from the Caribbean on Sunday afternoon. On the one-night-standers whose failure to call leaves you slightly insulted and vastly relieved. On the lovers from your past who telephone in the middle of the night and, after forty minutes of idle conversation, ask if they can come over.

I want to have a baby, but I can't think of having a husband.

Jennifer is standing in my doorway. She wants to see what I've done so far on Kanine Krunch. The problem is, my notes would make no sense to her. I've figured out the people but not the setting. There will be a semi-glamorous young woman with a little terrier on a leash, and a regular guy with a golden retriever running around in the background. And the guy will have an angelic little toddler sitting on his shoulders. I'm not sure what they'll say, though.

"Can you show me an outline?" Jennifer asks.

"I would," I say, "but I don't really work in outlines."

"There isn't much time left, Virginia."

In fact, there are five weeks. But Jennifer's leave starts soon and she's getting nervous. "I'll have something to show you next Monday," I say. "First thing in the morning."

She groans, and just as I am about to say, OK, Friday, she comes over to my desk, leans against it, takes my hand, and puts it on her stomach. "It's kicking," she says.

This is awkward, looking up at her huge round belly, so I stand up, leaving my hand where she's placed it.

"Wait," she whispers.

At first there is nothing, then I feel her take a quick, deep breath. "See?" she says.

"That was it?" I was expecting a real kick, aimed outward, fierce, sudden.

"That was it."

It was like a wave rolling across her stomach. It had a wonderful, mysterious feel, as if it were a tiny manifestation of some grand, universal movement. Her face is flushed, and I realize that this is due only partly to exertion. The rest is pride.

I smile at her. "I'll have the outline for you on Friday," I say.

I have a blind date tonight. My brother called me from Charlottesville, the location of his current school, and told me that a friend of his from the microbiology lab was coming to New York for a conference. He said the guy, whose name was Hank, didn't know a soul here, that it would be great if I could take him out, show him the town. That's how my brother talks: "Show him the town." It's as if he only

arrived in this country a few years ago, and his studies have prevented him from learning the language.

Dating, I often think, is like applying for a job. You go all out in
the interview, proving your intelligence, your reliability, your suit-
ability for this particular position, and then when—if—you are offered
the job, you realize that the actual work would be tedious beyond
measure.

Promptly at eight, the buzzer rings. The intercom is broken, but
I go ahead and hit the button that releases the door downstairs. Up
here on the fifth floor, I figure no one will bother with the climb
unless his purpose is legitimate.

I wait a minute or two, then start listening for his footsteps.
Nothing. I unlock my locks, poke my head out the door, and listen.
No one is on the stairs; I can tell. The buzzer rings again, and again
I push the button for the downstairs door. I stick my head out my
open door and listen. Nothing.

After a few minutes the buzzer rings again, and now I realize that
what I've always feared has happened. The wiring that enables me
to open the downstairs door from inside my apartment has worn
out, or whatever happens to wiring.

I fly down the stairs, composing apologies in my head. When I
reach the door, there is Hank; it can only be Hank. He has a distinctly microbiology look about him: tall and thin, with overly
large hands and a quizzical expression on his face.

"I'm sorry," I say, out of breath. "The thing must be broken, you
know, the door-opening thing. What happened, there was no little
sound, or did the door just not open when you pushed it?"

"Virginia?" he says.

I am standing here, holding the door open with my foot, pant-
ing. Who does he think I am?

"Yes," I say. "I'm Virginia, and you're Hank, right?"

He offers me a large hand, which I shake. "Nice to meet you,"
he says.

"You, too," I say. "Sorry about the door."

"Huh?"

"The door," I say. "When you buzzed, and the door didn't work. Was there a little sound at all? Or did it just not open when you pushed it?"

He looks confused for a moment. Then he says, "I heard a noise, but I wasn't sure what it was, so I just waited for you."

Oh.

"Did I do something wrong?" he says.

"No," I say, "not at all." I take a step backward. "Come on in."

He steps through the doorway, smiling shyly, and of course he didn't do anything wrong, anything at all. He's probably a perfectly nice guy. But I already know how this is going to end up: a series of small advances and retreats—his advances, my retreats—over cocktails, over dinner, over one last drink in a small, dark bar, until we are back here, at this very spot, negotiating an awkward goodnight kiss. Sometimes I don't even feel like going through with the interview.

Sam and I are having lunch. The place is full of people, most of them eating in groups of two or three. It is very noisy. The tables are quite close together, and with the extra room Sam needs the waitresses can barely squeeze between her chair and the chair of the person behind her. It makes me very uneasy, watching the waitresses, huge trays of food over their heads, edging behind Sam.

"Are you ladies ready?"

Our waitress is here, order pad out, already impatient.

"Let's see," Sam says. "I'll have a bowl of the cream of celery soup, and a house salad, and the breast of chicken with the milanese sauce, and an order of hot French bread. And a glass of milk."

The waitress scribbles on her pad. "Anything else?" she says, not quite sarcastically.

"That's it," says Sam.

She turns to me.

"I'll have the same," I say. "Except the milk."

Since the pregnancies, I have been giving myself small indulgences: extra time with the newspaper in the morning, full square meals at lunch, bed a little earlier than usual. Sam says that not even Josh has had such a sympathetic reaction.

When the waitress has left, I lean toward Sam. "Have you decided about breastfeeding yet?" I ask. She wants to, but she's worried about what will happen when she comes back to work. They have those pumps now, so you can extract your milk and leave it in a bottle with the babysitter, but Sam thinks that would defeat at least half the purpose of breastfeeding, which is having the baby actually feed from your breast.

She shakes her head. "I'm still not sure," she says.

"You will," I say.

She nods and looks away, and a kind of distant smile comes over her face for a moment. Then she turns back to me. "I'm not ready to throw away my huge 32-B bras yet," she says. "I'd better breastfeed for as long as I can."

The ad is coming along. I've decided on a setting: a park. The guy is taking his adorable little girl and his golden retriever for a walk. He's throwing a stick for the dog, whose name is Sunny. The dog's name may not actually figure in the ad, but it helps me to visualize the thing. The little girl's name is Lizzie. She's about two, with big blue eyes and soft blond curls. She's wearing a dotted Swiss dress, yellow with white dots, and little white sandals.

She is sitting on her daddy's shoulders, and suddenly she puts her hands over his eyes. Moments later the dog comes back with the stick, and the daddy can't see to take it from her mouth and throw it again. The dog is jumping around, the stick in her mouth, nuzzling the guy's leg, being cute and frisky.

Enter the semi-glamorous woman with the terrier. Sunny drops the stick and begins sniffing at the terrier. The woman is immediately drawn to Lizzie and starts talking to her. They have a cute few seconds of conversation, which the daddy enters with a mixture of friendliness and irony, because his eyes are still covered.

Finally Lizzie takes her hands away and the grown-ups start in on the dogs.

That's as far as I've gotten; now I just need to figure out how to bring in the product. The woman: "She's a happy-looking dog." Lizzie: "That's 'cause her name is Sunny." The daddy (laughing): "It's because she knows she's going home to eat soon." The woman: "Mealtimes aren't any fun at our house, are they, Fido?" (I haven't thought of the terrier's name yet.) The daddy: "You must not be using Kanine Krunch." Etc., etc.

Well, it's a start.

Babes in Arms just got in a new line of stuffed animals. They're just the right size: smaller, as we used to say when playing Twenty Questions, than a breadbox, but larger than a shoe. There's a wonderful, soft grey rhino; a plush brown bear with heartbreaking button eyes; an adorable, jaunty little penguin.

"They're sure to be very popular," says the saleswoman, chattily, arranging the animals on a shelf. She's gotten to know me a little.

I pick up a rhino; who could resist? But the bear is great, too. And I'm not even ready to buy.

"We're putting them on special this week," the saleswoman says. "Half off. It's a special promotion to introduce them. They're from Sweden."

Half off is a good deal. Stuffed animals, I have discovered, are not cheap. I put down the rhino and pick up a bear. I hold him to my face. He even smells good: fresh and clean and, somehow, good for you.

"I'm going to take a bear," I say. I'll give him to Sam; the mobile is a little too expensive, anyway.

The saleswoman smiles and moves to the cash register. She's probably afraid I'll change my mind, I'm in here so often. She takes my credit card, runs it through the little gadget, and hands me the slip to sign. She wraps the bear in tissue paper printed with little baby bottles and rattles and diaper pins. She carefully puts it in a shopping bag and hands it to me. "Enjoy," she says.

It's ten twenty when the phone rings, jolting me out of sleep so fast that I have the receiver in my hand before I can possibly speak.

"Virginia?" It's a hollow little sound, a vaguely familiar voice coming to me from far away.

"Hello?" I say.

"Virginia?" It's my brother. "Did I wake you up or something?"

"No, no," I say. "I was reading." I always feel guilty when the phone awakens me, as if I should apologize for being asleep when someone wants to talk.

"So, how are you?"

"Fine," I say, and then it occurs to me that he simply wants to chat, that it's still my turn. "How are you?"

"OK," he says. "I'm at the lab."

"It's almost ten thirty at night, what, do you live there?" It's actually easier to picture him on a cot next to the Bunsen burners than in his own apartment. I haven't been to Charlottesville, but when I visited him in Cambridge, when he was getting the M.A. in philosophy, he lived in a three-room apartment in which there was nothing but a bed, a table, and two chairs. What bothered me most was that he didn't have a bureau. Where did he keep his socks and underwear? On hangers?

"I've got some cells in a petri dish that need looking at every three hours," he says. "So, you know."

"Yeah," I say. I picture the cells getting restless, saying, *Look at me, look at me.* It's a mystery to me, what my brother does.

"So, how'd you like Hank?"

This is why he called. "He seemed very nice," I say evenly.

"He liked you, too."

Not this, please. "Yeah, well," I say.

"He said you seemed a little depressed."

"Depressed?"

"You know, a little down."

"Oh, no," I say. "Not at all."

"He said you were kind of quiet, so I figured, something must be wrong, Virginia isn't the quiet type."

I wonder what type he thinks I am. What type am I? "Well," I say, "I'm in a quiet phase, nothing to worry about, but thanks for calling."

"Oh," he says. "Someone's there, right? God, I'm sorry."

"No," I say. "No one's here. No one but me."

Jennifer wants me in her office—to talk, I know, about the ad. She's had my outline for four days now, and she hasn't said a word about it.

"Sit down," she says when I get there.

I sit.

She is wearing my favorite of all her maternity dresses. It's a soft teal-colored wool with a white lace collar and white cuffs. When she first started wearing it she was hardly showing at all, and the dress flowed in an elegant line from neck to hem. But it has accommodated her belly beautifully, filling out as she's filled out. I know it was expensive, but it does not seem to me in the least extravagant.

"Virginia," she says.

I smile at her. In three weeks, or, who knows, maybe less, she'll have a baby. I've narrowed it down to something from Tiffany. Probably a spoon. It's the kind of thing she and John would appreciate.

"Kanine Krunch, Virginia."

"Yes?"

"This," she says, taking my outline from her desk, "won't do."

"It won't do," I repeat, stupidly.

"No."

I suppose I should have anticipated this. The people aren't mellow enough, the ad does not adequately capture the spirit of understated coolness required by the executives.

"First of all," she says, "when you have a father and a little girl meeting a glamorous young woman, you invite speculation on whether the father is going to commit adultery with the young woman. Right?"

I feel my face color a little; I should have thought of that. But if I take the woman out, who will the father discuss the product with? "Right," I say.

"And," Jennifer says, "more to the point, why a little girl?" She stands up and begins to pace, her hands on her lower back as if to give herself a push. "This is supposed to be about dog food." She looks at me, pointedly, then returns to her desk and ruffles through my outline. "Lizzie," she says. "What's with Lizzie, Virginia? You don't put adorable little children in dog food ads, you put adorable little dogs. OK?" She gathers the outline together and hands it to me.

I am halfway to the door when she says, "Virginia?"

I turn and look at her.

"Dog food," she says. "Think dog food."

The women's magazines are full of advice on every subject you can think of. How to get a man, How to get rid of a man, How to say no to your boss, How to put the sex back in sex, How to look great in work clothes, How to look great in no clothes, How to throw a fabulous dinner party without even trying. What I like best is the advice on how to treat yourself when you are feeling down. There are, contrary to what most people think, workable remedies. Setting aside an hour, a full hour, of time when you will not think about your children or your husband or your job. You will just sit in your favorite chair (they always assume you have such a thing) and sip a steaming cup of herbal tea.

Or, if you prefer, what about buying a brand new bar of scented soap and having a nice, long soak in the tub? Make the water as hot as you can stand it. Light a candle and turn off that bright overhead bathroom light. Put your favorite concerto on the record player (of course you have a favorite concerto). Relax.

This is, of course, laughable advice. If you are depressed, you're supposed to feel *better* after sitting there for an hour with nothing but Lemon Mist tea for company? You're supposed to feel like a new person after a long, hot bath during which you stare, through the water, at the distorted shape of your hips and thighs?

Still, here I am, in the tub. The light is on; there is no music. My drain doesn't work right, or, rather, it works too well, and as I lie here the water level gradually lowers until bits of my body begin to appear, small and then larger islands in a porcelain sea. If I were pregnant, my stomach would appear first. Pale and huge, yes, but I would love it.

The trip to Indiana is in less than a month, and I have begun to dread it. The client will meet us at the airport, me and two of the executives. We'll be taken to our hotel and offered half an hour to freshen up, then it will be out to dinner. We'll go to a steakhouse. The lights will be low and we'll be shown to a big round booth. The waitress will be there to take our drink orders before we've had a chance to think about what we want. The client will have whiskey sours. The executives will ask for Glenfiddich, settle for Dewars. And I will be unable to think of anything suitable. Aside from wine, the only thing I really like to drink is Campari and soda, and it will be months too early for that since it's a summer drink.

I will be seated between two of the men in the light grey suits. They'll ask me questions about life in New York, about the cost of living, the impossibility of parking your car, the poor public schools. They'll ask, challengingly, what I will do when I want to have children. Move to the suburbs? Send them to private school?

To change the subject, I will ask about their children, and out will come wallets containing studio photographs, smiling families in front of fake fireplaces. They are of my generation, these men, only five or six years older than I am, and they will show me pictures of children in the fourth or fifth grade, of children, perhaps, in junior high. They will point to little blond heads, saying, This is Kerry, he's pitcher on his Little League team; this is Heather, isn't she pretty?

The client is probably a good father.

I've reached an impasse on the ad. I am keeping the guy, who, I think, will be out for a run; I am keeping the semi-glamorous young woman; I am keeping their two dogs. I am trying to think dog food. But somehow it's hard to go on, without Lizzie.

I decide that what I need is a fresh pad of paper. I head for the supply closet but stop, as usual, at Karen's desk, for a look at her knitting.

"I just have the sleeves left," she says, holding up the rest. "Donald's mother is going to do the crochet work around the neck."

"It's so pretty," I say, fingering the soft gown.

She puts it in her shopping bag and goes to the closet for her coat. It is only four thirty, but she's allowed to leave early these days, to ensure herself a seat on the subway. She lives way out in Brooklyn, twenty-three stops away.

She buttons up, then comes over to the desk to get her things. Suddenly she starts laughing, her hand over her mouth.

I turn, and there is Samantha, walking toward us in that funny pregnant goose step of hers. She is bundled up in her wool cape, ready for the walk home, and when she sees us, sees Karen in her big blue coat, she, too, starts to laugh.

"What's so funny?" I say.

"The two of us," says Sam. "We're so . . . pregnant."

Karen giggles.

"When I see other pregnant women on the street," Sam says, "we always exchange this little smile, like we have a secret the whole world can't guess."

"You do that, too?" Karen asks, laughing.

"Of course," Sam says. She smiles at me, the trace of an apology in her expression, then turns back to Karen. "I'm leaving too," she says. "I'll walk you to the subway."

We say goodbye, and they head for the elevators. I watch them for a moment. They are so entirely unalike—Sam is tall and auburn-haired, with an elegant, angular face, while Karen is hardly more than a child herself: short and small-boned, her blond hair pulled away from her face and held by bright pink plastic barrettes. Yet what I see first and most clearly is the fact that they are both huge— huge with child, as they say. Grand with child.

The red "down" arrow appears over the door to one of the elevators. They turn and wave to me, then they are gone.

The woman ahead of me in the movie line is pregnant. Six months, I would guess. She keeps turning around and scanning the sidewalk behind me. She is waiting for someone and she seems impatient. Every few minutes she glances at her watch. I wonder why she's so anxious; the movie doesn't start for nearly twenty minutes.

I look away and catch sight of a billboard bearing a Fitch Brown Llewellen ad. It's for a fragrance. A woman with carefully disheveled hair stands on the beach at sunset. One strap of her sequined gown has fallen from her shoulder; her high-heeled sandals dangle carelessly from her hand. She looks into the distance. The copy line reads, "You can't forget his touch . . . ."

I look back at the woman and find that she is looking at me. I start to smile at her; I can already feel the small, intimate smile we will exchange. But she looks away, and again ranges her vision over the sidewalk behind me. She is about to turn around when her expression changes to pleasure.

A man comes up from behind me and bends to kiss her. "Sorry," he says. He is tall and has curly brown hair and little wire-rim glasses. He is wearing faded Levi's that fit him wonderfully, a brown suede baseball jacket, and a blue and white striped dress shirt. From the shirt I deduce that he has a real job somewhere, but he's not so stuffy that he would wear his suit to the movies. When they're at home together, he's probably very sensitive to whether she feels like talking or whether she'd rather be left alone. He's sure enough of her, of them, that he's perfectly content to spend entire evenings in silence. But he's wonderful to talk to, when they do talk: he really knows her, and their conversations have a rich subtext of shared knowledge and experience. When he kisses her, it means something.

It's somehow worse actually to see men like this, to know they exist. It's as if he has been sent to remind me that the only men I might consider marrying are those who are already husbands.

He puts his hand on her rounded belly. "How's the baby?" he says.

Jennifer approved my new outline, her last act before starting her leave. She has been gone for a week now, and so far she has called in every day. I fill her in as quickly as possible, assuming she'll want to get back to hanging curtains in the nursery or whatever, but she lingers on the phone, asking about this meeting or that report. When I mention Sam—she's due "any day now"—Jennifer sounds impatient. I think she resents Sam for working all the way through her ninth month. It is somewhat surprising that Jennifer started her leave so early. Sam thinks she was afraid her water would break at work, which would not look business-like at all.

It is seven o'clock at night, and the office is empty except for me and Max, my art director. He is working up story boards, I am scripting. We sent out for Chinese.

To my surprise, my original tag line made the final cut. The last image will be the guy in his running clothes throwing the stick for Sunny, then turning to wave at the semi-glamorous woman as he heads out of the park. He stumbles, rights himself, looks sheepishly back at her, and she stands there, an amused smile on her face, and waves. Voice over, tag line: *Kanine Krunch—food for the dogs that people like you love.*

I dip my chopsticks into a carton of Hot and Spicy Shrimp, pull out a water chestnut, and put it into my mouth. The phone buzzes and I pick it up, thinking it must be Max, who is sitting across the hall eating Beef with Broccoli.

"Szechuan Kitchen," I say. "What's your pleasure?"

"Virginia?"

"Oh, hi," I say. It's Sam. "I thought you were Max. We ordered in Chinese."

"It's starting," she says. "I've had four contractions."

"Oh, my God."

"Just wanted to keep you posted."

"Oh, my God," I say. "Oh, my God." I've got this huge smile on my face, I must look ridiculous.

"Josh is making me get off the phone," she says. "He wants us to practice our breathing again."

"You've practiced a million times," I say.

"I know," she says, laughing. "Wish me luck."

It's a girl. I got the call at work late this afternoon. She was in labor for seventeen hours. Seventeen! Visiting hours go until eight thirty, so I finished what I was doing before racing to the hospital.

I am hurrying down the corridor, looking for Sam's room, when ahead of me I see a pair of swinging doors and a large sign that says NURSERY. There is nothing to stop me, no sign saying STAFF ONLY or even PARENTS ONLY. I push through the doors and into a darkened hallway.

No one else is here. A huge glass wall separates me from the babies, reminding me of those one-way mirrors psychologists use to study people.

The nursery is brightly lit, and there are, unbelievably, row upon row of babies. They are in cribs about two feet apart, their tiny red heads all pointed in the same direction. The cribs are numbered, 01 through 56. Only seven cribs are empty. What happens when there are more babies than cribs? The whole thing suddenly seems comical to me; ludicrous, even. I imagine baby after baby being born and brought to this room, an assembly-line gone mad. Babies making way for more babies, hospital cribs filling and emptying, filling and emptying, all over New York, all over the world.

All this time, going through Sam's pregnancy with her, it has seemed to me magical somehow. But it's just what happens: women have babies.

I push back through the swinging doors. The hospital corridor is brightly lit: clinical and matter-of-fact. I find Sam's room, knock on the open door, and go in.

"Virginia," Sam says. She is lying in bed, looking very pale and tired and happy. Josh is sitting on the edge of the bed, all wrinkled and unshaven. He is, I realize, still in yesterday's clothes. There is a look of bliss on his face. Or maybe it's exhaustion.

I lean down to kiss Sam. Her face feels damp and warm. "Virginia," she says, "you would have been proud. I made it all the way through without any drugs."

"Great," I say. That was one of the things we always talked about: would she be able to stand the pain? It was as if I were pregnant, too, I was so interested.

"I could have killed her," Josh says. "I was hoping they'd give me a little something."

"He was wonderful," Sam says, smiling at him.

"You were wonderful," Josh says, touching her shoulder.

There is a moment of silence. There are things I should be saying, but what are they?

"So, Virginia," Sam says, "what do you think of Isabel?"

Josh laughs. "Can you believe we changed our minds again?"

For the longest time it was going to be James or Sarah, there was no wavering, no doubt. But the past few weeks, Sam was coming in to work with new possibilities every day. Amelia, Susan, Laura. Henry, Timothy, Jacob.

"I like Isabel," I say. In a few days they'll take her home, and a new baby will appear in whatever crib she's in now. Maybe it'll even be Jennifer's baby, although I don't even know at which hospital Jennifer is going to deliver.

"Oh, look," Sam says. "Your timing was perfect."

I turn around and there, standing in the doorway, is a nurse, a little bundle in her arms.

Sam is radiant. "Her first real feeding," she says.

The nurse comes over to the bed. "Are you ready to see Mom?" she says to the bundle. "Are you ready to say hello to Mom?"

I look at Sam, but she doesn't seem at all amused by the nurse's little show. She holds her arms out, and the nurse gently gives her the bundle. Sam looks up at Josh and smiles. She turns to me. "See?" she says.

I lean in close, and there, in the midst of an elaborate system of soft white wrapping, is a tiny pink face. "She's very cute," I say. I look up at Josh, but his attention is fixed on the bundle. He touches the little nose, then puts his arm around Sam and buries his face in her hair.

"I should go," I say.

They look at me in surprise, almost as if they've forgotten that I'm there.

"Stay a minute," Sam says. "Would you like to hold her?"

She seems to want me to, so I sit on the bed and carefully take the bundle from her.

I look down at the tiny face. She's so little, but somehow she is remarkably heavy, substantial. There's a real body inside this blanket. A real baby. I touch her cheek; it's so incredibly soft and pink and warm. I can't believe how warm she is, how I can feel the warmth of her body, all the way through the blanket and through my clothes, all the way to my breast. Which one was she, in the nursery? How could I not have wondered? I can't help it; there are tears rolling down my face. In a moment this crying will find a voice, and I am afraid to hear it.

Someone, the nurse, takes the baby from me. I don't want to look at Sam, I'm so ashamed. But I do look at her, and when I see the way she's biting her lip, when I see the squint of understanding in her eyes, I let out a single, hoarse cry. Her arms come up around me and she pulls me close and holds me. She runs her hand down the back of my head, and I can imagine how it would feel to really let myself go, to sink against her.

But I don't. I pull away and stand up. I grab a Kleenex from the box on her table and dab at my eyes. "I've got to go," I say.

"No," she says, "Virginia—"

"I'm sorry," I say. "I'll call you."

Without looking at Josh or the nurse—or at Isabel—I hurry out of the room and past the nurses' station to the main hall. I hit the button and wait for the elevator to come and take me down.

I went back to Babes in Arms and bought the mobile for Isabel; I have decided to keep the bear for myself. He sits on my couch, a mute and pleasant companion. Lately I have been spending a lot of time on my couch, too. I read there, of course, and I nap there, but that's also where I eat, my knees bent, a plate of cheese and crackers in the hollow of my lap. I just can't be bothered to set the table.

In this city, there are dozens of pairs of sneakers, their laces knotted together, hanging from telephone wires and power lines. This city is Madison, Wisconsin, and Winch is trying to understand the sneakers because, a newcomer, he thinks they might explain something to him—tell him how to live here, whether to live here.

Winch sits on the porch steps of Luke and Sarah's apartment. He has forgotten his key again. He knows exactly where it is, too—in the little painted bowl Sarah keeps on the coffee table in the living room, where he sleeps. He put the key there last night because Sarah was trying to get Luke to talk about whether or not there ought to be something in the bowl—whether the bowl would look better with something in it—and Luke would not cooperate. Winch felt like a peacemaker, donating his key to the cause. When he saw the key in the bowl Luke snorted, a sound that Winch finds extremely disagreeable. He can't remember Luke ever making it before, but he makes it a lot now.

Sarah comes pedaling up the street on her three speed, her short hair flapping against her head. Whenever Winch sees her on her bicycle he can't help thinking of *Butch Cassidy*—that part when Paul Newman takes Robert Redford's beautiful girlfriend for a spin on a rickety old bike. Who played the girlfriend? Winch can't remember, but Sarah looks a bit like her. Winch thinks she should wear more long skirts, should try letting her hair grow.

"Are you locked out?" Sarah says, just stopping herself from adding "again." The way he sits there just kills her. He's so—passive. She refuses to feel guilty, though; the guy is thirty years old and ought to be able to keep track of a key.

"Yeah," Winch drawls. "I guess I am."

"Well," Sarah says, adjusting her pack and lifting the groceries from her bike basket, "I hope you haven't gotten cold waiting for me." She walks up the steps and past him to the door. She feels like some kind of dreadful nanny, chirpy and upbeat. She decides that after she's put the groceries away she'll hide out in her and Luke's bedroom for an hour or two. Not for the first time since Winch's arrival, she thinks it's too bad he couldn't have shown up next year, when, if all goes according to plan, their penny-pinching will have paid off and they'll have bought a house—with a guest room. Having Winch camped out in the living room is just one more reminder that they're still living like students.

"What do you think about those shoes?" Winch says. He's still sitting on the steps.

Sarah turns from the door. "Excuse me?"

Winch points at a pair of hightop sneakers dangling from the phone line.

"I think," Sarah says, "that someone's feet must be cold." But as she goes into the house she thinks, Why'd I say that? She's been wondering about the shoes, too—ever since they appeared, last spring. She's noticed a few other pairs around town.

Through the living room window Luke can see Winch sprawled on the couch, wearing his—Luke's—headphones. Winch is grooving to the music; Luke watches as his feet wiggle, as his arms beat time on his thighs.

Luke backs off the porch and down the steps, undetected. He makes his way around the house, looking in windows, until he sees Sarah lying on their bed, her arms crossed over her chest, staring into space.

He taps on the window and her body jerks out of position—both feet lifting off the bed, her arms flailing out in front of her. Immediately, she's raising the window.

"Don't ever do that again," she says. "Jesus, you scared me."

"Sorry." He waits to see whether he's instigated a bad mood, but she seems OK. "What're you doing?"

"Oh, nothing," she says. "Avoiding you-know-who."

"Me, too."

"He was locked out again. Sitting on the porch when I got home like some dopey-eyed stray."

"The guy is hopeless," Luke says. This feels vaguely disloyal, but he no longer cares. Whatever he's owed Winch has long been repaid. He looks at Sarah, standing in the lighted window, and gets a brilliant idea. "Can you slide the screen up?"

"You're going to climb in? Wearing your suit? You'll get it all dirty."

"No," he says, "you're going to climb out. I'll help you. Then we'll sneak out for dinner."

"Oh, Luke," Sarah says. "We can't do that. He's our guest."

Luke stares at Sarah. He wishes he could be certain that she's not just trying to avoid messing up her clothes. "Fine," he says. "I'm going around."

Winch is in the kitchen, his hand halfway into a box of Ritz crackers, when he hears Luke at the front door. Luke calls, "Hi, honey, I'm home," as he does nearly every time he enters the house: even if Sarah's not home and he knows it, even if Sarah's with him.

Winch grabs a handful of crackers and, hearing Luke's step, shoves them into his breast pocket. He puts the cracker box back and is at the sink, filling a glass with water, when Luke comes in. "Hi, honey," Winch says.

"What's up," says Luke. He pulls a beer from the refrigerator, twists off the top, and begins to drink. Winch would really love a beer, but Luke doesn't offer—maybe because Winch has the water.

"I said what's shakin'," Luke says. "What'd you do today?"

Winch thinks. Luke's after what job and apartment progress Winch made, but the answer is none: he went to see about a room in a house that turned out to be on a street with four pairs of sneakers hanging from wires, which was weird in and of itself; and then the people were nice but not quite right—the girl kept talking about group meals and schedules and the two guys were classic, wearing ironed shirts and sure to be uptight about stereos and shampoo and stuff. And Winch did nothing about a job today—wasn't into it. "Oh, I saw this cool exhibit," he says. "On State Street. This whole place was painted black and then there was furniture in it, but made of neon. It was cool. I mean, you couldn't sit on the chairs or anything, they were—"

"Air?" says Luke.

"Well, yeah, you know. And neon tubing."

"Sounds special," says Luke. He puts his beer down and opens the refrigerator. "What's that wife o' mine got planned for dinner, I wonder."

"She said something about spaghetti," Winch says. What Sarah said was "Maybe Luke will make spaghetti tonight," but Winch doesn't tell Luke this. He's not sure when it's going to happen, just that it is: Luke and Sarah are heading for trouble. Winch feels like the pan that's keeping the oil out of the fire.

"Did she?" says Luke. "Well then, who am I to say otherwise?" He pulls a package of hamburger from the refrigerator, sets a pot on the stove, and begins emptying the meat into the pot. "Hand me that spoon there, lovey," he says, gesturing with his chin at a wooden spoon in the dishrack.

Winch hands it to him. "I'm going to just go into the living room for a sec," he says. He's got to do something about the crackers in his pocket—stash them somewhere or eat them.

"You do that," says Luke. "I'll be right here."

Sarah's relieved to find Luke alone in the kitchen—she wants to get things on a better footing. She even put on a skirt, she's not sure why. Well, maybe she is: it's one he really likes and the last time she wore it he told her she looked beautiful. "If the second graders could see you now," he said, "they'd all fall immediately and hopelessly in love—they'd never give you another minute of trouble." So, OK, she admits to herself, she's after a compliment.

"Seduced into the kitchen by the heavenly smell of browning hamburger," Luke says. "I knew it would work."

"Where is he?"

"Having his cracker fix in the living room."

She laughs. "Telltale bulge in the shirt pocket?"

"I'm going to put a note in the Ritz box," Luke says. "'I'm on to you—a friend.' What do you think?"

"Too subtle," Sarah says.

"You're probably right. Something like 'Keep out, fucker' might work better."

Sarah doesn't respond. She gets onions and a green pepper out of the refrigerator and starts chopping. She wishes Luke would just relax about Winch. It's inconvenient having him here, sure, but it's not that bad. There's something sweet about him, really; he's like a child, eager to please but helpless when it actually comes down to pleasing. She remembers the first time she met him: she'd gone to visit Luke at school—their spring breaks hadn't matched up that year—and she was lying on his bed, reading, waiting for him to get back from a class, when there was a pounding on the door. She hurried to open it, fearing something awful had happened to someone, and there was this impossibly tall guy with wild blond hair and surprised eyes—Winch. "You've got to come with me, you've got to see this," he said, grabbing her hand and virtually pulling her out of Luke's room. She followed him out of the dorm and down to the creek: there, standing on the bank, were eight or ten tiny ducks watching their mother gliding on the water. Remembering this, it occurs to Sarah that Winch would be a good teacher. Better than she is, anyway. Ducks! If only she could take her class to see ducks. If only she knew where to find them, how, when.

Once the sauce is simmering, Luke heads back to the bedroom to change his clothes. He had just gotten over feeling like an imposter, wearing a suit and tie every day, when Winch showed up. During the two weeks that Winch has been here Luke's backslid to the point where he doesn't only feel ridiculous because of how he's dressed; he's started wondering again how anyone—his colleagues, other lawyers around town, even his clients—can possibly take him seriously. He looks like the kind of person his clients—boys fifteen, sixteen, and seventeen years old, and making their third and fourth court appearances—contemplate mugging when the bars close Saturday nights. One kid today said as much—Doug Kaiser, whose illegal activities strike Luke as especially unfortunate: he ought to be a starter on East High's defense. Explaining to Luke that he'd been minding his own business at the corner of Gorham and Bassett (at two o'clock in the morning, of course) when two frat boys came along and started hassling him, Doug said, "Those pretty boys had their heads up their asses. They're dumb shits. A guy that looks like you doesn't fuck with a guy like me." "Word to the wise?" said Luke. "Man," said Doug, "they were asking for it." "Right," said Luke. "But we won't mention that to the judge."

He pulls on jeans and a sweatshirt and looks in the mirror. When he was in college—bearded, and hollow-eyed from too many late nights—he could pass for thirty. Now that he is thirty what does he look like? A frat boy. A pretty boy. Dumb shit. He would not like to run into Doug Kaiser late at night anywhere.

Heading down the hall to the kitchen, he hears Sarah and Winch laughing. How is it, he wonders, that a guy with whom you once agreed about everything can become a measuring stick for your own self-delusions? He smiles to himself. Who better could there be for the job? Maybe Winch should settle in Madison—to keep Luke honest.

Sarah's so pretty when she laughs—Winch wishes she did it more often. He goes on with his story, lying now. "And the next night I went back and she'd carved this message into the table where we'd been sitting. It said, 'I'd like to coil around your winch.'"

Sarah cracks up. "No way—you made that up."

"Cross my heart," Winch says.

"You lie like a dog," Luke says from the doorway. Winch turns and looks at him. "I made it up—about ten years ago, remember?"

Winch can't tell whether Luke's angry or not. He shouldn't be, but these days Winch doesn't know how to read him; the one constant in dealing with Luke is that Winch is almost always surprised. "You nailed me, man," Winch says. He turns to Sarah. "So he's still got his bionic memory, eh?"

Sarah smiles at him. "When he wants to."

Winch feels the tension wires that run between Luke and Sarah start to jangle. He goes over to the stove and looks at the spaghetti sauce. "This smells good," he says.

When he turns back, Luke's smiling strangely at Sarah. "Well?" Luke says.

"What?" she says.

"What'd I forget?"

"Did you forget something?"

"Isn't that what you meant?"

"By what?"

"What you just said."

Sarah turns to Winch. "Did I say something? I don't remember saying anything. But then, I'm not the one with the memory."

Winch attempts a peace-making smile. What's he supposed to say? Luke faces him. "Women," Luke says, "have this uncanny way of making you feel ever so slightly insane. Keep that in mind, son, and you'll be OK."

Winch swallows uncomfortably. "So do you think maybe we should start the water boiling for the noodles?" he says. Then he remembers the thing he did today, the great idea he had. "Hey," he says. "I bought you guys some wine."

He goes into the living room to get it, and when he comes back something's changed. They're in precisely the same places they were, but the tension wires have, miraculously, gone slack.

Winch holds up the bottle. "Are you guys into red?" he says.

Sarah's too tired to talk. Sitting at the table, playing with her pasta, she tries in a desultory way to get a fix on the conversation. They're talking about drugs, though—tripping on some camping trip they took together—and the only things she can think of adding are in the teacher mode: Weren't you afraid that you might get separated? How could you have forgotten sweaters?

Or is that the mother mode?

At school today, the kids who'd had a brother or sister born in the last year—a remarkable twelve out of twenty-seven—brought in updated information for the New Baby at Home chart, an element of the Family Life unit that worries Sarah: what do you do when someone comes in with the news that little Susie died in her crib? The kids love the chart, though, and as Nan Mikelberg, the other second-grade teacher, has said, if it involves thumb tacks and a bulletin board, go for it. Sarah was helping Merry Clark pin up a new photograph of her baby brother when Merry said, "Mrs. Prinden," —they always call her Mrs., there's nothing she can do about it— "Mrs. Prinden, how come you don't have a baby?" and Josh Gold, who lives across the street from Sarah and Luke, said, "It's 'cause her husband's not really her husband." What Sarah finally managed to find at the bottom of his confusion was the fact that she and Luke don't have the same last name. But she wonders whether Josh wasn't, in his childish way, right. Did she and Luke forfeit something, living together all those years? It sometimes seems that the primary effect of actually getting married was to make the things that used to be annoying about the other person enraging now: you feel like you'll be voicing or stifling the same complaints for the rest of your life.

Sarah closes her eyes, and when she opens them Winch is saying, "Maybe we should get some acid for next weekend." Sarah turns to Luke, her mouth open. He wouldn't, would he?

"God," Luke says. "Relax. You look like we're thinking about robbing a bank."

Sarah shrugs. "Do what you want," she says.

Luke hates this. He wishes she'd just say what she's thinking—that it would really bother her. What bothers him is her just sitting there pretending not to be bothered.

Not that he has any intention of doing acid—with Winch, with anyone—ever again. Getting high now and then is one thing, but he's fried his brain enough, thank you very much.

He looks at Sarah. Poor, worried thing. It's funny how the very moment when he's most pissed off it can all just dissolve and leave behind nothing but tenderness. He leans across the table and touches her hand. "I don't want to," he says, smiling. "OK?"

"Whoa," says Winch. "I didn't mean to rock the boat here. Just a little nostalgia kicking in."

Luke sings, "We were so much younger then, we're older than that now."

"You guys are older," says Winch. "Maybe that's my problem."

Sarah turns to him—an eager, intimate look on her face. "What do you mean?"

Luke's not in the mood. He stands up. "I'll clear," he says. "Winch, honey, it's your turn to wash."

Winch feels terrible. He's so stupid! Sarah was always like this about drugs, which is fine, it's her choice—her loss, in his opinion. But he should have known better. Years ago when she'd come to visit Luke at school, Luke would always give Winch his stash for safekeeping, so Sarah wouldn't come across it and be bummed. In those days Luke called her The Schoolmarm—to her face, too; he didn't say it to be mean or anything—and even now Winch thinks it's kind of funny that that's what she ended up being. He'd love to go to work with her one of these days, sit in on her class, but he's already asked and she's already said no.

"Winch, please," she says now. "It's not a big deal. Don't look so hangdog."

He shrugs. "I guess I just have a knack for saying the wrong thing." This is such a pathetic thing to say, he can't believe the words came out of his mouth.

She stands up. "Shall we?"

He knows he should get up, go in and do the dishes. He watches as Sarah gathers up the empty wineglasses; he likes the way she holds them, stems between her fingers, the three bowls just touching each other in her outstretched palm. She picks up the salad bowl with her free hand and turns toward the kitchen, her skirt twisting around her legs for a moment.

"Sarah," he says, but when she turns back he's suddenly embarrassed, doesn't want to say what he was going to say—that he likes her skirt, thinks it looks good on her. "Here," he says, reaching for the salad bowl. "I'll take that."

Sarah wipes up spaghetti sauce spills on the stove while Winch washes and Luke dries. She wishes she hadn't reacted about the acid. Would it be so awful if they did it? Not really—not if she didn't have to be around them. She never wanted to be so conventional; it's crept up on her, all the more insidious because it's so surprising. After she straightened out Josh Gold's misunderstanding this morning, she found herself thinking that maybe she should have changed her name. Sarah Merrill, though—it sounds like a game show hostess.

She turns from the stove and watches Luke and Winch. It's funny how, just looking at them from the back—both of them in jeans, both with fairly short hair—you can tell that Luke's the one with a job and Winch is the drifter. Sarah thinks that Winch would be shocked if he found out about the time she dropped acid. Luke's the only one who knows, though: Luke and her sister, who was there—who made her do it, Sarah's always thought.

Then suddenly Sarah realizes that she's been unfair, blaming Becky. Thinking back now, for the first time in years, the whole episode shifts, as if she were looking through a kaleidoscope and had just realized you could turn the end and get an entirely new view. Sarah was fourteen, Becky barely sixteen: where was it written that Sarah had to accept Becky's offer? She could have done what she'd planned that day, gone to the beach with her friends. She sees now that Becky must have been scared—must have given Sarah the second black pill because she wanted Sarah's company, not to test her. And when they walked home from the park late that afternoon, and Becky took Sarah's hand—couldn't that have been for her own comfort? Remembering that endless walk home, Sarah has always connected the terrible feeling of there being fur growing on her shoulders, of her lips being grotesquely swollen and her eyelids puffy, with the shameful notion that her sister was holding her hand because otherwise Sarah might never find her way home.

"Sarah," Luke says for the third time, and finally she looks at him.

"You were a million miles away," says Winch, and Luke wishes to hell he were alone with his wife. It takes the greatest effort to stay where he is, holding the damned dishtowel, to not cross the kitchen and put his arms around her.

"Are you OK?" Luke says. He puts down the dishtowel and does cross the kitchen, but settles for touching her shoulder.

She appears to be on the verge of tears and although she nods, he feels a kind of panic start up through his legs. He thinks it must be about the acid and he says, "You know what *I* was thinking we should do next weekend?"

Sarah doesn't respond and Luke turns to Winch; he just wants

someone to say "What, Luke?" But Winch has gone goony; his
mouth half-open, he stares at Sarah.

"I was thinking," says Luke—but he wasn't thinking anything. "I
was thinking we should all go to the zoo."

Too late he remembers that Sarah hates zoos—they make her
self-conscious, she says, as if she were in the cage with the animals
watching her. But she smiles and says, "That might be fun," and
Luke's so relieved he just lets it go.

"Oh, man," says Winch. "They've got a great zoo here. I was there
a couple days ago, they have a very cool panda at that zoo. I'll bet
you guys have never even been, have you? That's an excellent idea."

Luke allows himself to wonder what Winch was doing at the zoo
when he's supposed to be looking for a job. Maybe he *was* looking
for a job. Monkey feeder, shit raker, bird man: so many possibilities.

"You know what's weird about pandas," Sarah says. Luke looks at
her. She's smiling—she's got something up her sleeve.

"They don't breed in captivity," Winch says. "I, for one, can't really
blame them."

Sarah shakes her head. "No, listen," she says. "They're huge, right?
Get this: it's not unusual for them to give birth to babies the size of a
stick of butter."

"I think I'm disgusted," says Luke.

Winch goes to the refrigerator, gets out a stick of butter, and
comes over to where Luke and Sarah are standing.

"I don't believe this," Luke says, glancing at Sarah.

Winch takes Luke's hand and puts the butter in it. "I think you
should be ashamed," Winch says. "The animal kingdom is a beautiful part of our world. Who are we to judge its mysterious ways?"

Luke laughs uncomfortably.

"Pet the baby," says Winch.

Luke looks at Sarah and rolls his eyes.

"Pet it," says Winch. He says it again, and Luke strokes his finger
over the waxy paper. It's pleasantly cool and firm.

Winch isn't sure what just happened between Luke and Sarah. She's better, right? It's exhausting, this going back and forth.

"Satisfied?" Luke asks him, making his snorting sound.

Winch takes the butter and taps Luke's shoulder with it. "You sound like a hog, brother," he says. He returns the butter to the refrigerator. When he turns back Luke's staring at him. "What?" Winch says.

"What did you just say?"

Winch tries the snort himself.

Luke turns to look at Sarah, but she's staring at Winch, a disgusted look on her face. Is she disgusted with Winch or with Luke? He didn't mean anything by it—the snort just bugs him.

"You've got this noise you make, man." He does the noise again himself. "Like that."

"He's laughing," Sarah says coldly. She continues to stare at him.

"Well," Winch says, "nice laugh." He feels very peculiar just now —almost as if he were high, only decidedly unrelaxed.

"Well," Sarah says, "we're sorry it bothers you. Is there anything else we can do to make your stay more pleasant? Change the way we cook your dinner, maybe, or how we—"

"Sarah," Luke says, putting his hand on her arm.

She pulls her arm away and leaves the kitchen.

Luke stares at Winch.

"Oops," Winch says.

"Oops?" Luke says. "You say *oops*?"

Winch doesn't know what to say.

Sarah's in the bathroom, door closed, running cold water into the sink for no good reason. She feels reckless, like breaking something—hurling something heavy and expensive through the big living room window. At the same time, she knows that she is someone who could never do something like that. She'd be unable to stop herself from thinking beyond the exhilarating crash to the broken glass on the floor, the room sucking in the cold autumn wind, the repairmen summoned.

There's a knock at the door, and Luke's voice asking her what she's doing.

She reaches into the tub and turns on the hot water. "Taking a bath," she says.

"What?" he calls.

She opens the door a crack. "I'm taking a bath," she says, and closes the door before he can respond.

She's not someone who takes baths, and the tub is not exactly clean, but she finds an old envelope of rose-scented bath salts, puts the rubber disk over the drain, and takes off her clothes.

Luke finds Winch in the living room, his tall frame folded into a low, narrow chair, his elbows held awkwardly at his sides. Luke sits on the couch and with the remote switches on the TV. Someone has turned the volume all the way down, and the football game on the screen seems absurd without the attendant noise—strange green shapes trying to knock over strange white shapes. When he reaches forward to put the remote back on the coffee table, he sees Winch's key right where he left it last night—in the little bowl. Luke fishes the key out and holds it up. "Look familiar?" he says.

Winch nods. "I forgot it this morning."

"I heard." Luke puts the key on the table and slides it toward Winch, but with too much force; the key goes off the table and lands near Winch's foot.

Winch doesn't move for a minute, and Luke's about to reach over and pick it up himself when Winch says, "Maybe you should keep it." He picks up the key and tosses it to Luke.

It's what he's been wanting, but Luke doesn't feel the relief he expected. Instead, he's worried—honestly worried—about what on earth will become of this man. Watching Winch sitting there in the too-small chair, Luke finds himself thinking back to the summer after their junior year, when he and Winch housesat for Winch's advisor in the English department. Luke had been nervous about

accepting Winch's offer of a free place to stay—he saw himself following Winch around, picking up towels and abandoned sandwich
halves, putting coasters under Winch's beer bottles. But Winch was
so excruciatingly fastidious that Luke took to leaving his own bed
unmade, to waiting a day or two to wash dishes, just to keep some
balance in the house. By the end of the summer Luke was wondering whether Winch had decided to abandon his direction—or his lack
thereof—to become, after all, the thing his parents wanted him to
be: someone who wouldn't be ashamed to call himself by his given
name, Lewis Winchell, Jr.; someone who would take the trouble to
graduate with honors; someone who would throw away his half-fin-
ished, water-logged copies of Dickens and Hardy, and move back to
Buffalo, and get a respectable job.

Looking at Winch, Luke wonders, not for the first time, what it's
cost his friend to go on rebelling long past the point where the re-
belled against could possibly give a damn.

In his mind, Winch is drawing a map of the Midwest. He lived in the
Twin Cities for eight or nine months once, but for the life of him he
can't figure out what's on the other side of Minnesota. Montana and
Wyoming and Nebraska, but in what configuration? He's thinking
west might be a good direction, with winter approaching: he likes
the cold. Hitching, he could probably make it to Minneapolis in a
day or two, and he's pretty sure some of the people he knew there
would put him up for a while. And then—the Dakotas! That's what's
west of Minnesota. After Minneapolis he could head for South
Dakota. It's not something he would tell anyone, but he's always
longed to see Mt. Rushmore.

He looks at Luke, who's looking at him. "Got to keep rolling,"
he says.

"Listen," says Luke, "you don't have to be in any hurry to leave."
He leans forward, fiddling with the key. "Tonight was just, you
know, weird. But if you're on to something job-wise, or if you think

Madison's the place for you and you want to work on getting set up here ..." His voice trails off and he shrugs.

"I don't know," Winch says.

"In fact," Luke says, "I know this'll sound strange, but did you ever think of working at a zoo? I was thinking before—I mean, don't you kind of like animals?"

"They're OK," Winch says. He stands up and stretches. It's funny—but sad, too—that Luke of all people would suggest this. Working at the zoo! It's the kind of last-ditch idea people give you when they try to put themselves in your position and can't bear the desperation they feel. One thing Winch can say is that he's never felt desperate. Not ever.

Sarah leaves her clothes on a chair in the bedroom and, in her bathrobe, heads toward the front of the house. She feels like a little girl going to say goodnight to the grown-ups. Then she thinks of Winch saying "You guys are older—maybe that's my problem" and she wonders whether it can be said that any of them are, after all, grown-ups. She and Luke are just doing a better job of pretending.

Winch is squatting next to his backpack, looking through an outside pocket. Luke gives her a look she can't quite read: something's up.

"Taking a bath is kind of nice," she says. She sits next to Luke on the couch.

He leans over. "You smell good," he says. "Sort of like carrot cake."

"Luke." She gives him a friendly push. "Wild rose bath salts."

"They obviously marked it wrong at the factory." He takes her hand and holds it in his lap.

Winch stands up, a tiny red book in his hand. "What's that?" she says, smiling at him.

He won't meet her eye. "My bible."

"His address book," Luke says. "Winch is thinking about moving on."

Sarah looks back at Winch. He holds the address book in his palm and tosses it up just far enough so it can flip over before he catches it again. She moves to stand up, but Luke still has her hand and won't let go. "Winch, you're really welcome to stay," she says. "I apologize for what I said. I—I had a bad day."

He tosses the book again, and again. "Well, I'm thinking I might go back to Minneapolis."

Sarah looks at Luke, who shrugs. "Not right away?" she says. "Not tomorrow?"

"I think tomorrow might be good," Winch says. "Get there by Wednesday night."

"I feel terrible," Sarah says.

"Don't," Winch says.

"No," Luke says, tightening his grip on her hand. "Don't."

They say goodnight to Winch, promising to send him off with a big breakfast. Luke follows Sarah to their bedroom, his hands on her shoulders.

"I do feel terrible," she says, once the door's closed.

"But not that terrible?" Luke says.

She sits on the bed. "I never say things like that to people. I felt so strange afterward—too powerful."

"It's a lot easier being the victim," Luke says. "Isn't it?" He takes off his sweatshirt and jeans and drapes them over a chair. He stretches, yawns. She's got a strange, intense look on her face—as if she were trying very hard to hear something in another room. "You know what?" he says, going over to the bed. "I'm not going to brush my teeth tonight." He gets under the covers; she hasn't moved. "What do you think about that?"

"Vile," she says, standing up. "Disgraceful."

She goes over to the chair where his clothes are and starts picking them up. He's about to tell her that she shouldn't be putting his clothes away when he realizes she's not: she's getting hers out from under them. She shakes out her sweater, folds it, puts it in a drawer. Then she picks up her skirt and shakes it out, too.

"Hey, is that new?" he says. "I like it."

She doesn't say anything for the longest time. She just looks at him. Then she gives him a peculiar smile. "Thanks," she says.

She hangs up the skirt, takes off her robe, and climbs into bed. "What do you suppose he'll do in Minneapolis?" she says.

Luke thinks about it for a while. Over the years he's gotten dozens of postcards from Winch, and from the strangest places, but they never really say anything; they make jokes. The one announcing Winch's imminent arrival came from Texas and featured a man standing next to a giant replica of a ten gallon cowboy hat. On the back Winch had written: "Everyone here's got a swelled head. I tried to get work ropin' cattle but the damn outfit didn't look good on me. Watch your front door."

"Maybe he has a girlfriend there," Sarah says.

"A port in every girl," Luke says. Then, before she can respond: "Sorry." He takes her hand.

"I have a question," she says. "Say—just say—you guys had decided to drop acid this weekend. Where would you have gotten it?"

Luke loves that she said "drop": it's so her. "Well, honey," he says, "a man just knows a thing like that."

"Come on."

"I don't know," he says. Then he remembers something Doug Kaiser told him the last time he was busted. "You know those sneakers you sometimes see hanging from power lines? They're supposed to mark dealers' houses. I guess we could've just knocked on doors until we got lucky."

"What?" Sarah says. "You're kidding. There's a pair outside our house. Jesus."

"Well," Luke says. "It's not me. Is it you?" He rolls onto his side and brings his hand up to touch her hair. "I always had a funny feeling you weren't telling me something."

Winch can't sleep. For one thing, the couch is too short for him—he won't miss it. But he's also got agitation of the brain: he feels like he's just on the edge of understanding something important. He starts running through some of his more long-standing questions; but he still doesn't know why people in the south pretend to be so friendly when they're really not; or why so many women who sit next to him on busses act so cold for the first fifteen minutes and end up pressing legs with him for the better part of the trip; or why, when he gets picked up hitchhiking, guys in hats usually wind up angry at him for some reason. He still doesn't know why six months working outside somewhere is OK while six months indoors cooks his goose. Or why being really cold is kind of pleasant but being really hot is like being visited by a terrible illness. And he still doesn't know why his parents continue to send him money to go home for Christmas, or why he continues to go.

He sits up on the couch, swinging his sleeping-bagged legs onto the coffee table. Thinking of Luke and Sarah, Winch decides that the next time he's in love he will pay closer attention. To make it last maybe all you've got to do is be super vigilant, stand there looking for the small, misleading shapes of problems that are destined to grow. Or maybe what you've got to do is turn your back on them: whistle past those graveyards.

The plastic thing on the cord of his sleeping bag has worked its way into the small of his back. He twists out of the bag altogether and stands up. On tiptoe, he goes to the kitchen and fetches a beer. He waits until he's back in the living room to open it; then he pulls on his jeans and goes out to the porch. He sits on the top step. The cold beer and the wind on his bare chest feel just right. He looks up at the shoes dangling from the wire, and he's happy to find that he no longer really cares what they mean. If he were someone else he might take them as a signal: Walk. But he's going to walk anyway—just because he wants to.

When I entered the ninth grade I had just turned fourteen and I wanted more than anything to be a pompon girl. My desire had formed over the course of the summer: my friends and I customarily ate lunch on the benches near the English office, but during the long idle months I had taken to imagining myself moved as if by magic to the picnic table in front of the snack machines, which was handed down, with all the arrogance and inevitability attached to the turning over of a monarchy, from one pompon squad to the next. Our school colors were red and yellow—crimson and gold, we called them —and by the end of the first day of school the idea of owning one of those short, flip-skirted red and yellow dresses had taken over my mind. The football season pompon girls had shown up in their new outfits, and I was enamored even of the spotless white Keds they wore. Tryouts for the basketball pompon squad weren't until the beginning of October, but within days I had cleared out our garage and claimed it as my practice area. I set up my record player on the shelf where my mother kept the tools, and I listened to all of my albums, over and over again, in an effort to find a song that would inspire me to make up a winning routine. The routine, according to the printed rules I got from the girls' P.E. office, would be composed of a series of "steps"—dance steps, I decided—of my devising. The only fundamental thing about pompon was pompon step itself, a kind of miniature running in place that would form the basis of everyone's routine. The rest was up to me.

One Saturday morning, as I passed through the kitchen on my way to the garage, my mother cleared her throat and said she wanted to talk to me. She was sitting at the table, stacks of envelopes and her big, ledger-style checkbook lined up in front of her. She was paying the bills.

She pulled her reading glasses down onto the tip of her nose and looked up at me. "Found a song yet?" she asked evenly.

"Not yet," I said.

She nodded, and I wondered whether she was finally going to condemn my pompon dreams. So far, she hadn't come out against them—she hadn't, for instance, told me that she thought the whole concept was sexist or exploitative or elitist or even just plain silly—and because of her very neutrality I'd been assuming the worst. It wasn't like her not to comment.

"I got a call last night from Jim Baranski," she said, naming our down-the-street neighbor, who coached basketball at the local college. "One of his players needs a place to live and Jim thought we might let him have the guest room."

"Why would we do that?" I said.

"That's what I asked Jim. I'm not looking to be anybody's frat mother."

"So that was that?"

"The poor guy was supposed to have a full scholarship, but it fell through. If he can't find a place to live for free he's going to have to leave school. Jim says he's willing to do yardwork in exchange for a room."

"If we need yardwork done," I said, "maybe we should just get a gardener."

"We're not exactly rich at this point," my mother said, her voice tight and controlled. She cleared her throat and went on in a friendlier tone. "Jim said it might be nice for Danny to have a guy around. You know, an older guy—someone he could do things with. Play basketball and stuff."

Now I understood; and I understood that she wasn't asking my opinion so much as pleading with me not to say no. My father had died a year earlier, a heart attack at forty-five, and my ten-year-old brother Danny had become a big source of worry to her. He spent all his time in his room, reading Planet of the Apes books and drawing highly detailed maps of outer space. The maps were really good: all the lines were meticulously drawn; the planets were colored in to look like real spheres; and everything was carefully labeled in his tiny, scientist's script.

"When's he moving in?" I said.

"Elizabeth."

"Well?"

She began flipping through the bills. "I told Jim we'd try it for a month. And if any of us doesn't like it that'll be that." She looked up at me, a small, desperate smile on her lips. "His name's Bobby. He's going to bring his things over tomorrow."

"OK."

"Really?"

I forced a smile. "Sure," I said. "It'll be good for Danny." But I thought, a basketball player? It seemed like an insult to my father's memory: he had taught philosophy at the college, and his favorite and only sport had been speed-reading paperback mysteries.

The guest room was right next to my room, and I got up early the next morning to take a last look at it. My room had been decorated —very decorated—according to my specifications six or seven years earlier; it was all pink and white, and whenever I felt the girlishness of it too keenly I would go into the guest room and lie on the bed in there. It was a big, square, airy room, full of plain oak furniture. The only adornment was an elaborate cut glass water pitcher on the dresser; anywhere else it might have looked gaudy, but it was the perfect touch in that austere room.

I stood in the doorway and tried to imagine a college basketball player living next door to me. The room was empty except for when my grandmother came to visit, and although I could never really hear her, I always felt aware of her when she was there—of her breathing, of her sighing, of her rolling over in bed in the middle of the night.

I went down to the garage and, as I had every day for the past two weeks, I worked on my pompon step. It wasn't, I had quickly learned, as easy as it looked. You had to jump from foot to foot, pointing first your left toes, then your right toes, then your left toes, then your right toes, and all the while you had to keep your hands at your waist, but not around your waist: they had to be bent at the knuckles so your fingers and thumbs wouldn't show. It was a little boring, but I didn't mind spending so much time on it because the next thing I had to do was settle on a song and start working on my routine. I knew it would have to involve some kicking, some little flips of the shoulder, and, most important, the splits, and although I'd been stretching every day I could only get down to about eight inches off the ground.

Early in the afternoon, a car came up the driveway and stopped just on the other side of the garage. I turned off my music. A couple of doors slammed; then I heard a deep voice.

"Nice deal, Bobby. Maybe they'll go away a lot and you can have some parties."

"Quiet." His voice was clear and rather high for a man's. "They might be able to hear us."

I lowered the arm of the record player back onto the album I was playing, turned the volume up, and sat down on the garage floor, my bare legs touching the cold concrete. I listened to the muffled sounds of people going back and forth, from car to house, for the next five or ten minutes. After a while the commotion stopped, and I knew my mother and Danny were talking to Bobby and his friend. She had probably offered them iced tea, maybe even sandwiches. The only thing I had with me to read was the pompon tryouts instruction sheet, and I read it through several times, trying to concentrate on all the details—what kind of gloves you were supposed to wear, how long your routine should be, when the winners' names would be posted. There was one paragraph that I kept going back to. It said, "The pompon girls represent everyone at Murphy Junior

High. They are our ambassadors to schools all over the county. Even when they're not in uniform they feel like pompon girls, and it's important that they look that way, too. This means extra special attention to personal hygiene and grooming. Any girl who doesn't know what this means should speak to Mrs. Donovan in the P.E. office as soon as possible."

I didn't know what it meant—I assumed it had something to do either with shaving under your arms or getting your period—but I wasn't about to ask Mrs. Donovan. With my mother I had only recently managed to shut down communication about such things; as far as I was concerned, we had covered what needed to be covered. The occasional appearance on my desk of pamphlets entitled "Your Changing Body" or "A Single Egg" suggested that she disagreed.

Finally, I heard the car starting up again, and I turned the music off in time to hear the low-voiced guy say, "Later, bro."

"See you at practice," Bobby said.

They said a few more things, but in voices pitched so low I couldn't hear them. I imagined they were talking about me: saying how strange it was my mother hadn't made me say hello, that I must be one of those shy girls who couldn't look anybody in the eye. Either that, or they were wondering what I looked like, what color hair I had. What my body was like.

At six Danny came out to tell me dinner was ready.

"What are we having?" I asked.

"Steak," he said. "Baked potatoes with sour cream. Corn on the cob with butter. Chocolate cream pie."

He was joking. All we ever had now was fish. Sometimes she put a sauce called Mock Hollandaise on our vegetables, but usually it was just lemon juice and pepper. There was no salt in the house anymore, no butter.

I laughed. "What'd you read today?"

"I didn't really read."

I turned from him and began stacking my records together.

"She invited him to eat with us," he said.

I didn't reply.

"That guy. Bobby."

I wheeled around. "I know who you mean. What do you think I am, stupid?"

His face turned a delicate shade of pink, the color he used to get when he had a fever. He was wearing a nerdy little plaid shirt with a too-big collar, and his head looked unbearably small to me.

"I'm sorry, Dan," I said. I took hold of his shoulders and pulled him to me. "You're almost as tall as I am, sonny-boy."

"Won't be long now, moony-girl." He pulled away from me and I followed him into the house.

Bobby Johansen was very tall: six foot four, I later learned. His hair was pale blond, almost colorless. He was leaning against the kitchen counter, wearing shorts, and I thought his legs would probably come up to my chest if we stood close.

My mother was washing lettuce. "*Here* she is," she said, as if my whereabouts had been a mystery. "Elizabeth, this is Bobby Johansen."

"Hi," I said. The table was set for four, and my mother had even used cloth placemats; lately even the usual woven straw ones had gone missing more often than not.

"Hey, Elizabeth," he said. "How's it goin'?"

I looked up at him and shrugged. "OK."

He didn't seem to know what to do with his hands. First they were on the counter behind him, then they were clasped in front of his fly, then crossed tightly over his chest. "What do you go by?" he said. "Liz? I've got a cousin Liz, just about your age."

"Elizabeth," I said.

"We used to call her Bit, though," my mother said. "Didn't we, honey?"

"We?" I said.

She pursed her lips. "Danny did. He couldn't say Elizabeth, he said *Elizabit*. Then it was just Bit. Right, Dan?"

"A few hundred years ago," Danny said.

"Well, anyway," my mother said to me. "We were thinking maybe after dinner the four of us could play a game. Monopoly or something."

"Can't," I said. "Math test tomorrow."

My mother yanked a square of paper towel from the roll and began arranging the wet lettuce leaves on it.

"I used to be pretty good at math," Bobby said. "If you need any help."

"That's OK," I said. It was in my mind to say, I'm pretty good at math, too; but I managed to stifle it. "Thanks, though."

There was a silence. I was still holding my records, so I went upstairs to put them in my room. The guest room door was ajar and I pushed it open. A couple of worn-looking green duffel bags were lying on the bed, with T-shirts and sweat clothes and towels spilling out as if they were someone's cast-offs at a garage sale. I tiptoed across the room and opened the closet door. It was empty except for three pairs of high-topped white leather sneakers arranged in a row on the floor. I bent over and picked up a shoe. It was longer than my forearm and it smelled: of dirty laundry and of sweat, but of something else, too—a sharp, leathery scent. It was, I decided, the smell of arrogance.

The following Friday, at the lunch-time rally that was the official end of the school day—during football season we got out early for away-games—I stood by myself and studied the football pompon girls' new routine. They would do it again at half-time later that afternoon, but I wasn't going to the game; none of my friends ever went, and I was too shy to go to an away-game alone. If I'd been asked why I wanted to go, I would only have been able to say that it had something to do with my father dying: that it wasn't the game so much as the way everyone looked after the game as they poured onto the field from the bleachers, uniform expressions of joy or despair on their faces.

I rode my bicycle home through the college, thinking that I would have the house to myself for the afternoon. Students were lying on the grass in little groups, and I looked at them more carefully than usual, wondering if Bobby was among them. I hadn't seen him since the day he moved in. He had a meal plan at one of the dorms and he studied at the library, so all I knew of him so far was the sound of his footsteps on the stairs as I was falling asleep. He didn't even leave his toothbrush in the bathroom.

The guest room door was closed. I went into my room, put my books on my desk, and lay down on my bed. I closed my eyes and waited to see what would materialize—the glittering ballroom, the dark restaurant, the umbrella-shaded outdoor cafe: at that time the arena of my fantasy life was limited to places where I would not be alone with the object of my idylls. After a moment, the restaurant hovered into view. The walls were lined with smoky mirrors, the tables covered with pale pink linen and set with gold-rimmed china. I was tall and sleek in a clingy silver gown sewn all over with shimmering little beads. A handsome, square-jawed man with whom I never, in all the adolescent hours I spent in his company, exchanged a word—met me at the door and guided me to our secluded table, his hand in the small of my back. (I had just learned about the small of your back; it was where you were supposed to aim your tampon, and although that was nearly as unpleasant to think of as it was to do, the idea of that spot had a kind of power over me. It suggested romance—not the candlelight and flowers kind, but something easier, more intimate.)

I heard a noise from Bobby's room. It wasn't much of a noise: low and repetitive and only vaguely vocal. But before I was really even aware of the sound, I'd convinced myself that sex was taking place on the other side of the wall.

I turned my radio on, loud, and sat at my desk looking at my

Latin book, my heart pounding. A moment later I got up and clomped past the guest room and down the stairs. I paused in the kitchen, but the idea of the two of them—Bobby in pajama bottoms, a tousle-haired girl in the matching pajama top—coming down in search of something to drink sent me out to the garage.

Leaning against the wall was a brand-new basketball hoop attached to a backboard. I looked it over for a minute or two: the backboard was white with jaunty red trim; the basket itself was a metal circle from which hung a flimsy-looking white net. I bent my knees and tried to lift it, but it was surprisingly heavy.

"Careful with that, it's heavier than it looks."

I turned around and Bobby was standing in the doorway, his long arms dangling by his sides.

"I was going to put that up for Danny this afternoon," he said. He was wearing gym shorts and a grey T-shirt, and there were big dark stains where he'd been sweating. I must have been staring, because he said, "I was doing sit-ups."

"Danny's not much of an athlete," I said.

"Everyone likes to shoot baskets."

"Does my mother know?"

He gave me a funny look. "She bought it."

I turned from him and examined the hoop again. "These strings don't seem too sturdy," I said.

He laughed and came over to where I was standing. "They're not meant to hold any weight. They hug the ball when it goes through so it'll drop down gently instead of flying all over the court. Stick around while I put it up and I'll show you."

"I have homework," I said.

He nodded. "More math?"

"Latin."

"Can't help you there. The only Latin I know is pig."

I edged toward the door. "Well," I said. "See you later."

"O-say ong-lay," he said with a smile.

A few nights later my mother came into my room on her way to bed. I was rearranging my closet, and she sat at my desk and watched me.

"I guess we should get you a new parka this year," she said.

"This one's OK." I hung it on a hook inside the closet door.

"Maybe a down one," she said. "I was thinking we should go up to Tahoe in February. Try again." When I was eight or nine the four of us had spent a miserable weekend trying to learn to ski; we'd never gone back. My father had liked to say that we were the only family in California who *didn't* love the fact that the mountains were only five hours from the beach.

"Down jackets aren't good for skiing," I said. "Too bulky."

"Elizabeth," she said. "Why do you have to be so difficult?"

I looked at her; her lips were pressed into a narrow line. "I'm not being difficult. I just don't happen to want a down jacket."

"That's not the point," she said. "I mention skiing and you don't react at all. Can't you at least say, 'Yes, Mother dear, a ski trip would be lovely,' or 'No, Mother dear, the idea of trying to ski again makes my legs turn to jelly'?"

I turned back to the closet. Very quietly, I said, "I'll go if you want me to."

"I want you to have an *opinion*."

I shrugged, but suddenly there were tears running down my face. I stared at my clothes.

"Eliz?"

"I can't."

She came over and touched my shoulder and I turned around. "What is it?" she said. She pulled me close and held me, and my shoulders started to shake. "What is it?"

I shook my head.

She ran her hand up and down my back. "Tell me," she said. "Poor baby, to have such a brute of a mother. Tell me."

I pulled away from her, got a Kleenex from my desk, and blew my nose. "Why do you have to get so mad at me?"

"I'm sorry." She sat down on my bed and shook her head. She looked very small, sitting there; small and tired. There were wrinkles around her eyes and mouth, and her hair looked thin and lifeless.

I heard the sound of someone—Bobby—opening and closing the front door and coming up the stairs. A moment later, the guest room door closed.

"I'm sorry," my mother said again. "I'll try to be better."

I held my forefinger up to my lips, then pointed at the wall dividing my room from Bobby's. *He can hear us*, I mouthed.

She smiled at me. "He doesn't care," she whispered.

"Well," I whispered back, "I do."

With the coming of the basketball hoop Bobby was around more, and I had to find a new place to work on my pompon routine. I moved down to the basement, and against the muffled yet insistent sounds of the basketball bouncing on the asphalt and—thud—hitting the backboard, I settled on the Beach Boys' "I Get Around," and began to choreograph my moves.

Late one afternoon, when my routine was going badly and the Beach Boys' falsettos were all but drowned out by the hammer of the basketball, I decided that I'd had enough. I marched up the stairs and out to the driveway, icily polite equivalents to WILL YOU PLEASE SHUT UP running through my mind. But when I saw Danny standing there looking at the ball, which seemed bigger around than he was, I couldn't say anything. I watched.

"OK," Bobby said, glancing at me, "dribble a couple of times and then when you shoot try for some backspin." He held his hand up, palm to the sky, and flicked his wrist a couple of times. "Roll the ball up your fingers."

Danny bounced the ball, then threw it at the basket; it hit the rim with a metallic clang and careened past me. I turned and ran after it, then carried it back and handed it to Bobby.

"Want to try?" he said.

I shook my head.

He gave the ball back to Danny. "That was better," he said. "Try again."

On the fifth shot, the ball hit the backboard, rolled around the rim, and went through the net. "Great," Bobby said, giving Danny's shoulder a little shake. "That's the stuff."

He took the ball and without looking at me backed up so that he was standing just a few feet from me. Without seeming to aim, he tossed the ball and it sailed through the air and went cleanly through the basket without touching the backboard or the rim. "Swish," he said.

Danny caught the ball and came running over. "Can we play HORSE?" he said.

Bobby looked at me and smiled. "Only if your sister will try a shot first."

"Blackmailer," I said.

Danny handed me the ball and I moved closer to the basket. I held the ball in front of my face, closed my eyes, and threw.

"Two points," Bobby yelled. "Whoo!"

Danny clapped and called, "Maybe you should try out to *play* instead."

"Ha ha," I said. I tugged at my shirt, which had ridden up and exposed my stomach when I threw the ball.

"Play HORSE with us," Danny said. "Please?"

"HORSE?" I glanced at Bobby; he stood there with the ball tucked under his arm, looking at me. "I don't think so, Dan."

"You don't even know what it is. Let me at least explain it to you." Danny held out his hands and Bobby threw him the ball. He bounced it and looked up at the basket. "Say I go first. I stand wherever I want and try for a basket. If I make it, the next person has to stand in the same spot and shoot. And if they don't make it they get an H. And you keep moving around and whoever spells out HORSE first loses. Get it? They're a horse. Come on, it's fun."

"Sorry, kid," I said. "Got to practice. I have no time for this 'fun' of which you speak."

"Your graciousness," he said, and bowed to me.

"Your majesty," I said, bowing back.

I turned and headed for the house. "Bye, Elizabeth," Bobby called to me as I reached the kitchen door. "Nice to see you again."

I needed some white gloves. My mother had said not to worry; she had several pairs I could choose from. The Saturday before tryouts I asked her to let me see them.

She led me up to her bedroom and pulled a shoebox from the back of her closet. "I know you can't believe it," she said, "but your mother used to be the picture of elegance."

We both laughed; she was wearing blue jeans and an old checked shirt, her usual weekend attire. Even when she went to work I thought she looked a little mannish—she dressed in somber colors, never wore jewelry.

She slipped the top off the box and pulled away some tissue paper. "God," she said.

I looked into the box, and it was a strange sight: over a dozen gloves, some white, some beige, even a single navy blue one, all lying in a tangle. "How orderly," I said.

"Don't give me any lip, kid," she said, smiling. She set the box on the bed and we began sorting through it, putting the gloves in pairs.

"Where's the other blue one?" I said.

"Long gone." A dreamy look came over her face and for a moment I thought she was going to tell me a story. But all she said was "Lost to another era."

There were four pairs of white gloves in all, but none of them seemed right to me.

"What's wrong with these, Elizabeth?"

"The rules didn't say anything about buttons."

"Well, what about these?"

"There's a huge stain on the left one."

"It's on the palm, no one'll see it."

"Mom."

"These?"

"Too long."

Finally she sat on the bed and looked at me, her mouth in a half-frown.

"I'll ride over to the shopping center and buy some," I said. I began piling the gloves back into the box.

She grabbed my wrist. "Elizabeth, for God's sake, you're only going to wear them for ten minutes."

I shook her hand off. "I want to look nice."

She stood up and cut me a disgusted look, then stalked out of the room. I hurried after her and caught up with her on the stairs.

"Why shouldn't I get new gloves?" I said. "What do you care? I'll pay for them."

"I don't care," she snapped.

"Mom," I said.

We reached the bottom of the stairs and she turned to face me. "It's just so silly, Elizabeth," she said quietly. "It's beneath you."

I opened my mouth, but nothing came out.

"Your father would—"

"Well lucky for me he's not here to see it!" I jerked open the front door and hurried out of the house. My bicycle was locked, and I had to twist the dial several times before I got the lock to open.

Twenty minutes later I was at the shopping center—without a cent. I decided to look around anyway; when I found the gloves I wanted I would ask the saleslady to hold them for me, then go back home for my wallet.

I went into Penney's and found the glove department. There was no one behind the counter, so I circled the glass case, looking. There were leather gloves and wool gloves and gloves made of bright red satin, but I couldn't find a single pair of white gloves.

"Can I help you?"

A woman stood behind the counter, blue hair piled on top of her head. I told her what I wanted and she said, "Oh, we haven't carried white gloves in ten years, dear. Is it for Halloween?"

"Um, no."

"Prom?" she asked, cocking her head gaily.

"No, I just need them for school."

She raised her eyebrows. "School play?"

"No, I—thanks anyway." I turned and hurried away.

"You might try Peaches and Cream, dear," she called after me.

I got outside the store and leaned against the wall. My face felt hot. At the other end of the shopping center was Bullock's, where my mother took me twice a year for school clothes. I decided to go there first, even though Peaches and Cream was on the way; Peaches and Cream was a shop full of breakable knickknacks and precious little silk flower arrangements, and although I'd never been in it I had always held it in a kind of contempt: it seemed to have nothing to do with real life.

But Bullock's didn't have white gloves, either. I wandered around the ground floor of the store, and, as if I were languishing in a boat on a hot day and needed the feel of the water, my hand trailed behind me, touching whatever I passed: wool, leather, chrome. In the makeup department I slowed even more, studying the nail polish and lipstick at first one counter, then another. A young woman in a salmon-colored lab coat caught my eye.

"Free makeovers today," she said. "Would you like one?"

"I don't have any money," I said.

"They're *free*."

"But I won't be able to buy anything after."

She patted the seat of a chair set against one of the counters. "You'll feel better."

I glanced around the area; it was nearly empty. I climbed onto the chair.

"I'm Kristen," she said. "Tell me a little about what you usually wear. Makeup-wise, I mean."

"Oh, just a little eyeshadow and lip gloss," I said, although in truth I never wore a stroke of either.

"What's your name, honey?"

"Elizabeth."

"Well, Elizabeth, I'm going to start with a little foundation." She unscrewed the top of a small white bottle, tipped some liquid onto her fingers, and began dabbing the stuff onto my face.

Another salmon-coated woman appeared. "Oh, *fun*," she said. "Wild Sage on her lids, don't you think?"

"I was thinking Midnight Velvet," Kristen said.

They joined forces. They mixed colors. They tried a little of this and a little of that. Half an hour later Kristen offered me a hand mirror. "You're going to love this, Elizabeth," she said.

I searched the image for signs of myself, but I looked like a stranger —not just someone I didn't recognize, but someone who wasn't quite human. My cheeks had unnatural-looking hollows, and across each cheekbone was a slash of pink. They had used so much mascara it looked as if I were wearing false eyelashes.

"Well?" Kristen said.

"She has to get used to it," the other woman said. "It's a change."

I handed Kristen the mirror. "It's a whole new me."

She gave me a wide smile. "I knew you'd like it."

I thanked them and left the store. There were some benches arranged around a fountain and I slumped onto one. I closed my eyes and felt the sun on my hair and skin. My face felt odd, as if I'd washed it and let it dry without rinsing the soap off. I thought about the pompon tryouts instruction sheet, the part about hygiene and grooming. I wondered whether everyone else would be wearing a lot of makeup for the tryouts: I knew that the other girls who were trying out were the kind who *did* wear eyeshadow and lip gloss to school every day. I imagined myself in the girls' gym on the day of the tryouts, standing there in my forest green polyester one-piece gymsuit and my white gloves, waiting for my turn; my stomach did a queasy dance. Then I thought about what my mother had said, and I stood up, ready to try Peaches and Cream.

And there was Bobby.

He was coming toward me, but he hadn't seen me yet. I thought of running, but I knew that would attract more attention than anything. Hoping I would somehow be invisible to him, I sat down on the bench again and stared at the ground.

"Elizabeth?"

I looked up. "Hi."

He did a quick double-take, so subtle that if I hadn't been looking for his reaction I might not have noticed it. "What are you doing?" He put his foot up on the bench next to me.

"Shopping."

"What have you bought? I need socks."

"Nothing," I said. "I forgot my wallet."

He laughed. "Window shopping, more like, huh?" He turned and sat on the bench, a few feet away from me.

"I guess so."

We sat there staring straight ahead, not talking. I was certain that he thought I was the most pathetic person on earth, that he felt too sorry for me to make a get-away.

"So," he said.

"So," I said.

"Can I ask you a question?"

I turned to look at him.

"What happened to your face?"

I felt, surprisingly, that I had a choice: I could die of embarrassment or not, it was up to me. I smiled, and a moment later we were both laughing. "I had a make-over," I said.

"In there?"

I nodded. "There were two of them, Kristen and someone else. It took half an hour. It was free."

"What a bargain," he said, and we both laughed. "I don't know, I think Kristen and her friend are in the wrong line of work."

"What?! You don't think they're artists?" I stood up and struck a pose.

"More like morticians."

"So that's why I couldn't recognize myself in the mirror. I look dead."

We both started to laugh again, but a shadow of unhappiness fell over me and although I kept laughing, I was thinking about my father; we'd had an open casket, against my wishes, and when I saw him lying there, a false rosiness on his waxy cheeks, I felt a tiny pinprick of shock, as if I had to learn all over again of his death.

I looked at Bobby and he was biting his lip. He smiled quickly and stood up.

"Maybe I could help you buy your socks," I said. "I mean, I'm sure you don't need help, but maybe I could go with you."

"Actually," he said, "I do need help. I can never decide on colors. Red and yellow or blue and green."

"You wear red socks?"

"No, no," he said, laughing, "the bands on top. I need tube socks. For practice." He dribbled an imaginary basketball, then shot it into the sky.

"Would you like to go to a movie tonight?" my mother said at dinner that evening. I'd been back and forth to the shopping center until the middle of the afternoon—I'd finally found some gloves at Peaches and Cream—and since I'd gotten home she and I had been distant and polite when we'd seen each other, as if we were strangers whose paths kept crossing in some foreign city.

"No, thank you," I said. "I've got to spend some time on things that are beneath me."

She colored, and Danny looked down at his plate. "I'm sorry, honey," she said. "I didn't mean it, it was a dumb thing to say. I just don't want you to be disappointed."

"When I don't make it?" I asked, standing up to clear the table.

Danny all but leapt from his chair and hurried from the room.

"Oh," my mother said quietly, and covered her mouth with her hand. She shook her head, and I could see she was fighting tears. After a moment she turned and faced the door, following Danny's path with her eyes. "Should I—"

I went over to her and held her head to my chest. "He's OK," I said. "I think we should just leave him alone."

"The old laissez-faire attitude was never my strong suit," she said. The vibrations her jaw made against my stomach as she spoke felt strange. She sighed and put her hands on my hips and I moved away. She looked up at me. "Show us your dance, honey," she said. "I think it would mean a lot to Danny."

I nodded. *Dance*, I thought.

"And to me, too, of course."

"Tomorrow," I said.

But the next day, a Sunday, Danny had been invited by a friend's family to go to San Francisco, and it wasn't until Monday night, just two days before tryouts, that I allowed my mother and Danny into the basement to watch me run through my routine.

"OK," I said when we got downstairs, "I'm going to pretend you guys are the judges."

Danny had perched on the washing machine. My mother leaned against the dryer. "How many are there?" she said uneasily.

"Six," I said. There would be Mrs. Donovan; Coach Simpson; Sally Chin, the head pompon girl for the football season; two guys from the basketball team; and Miss Rosenthal, a Home Ec teacher— *my* Home Ec teacher, as it happened, and it was she who worried me most. We had somehow, already, not hit it off; the other girls in the class were already on their A-line skirts, but I just couldn't finish my pot holder. I was afraid she would take it out on me in the judging.

"Six?" my mother said.

"The competition is going to be tough," Danny said. "We've got some very critical judges, ladies and gentlemen, and only five of these fifty beautiful young ladies will be selected. Sam, tell us a little about how the competition works."

"Fifty!" my mother said.

"He's joking, Mom. It's twenty-two."

"Oh, that's not so bad," my mother said. "Five out of twenty-two." But she looked unhappy.

"And now, from our own Manzanita Drive, it's Elizabeth Earle," Danny shouted.

"Quiet," my mother said, elbowing him.

I winked at Danny and turned to start the music. I stood with my back to them, my hands at my waist, my right knee bent. Then, on cue, I whipped around and started the routine.

It was the first time I had done it in front of anyone, and the thing I was most conscious of was the fact that I could not keep a smile on my face: Smile, I would tell myself, and my lips would slide open, and I would think about the kick I was doing (was my knee straight? were my toes pointed?) and I would realize my mouth was twisted into a tight knot again.

I finished with the splits, my arms upstretched in a V for Victory.

"Yes," Danny cried, leaping off the washing machine. He high-fived me and ran up the stairs to the kitchen.

My mother smiled at me. "Very nice," she said.

I sighed and turned around.

"Really, honey," she said. "It's good—you got all the way down on your splits. I'll bet most of the other girls can't do that."

Danny came running back down the stairs, waving a piece of paper on which he'd written "9.9" with a thick pen. "An amazing routine from Elizabeth Earle," he cried.

"Thanks, Dan." I looked at my mother. "Well, it'll all be over in two days."

"Who knows?" she said. "Maybe it'll just be beginning."

They went upstairs while I took the record off the turntable and put it back in its paper sleeve. I wiped my sweaty palms off on my shorts—I'd decided not to wear the gloves for practicing, to keep them clean—then I turned the basement light off and climbed the stairs.

My mother and Bobby were sitting at the kitchen table. When my mother saw me she said, "Elizabeth's got her tryouts day after tomorrow."

Bobby looked at me. "Nervous?"

I nodded.

"Twenty-two girls are trying out for five spots," my mother said.

"OK, Mom." I looked at Bobby's feet. "Are you wearing your new socks?"

He pulled up one leg of his jeans to display the bright red and yellow bands around the top of his sock. "Listen," he said, "try not to be too nervous. It'll show, and that'll be the thing that gets you. Know what I mean?" He turned to my mother. "They totally watch for whether the girl has the right look. You know, smiley, bouncy. Believe me, I was once a judge for one of these things."

"Maybe you should do your routine for Bobby," my mother said.

"Absolutely not." His words had sent my heartbeat out of control. Eyeshadow and lip gloss, I thought, like it or not.

"Please?" he said.

I shook my head.

"Well, just remember," he said. "You've got to smile."

I felt my face fill with color.

My mother coughed and said, "You know, honey, you did look a little fierce down there."

I gave them a frozen grin. "Like this?" I said through clenched teeth.

"That's the one," Bobby said. "Glue it on."

"Goodnight," I said. Without looking at either of them, I got myself a glass of water and climbed the stairs.

"Elizabeth?" Danny called from his room.

I stopped in his doorway. He was lying on his bed, our giant world atlas open in front of him. "Planning a trip?" I asked. I sat down next to him and glanced at the atlas; it was open to a page showing the whole of Africa. "They say Morocco is nice this time of year."

"It was good," he said. "I'm sure you'll make it."

I shrugged. "Not according to Mr. Basketball down there."

"What did he say?"

"Nothing. I can just tell. He thinks I'm not pretty enough."

"God," Danny said. "He does not. You are so puerile sometimes."

"Puerile?" I laughed and reached over to tickle his neck. "Little Mr. Vocabulary."

"Don't call me little." He scrambled off the bed and assumed a body-builder's stance. Then he put his hands on his hips and began mimicking my pompon kicks. "Do they have pompon girls in Morocco?"

"Danny!"

He started wiggling around, his arms snaking out from his sides. "I'm a Moroccan pompon girl," he said. "Elizabethahad Earlakim."

"Danny," I said. "Stop, tell me the truth. Did I look fierce?"

Of course I didn't make it. Ten or twelve years later, at parties, I would offer up the comic spectacle of myself standing in the girls' gym, my back to the judges, my eyelids powder blue, my white-gloved hands clenched into fists, my right knee bent: my hopeful, embarrassed self waiting for the music to start. I would say that as I slid down into the splits at the end, my arms in their V, I caught Miss Rosenthal's eye and mistook her horsey grin for congratulations on a job well done, when in fact she was trying to get me to smile. I would perhaps also say—although this wasn't true, I was far too nervous for such fancies—that as I stood in the locker room changing out of my gymsuit, I had a triumphant vision of myself on the floor of the basketball court at half-time, facing the crowded bleachers in my crimson and gold dress, and that I felt a thrill of fear at the idea of doing something so marvelously alien. I would say, in closing, that I was lucky: no one could admit to actually having been a pompon girl. The cachet was in having wanted to, and failed.

Here's what I never said: After the list was posted I telephoned my mother to come pick me up; it was nearly six o'clock and the afternoon light was fading. I was sitting on the curb in the parking lot hoping that Bobby wouldn't be around when I got home, when the memory of my mother's voice came to me. "Your father would—" it said. Your father would, your father would . . . And I was filled with sickness because I realized that she might have been wrong. Wouldn't he, after all, have been on my side? What would he have thought? *Well lucky for me he isn't here to see it.*

A little while later my mother arrived; neither of us spoke on the way home.

As we turned into our street, I saw that Danny and Bobby were outside the house, shooting baskets. "No," I said, turning to her. "Oh, please."

"What?" She put her foot on the brake.

"I can't face him right now. Can't we go to the store or something?"

"You look fine, honey."

"Mom," I said. "It's not how I look. He'll think I'm such a loser. He'll try to get me to play basketball. Please."

She steered the car to the curb and cut the engine. She turned to face me. "You don't get it, do you?" she said. "He doesn't think you're a loser. He's scared of you."

"Bobby?"

"Terrified. You're what's standing between him and a place to live. Next week his month is up, and if we say he can't stay he's in big trouble. He's scared you want him out."

My mouth fell open. "He told you this?"

"Elizabeth," she said. "Believe me. No, he didn't tell me, but I know. You can be—formidable."

I looked out the window at our house. Dusk was coming on quickly now, but still they played. I watched Danny make three baskets in a row. Then Bobby took the ball, backed up to the foot of the driveway, and drove in for a lay-up. "That was a good shot," I said. I turned back to my mother.

She had picked up my gloves, which I'd thrown onto the seat between us, and was pulling them on. She held her hands up in front of her face and looked at them. Then she reached out and ran her finger down my cheek, a soft, velvety touch. "I'm sorry you didn't win," she said.

I sat without speaking for a while. Then I took her hand and pulled at the fingertip of the glove. "What am I going to do with these?"

"I know of this shoebox," she said. She smiled at me; then she started the car and drove the last hundred yards to our house.

When they saw us, Danny and Bobby stopped playing. I got out of the car, and for a moment neither of them said anything. Then Bobby said, "I'm sorry, Elizabeth—it's too bad." He brushed the hair off his forehead and I could see he was trying to think of something to add.

"Thanks," I said.

Danny bounced the basketball a couple of times. Without quite looking at me he said, "We could play one game of HORSE before dinner."

"I'm kind of tired, Dan."

He bounced the ball again.

"We could just play GOAT," Bobby said. "That would be quicker."

"Or DOG," Danny said, smiling.

I set my books on the trunk of the car. "Jeez, guys—I'm not in a hurry. Let's play RHINOCEROS."

"All right," Danny said, jumping up and down. "You'll play."

I looked at Bobby and we exchanged an amused smile.

"I know," Danny went on. "I have a great idea. Let's play ANTI-DISESTABLISHMENTARIANISM."

"What?" Bobby said.

"Antidisestablishmentarianism," Danny said. "It's the longest word in the English language."

That was something he'd gotten from our father. As a game at dinner we used to have these sort of spelling bees, and Danny always insisted that the longer a word was, the harder it would be to spell; our father gave him "antidisestablishmentarianism" once to show that he was wrong.

"Danny," I said, "spell 'puerile.'"

"Hold on, you two," said Bobby. "I think it has to be an animal."

Thomas picked our house because of the view, but there is something cruel in it to me: the sliding glass doors, the redwood deck, that sudden plunge of green; you could die falling out of our view. We live on a steep hill about an hour's drive south of San Francisco, and way below us, in the muted colors of a lovely old rug, is a sweep of neighborhoods and highways and trees that reaches all the way to the silver strand of the Bay. We have floor to ceiling windows on three sides, pristine white walls, and exposed beams, and there are rugs for warmth and a big, open fireplace. But it's a chilling house to live in. A man killed himself here.

It's seven o'clock and Thomas is up and gone. He's working very hard these first few months; he says he'll cut back a little once he gets his footing. This is something of a pun: his new job is to manage the finances of a company called ColoRun, which is about to introduce into the marketplace a revolutionary new running shoe.

I'm smoothing the bedspread over our bed when I hear Jenny calling for me. Her room is on the side of the house and looks onto a small clearing; most mornings I find her standing in her crib, looking out the window at one of the small delights of our life here: a rabbit trembling in the wet grass, a deer moving along the edge of the woods. Today, though, she's still lying down.

"Mommy," she says, reaching for me. "Up."

I lift her as if she's still a baby and that dependent on me; in fact, she just turned two.

"Eskimo kiss me," she says, butting at me with her nose. When I lean toward her, though, she wriggles loose and starts to sing a little song she made up a few days ago: "Mommy, Mommy. Mommy and Tommy. Tommy, Tommy. Tommy and Mommy." Although I've never told her to and I'm sure she doesn't yet understand that he isn't her father, she has always called Thomas Thomas. Now there's a little boy down the street named Tommy, and this coincidence has been a source of intrigue and delight to her.

"Thomas went to work," I say. I go to her dresser and pull open a drawer. "What are you going to wear today, Jenny?" Without hesitation she comes over and reaches for her yellow overalls. It amazes me, how clearly she knows what she wants.

In the kitchen, I settle her into her highchair, then slice a banana onto her tray. "Breakfast," I say.

I pour myself a cup of coffee and when I see that she's eating contentedly, I wander out of the kitchen and through the living room, to the doorway of Thomas's study. At some point every morning I seem to end up at this spot, staring at the magazines and papers on his desk, looking for last night's old-fashioned glass or tea mug and hoping to learn from these artifacts how he is doing, to discover just who it is I have married.

I'm standing at the door eyeing a yellow pad on which he has scribbled half a page of notes, when suddenly the feeling comes over me—like the floor has vanished from beneath my feet and I am falling.

Where? How?

I wheel around, expecting a vision, an answer.

Did his wife find him?

My heart is beating too fast. I try to fix my concentration on the sliding glass door that leads to the deck: through the glass I can see that the early-morning fog is thinning and the sky is turning a watery shade of blue.

Thomas tried to joke me out of it at first. "In the billiard room with a lead pipe," he would say when I brought it up. "Colonel Mustard in the hall with a revolver." I'd laugh, but I would never be able to stop myself from reminding him—as if he didn't know it all too well—that we knew *who* did it. Not Colonel Mustard, not Miss

Scarlett, but a man of our time. A man defined to us by an act that
must have undefined him to everyone who thought they knew him.
We have lived in his house for seven weeks now. We have been married for sixteen.

"Mommy," Jenny calls from the kitchen. "Mommy!"

"I'm coming," I call back. You'll never know, I tell myself. It's not
something you'll ever know.

Jenny's father didn't want to be her father, or perhaps it was my husband he didn't want to be; I told him about her at a Chinese restaurant in the college town neither of us had managed yet to leave, and
he lowered his forehead into his palms and shook his head. His face
was as crimson as if I had shouted at him, or he at me, but for the
longest time he didn't say a word. Finally he called the waitress over
and asked for the check; she had to make room for it among the
plates of untouched food. It was anchored on its little tray by two
fortune cookies, and I thought, He won't open his, and he didn't.

I went home to have the baby and ended up staying for well over
a year; I began to feel guilty, but every time I suggested that I should
get a job, that Jenny and I should move into our own place, my parents would get twin hurt looks on their faces and my mother would
say, "But Claire, we're your parents," and my father would say,
"We want to help you," and then together, in their uncanny uni-
son, "It's our pleasure to have you here." And I know it was. But
somehow—perhaps because I'm their only child, born when they
were both nearly forty—although they've always made me feel
loved, I've never quite felt a part of them; they've got those twelve
years of history on me. When my mother's sister invited me and
Jenny to use her apartment in Rome for a month, I think we were
all relieved.

The airport in Rome was dizzying—everyone rushing around,
dark and full of purpose. With Jenny on my hip I had managed to
maneuver us and the metal luggage cart on which I'd piled our

suitcases into a corner, and I was feeling in my purse for the envelope of lire my father had given me, and going over and over in my mind the phrase of Italian I'd memorized to give the taxi driver, when Thomas saw us. He told me later that it was my calmness that attracted him, but I know he was teasing me: I've always thought it was a vision of himself as my white knight that made him follow me and, only two months later, marry me.

How marvelous, how mysterious, how brave! people exclaim. It must have been like marrying a stranger! And of course it was; but that stranger is the man I live with, and to my astonishment he isn't much clearer to me now than he was on the day we stood in front of the justice of the peace and he said those words to me: I, Thomas. I thought we would live inside each other; but we live next to each other, in a glass house.

On Saturdays Thomas is a family man. We go to the San Francisco zoo, we drive down to the Bay to feed the gulls, we cross the mountains to walk along the cold edge of the Pacific.

Driving back from the beach today, we took a new road. When we were back on our side of the mountains and nearly home we came around a sharp bend and through a space between the pines I saw a huge, sunlit meadow and a big yellow house. It was gone so quickly and the pines were so thick along the side of the road, I wasn't quite sure what I'd seen. I asked Thomas to turn back. He drove slowly, and when we came to the break in the trees he pulled over and we got out of the car.

I have seen grander houses, but perhaps none so perfect. It was set way back in the meadow, a house the color of yellow roses, with white shutters on every window, a chimney at both ends of the roof, a garden on one side, and, in the middle of the meadow, a quivering green pond. It was absolutely still, enclosed by woods, a house someone must have invented in a dream, then found through sheer force of will. I looked at Thomas and I was terrified that he would

say something and terrified that he wouldn't. Then Jenny woke
from her nap in the back seat of the car and called for me, and it
was over.

It's black out. I can see the lights of the valley, then the absence of
lights that is the Bay. The remains of Thomas's chili dinner are still
on the table. Jenny has been quiet for half an hour now, so she's
asleep. We are lying on the rug, playing gin rummy.

"It was beautiful," Thomas says.

"What?"

"That house this afternoon."

Ah, I think, at last, at last. I look up, expecting to lock eyes with
him, for this moment to be the beginning of something. But he's
staring at his hand, rearranging cards.

"Thomas!" I exclaim. "How did you— I was just thinking about
that house."

"I know," he says, shrugging. "That's why I said it."

"You knew?"

"Sure. Is that such a big deal?"

"Oh, Thomas," I say. "Imagine if we lived there."

He is silent.

"I could have an herb garden, and Jenny would have all that space
to play in."

"We have a house," he says.

I stand and walk to the window, peer out into the night. Without
even touching it, I can tell how cold the glass is. I turn around. "He
could have hung himself from that beam," I say. "How can you not
care? He could have shot himself, there could be bloodstains under
the paint!" I run into the kitchen and start cleaning, putting the
sour cream away, finding a Baggie for the unused half of the onion.
But there on the cutting board is a long, sharp knife, and I can't
bear the sight of it. I turn to find Thomas standing in the doorway.
He holds his arms out for me, and I think, No, it's only a body to
hide against; but it's no use, I'm already there.

He's been bringing me flowers—pink roses one day, lavender freesia the next. I'm running out of vases and still he brings them, splashing the house with color and scent. He hands them to me sheepishly, as if each bunch in its waxy green paper is a specific apology. But for what? It's like Italy again, all those small gifts—wallets stamped with gold fleur de lis, silk scarves in rich reds and browns. I'd open them with exaggerated care, thinking it was all practice for the day he'd hand me his soul wrapped in white tissue paper and I'd peel away the layers and know I was holding something I was meant to keep.

"It's because I'm working too much, isn't it?" Thomas says.

I knew he was awake. I've been awake for hours. It's three or four in the morning, the dead center of the night, and I've been imagining the things I could do if I got up: write a letter to my parents, get out the sewing machine and work on the dress I'm making Jenny, look through recipes for something Thomas might especially like. I've been picturing myself doing each of these things, then finding reasons to reject them, but the real reason I don't move is that I simply can't.

He puts a hand on my shoulder. "Am I right?" he says. "Is that what's bothering you? I'll slow down after the New Year, I promise."

I want to answer him, but I can't think of the right thing to say.

"Claire?" He pulls me into his arms. "Claire?"

"When you married Beth did you have a feeling in the back of your mind that it might not work? Did you say to yourself, Well, we can always get divorced?"

He laughs. "Of course not. What kind of way to get married would that be?"

I lie still. I can feel his heart beating against my shoulder. He doesn't like to talk to me about Beth; he'll answer questions if I press him, but then he always changes the subject. He says he doesn't understand what it is I'm trying to find out. I'm not sure either—just that I'll know it when I hear it.

"Do you want me to say I had some sense of predestination about you?" he says. He presses his lips to my forehead. "Beth and I were happy together for a while, and then we weren't. There's not much more to it than that."

I wonder what she thought. From what distance she saw it coming, and whether she turned from the sight of its approach, or welcomed it because she had always known it was just a matter of time. I've never met her, never so much as seen a picture of her, but I'd like just once to witness her, to watch her for a few minutes from a distance. I think that would tell me something.

He reaches a hand up and touches my hair. "Try to relax," he says. "Try to sleep."

I'm cleaning. Room by room. I bought huge, budget-sized containers of ammonia and Fantastik, and a package of bright green sponges, each one bigger than my hand. The sharp, chemical smells please me. We had the house professionally cleaned and painted before we moved in, but there's something about doing it yourself—getting down on your knees and scrubbing until your elbow aches. Thomas says it's like a dog leaving his mark, but in reverse.

"Thomish," Jenny says, stretching her arms up from the living room floor where she and I sit among building blocks. It is dusk, the time of day when I feel loneliest, when the sky is a thick, dark purple, but not so dark that I can't see the black shapes of the trees.

He swoops her up and down, way up and down, then gently sets her back on the floor. It's my turn. I stand, and he kisses me once, twice. "And what did you do today?" he asks as he moves into the kitchen to make our drinks. This is how it always is, the unfolding of ritual. This is how it's supposed to be.

Today, though, I have news. "I met a woman," I begin when he returns, and he smiles too soon; he wishes I would make a friend and I wish I didn't understand this to mean that he cannot be the friend he thinks I need. "Down at the Safeway," I say. She tapped me on the shoulder, a tall, grey-haired woman in a red silk blouse, and introduced herself, saying she recognized me from the neighborhood, saying with an ironic laugh that she was sorry she hadn't come over with a casserole or something.

"She knew them," I say.

"Knew who?" He has turned from me slightly; he is glancing longingly at the headlines of the afternoon paper.

"The people," I say. "The man."

He nods, still looking away, but I have his attention now.

"He was a judge. John Mehring. He was forty-one."

Thomas is forty. He looks up at me, his wide, clear brow etched with three deep wrinkles, wrinkles that are there even when his face is at peace. "Really," he says, and it is not a question.

I pick up Jenny. "He wants his dinner," I say, bouncing her a little, "and it's bed-time for you."

I have pot roast for him tonight, and he is very sure to praise it, it's perfect, the salad is perfect, the perfect dinner, the perfect home.

We do the dishes together, not talking, but when the water is off he takes my hands and says he is sorry he ever told me about the man. It was something the realtor accidentally let slip—the people who owned the house right before us didn't even know.

"Of course you should have told me," I say. "It would have been worse if you hadn't."

"Worse how? You'd be better off not knowing."

I pull my hands from his. "You don't understand," I say. I turn from him and start sponging off the counter. He stays still for so long I wonder whether he's waiting for me to speak. Finally he touches my wrist, and I look up at him.

"Maybe I don't," he says, "but I'd like to."

"Don't you see?" I say. "If you hadn't told me, it would have been between us." I press my lips together; I'm afraid I might cry.

"Claire," he says.

His eyes are red with fatigue, and for a moment I can see how it must be for him, wondering how his wife can spend day after day thinking about something he hasn't lost a minute to. I raise my hands to his neck, slipping the fingers of one hand into his collar, sliding the others along the soft skin under his hair. He lifts his hands and takes hold of my shoulders, but gingerly, as if they might be hot to the touch.

He never asks me about Jenny's father. That's how he refers to him when he has to mention him: Jenny's father. As if he doesn't know his name. It's rubbed off on me, so that I rarely think *Ben*. I rarely see him in my mind's eye, the way I used to during the months at my parents', when I would sit out by the pool in my navy blue maternity bathing suit and imagine that in five or ten minutes he'd come around the side of the house carrying a six-pack of beer and a dog-eared paperback. It got so I would tense up with waiting for him, with the expectation of seeing him in one of his ripped T-shirts, his bony bare feet.

I found a morning playgroup for Jenny; today is her first day. I was planning to stay, to sit on the sidelines in case she needed me, but the woman who runs the group told me it would be harder that way. For both of us, she said.

So I'm on my way to town. I would have preferred to take a walk until the playgroup was over, but there are no sidewalks up in our neighborhood—just gravel shoulders, and small cars whipping the curves. It's October, and the hills are still the same grey-brown color they were when we arrived. It's hard to believe that rain will come and change things.

I park in front of the travel agent's where the grey-haired woman works. Part-time, she said. I get out of the car and stand at the window with my hands cupped around my eyes and yes, there she is.

The door chimes as I go in. She gives me a formal smile.

"I said I'd stop in some day," I say, not sure she recognizes me, not sure what I'll say next. It doesn't seem possible to just ask what I want to know.

"Of course," she says, a little distantly—and it was only a week ago that we met. A pair of glasses hangs from a chain around her neck, and she unfolds them and puts them on. "Of course," she says again, smiling now. "Claire, nice to see you. Are you planning a trip?"

I sit in the chair in front of her desk. "Yes," I lie. "We want to spend Christmas in Chicago with my parents if Thomas can get away."

She asks for dates and I invent them. She taps them into her machine.

"I just want to make reservations for now," I say.

She looks up at me and purses her lips. "Then you can't get the good fares," she says. "The airlines won't let you reserve without paying."

"Oh, dear," I say. "Thomas doesn't know—"

"Maybe you should come back when your plans are more definite?"

"Yes," I say. "I'll come back." I stand up and turn away, then turn back. "Oh, I almost forgot. Thomas is so curious about the Mehrings. His wife. Widow. Did she leave the area? I thought she must have, but—"

"She's down here in the valley somewhere," she says. "I'm afraid I've rather lost touch."

"Was it violent? Of course it couldn't be less our business, but—"

"I don't know the details," she says. "He had cancer."

"My God," I say. Something inside me shifts, clears. "I didn't realize he was sick."

"Well," she says. "I heard they were giving him at least a year."

A fist closes back around me. I turn for the door, thanking her for her help. I hurry to the car, wanting very badly to get back to Jenny.

There's only one Mehring in the phone book; it can't be that common a name. 7237 Loma Vista. It's listed under John, too, which I guess is understandable. She wouldn't want people thinking she was a woman living alone. Is she a woman living alone?

In a tiny, dark house.

The local paper is indexed at the public library. It's a raw, grey morning, and I'm the only one here, aside from the librarian. She explains the system graciously enough, but behind her tortoiseshell glasses her eyes are curious. I said I was a student over at Stanford, and certainly I look young enough to pass; perhaps I look too young to pass. Perhaps she thinks I'm a high school girl, playing hookey. Thomas is prematurely grey, and at restaurants in Italy men used to nudge each other, even wink occasionally. I was twenty-four, and at night I would stand and stare into the mirror, looking for a sign that something, Jenny or Thomas, had put some age in my face.

There are a number of entries under his name, and I twist through the microfiche, looking. His appointment to court, judgments, sentencings, and finally I find it, October 24th, 1979, the obituary. "Judge John Mehring was found dead in his home last night . . . cause of death was not stated . . . survived by his wife, Alice, and two daughters, Carol, 8, and Cathy, 14." There is a picture of him in his robe, smiling, wearing wire-rimmed glasses. I stare at it, trying to read the eyes, the mouth.

He says we should get out more. He suggests the opera, the symphony, he learns about out-of-the-way restaurants, Italian, always Italian, he offers a weekend in Mendocino, at Tahoe, on our own in an elegant small hotel in San Francisco. But I don't want to leave Jenny.

I drive slowly, looking at the numbers on the mailboxes, until I find it. 7237. It's a medium-sized pea-green house, identical in nearly every detail to the grey one on its left, the white one on its right. It's mid-morning, and the street is quiet. I can tell just by looking that no one is home. She works, of course. Alice.

Surely Cathy has grown up and moved away, but Carol must still live here, a high school student alone with her mother, eating TV dinners in silence, going early to her room, her books, her telephone.

I accelerate until I am around the corner, then I park and walk back. I stand on the sidewalk for a few minutes, just looking. There's a picture window that must be the living room, but there's too much glare and I can't see in. I look around. There's no one on the street, no cars coming as far as I can tell. I take a step up the walk, then another, until I'm too close to turn back; then I hurry forward, squeeze between the bushes and the house, and cup my hands around my eyes.

A couch, a couple of chairs, a TV. A bookcase full of books. A doorway leading to a kitchen. What did I expect? But I'm glued here, straining to read titles, to see what's in the one frame hanging on the wall—a painting or a mirror. It's too dark to tell.

"Dear Thomas," I write. "What I have to say is this. It's not so much that you don't know me, as that you don't seem to know that you don't know me." I cross it out.

"Dear Thomas," I write. "We need to talk—we need to *have* talked." No.

"Dear Thomas," I write. "I feel like I'm holding my breath. I feel like something is going to shatter."

Dear Thomas, I can't write to you.

The street looks different at night. Living room lights are on; there are cars in driveways; and inside, although I can't see them, people are getting ready for dinner. It makes me wish I lived in a house where you could see your neighbors' lights.

I brake across from 7237. Jenny starts playing with the belt on her car seat and I tell her no, we're not getting out. We're just looking.

All the lights are on and I can see the back of someone's head above the couch against the living room window. The TV isn't on; maybe she's reading—or just thinking. Today's the 28th of October; he died eight years ago last Friday. Does she think *died* or *killed himself?*

"Mommy," Jenny says, impatiently. She's not used to being out at this hour; neither am I. But Thomas has a dinner meeting tonight.

"In a minute, Sweetie," I say. I lean back and kiss the top of her head. I love it when I pull my mouth away and some of her silky hair comes with it.

When I look back at the house I see that someone else has come into the living room. I take Thomas's binoculars out of their case and train them on the window.

It's a teenaged girl. Carol. She's tall and pretty, with shoulder-length blond hair. She's talking, smiling, waving a hand for emphasis. Her mother, whose hair is short and dark, nods once or twice. Then the girl turns and walks through the doorway to the kitchen.

After a moment I realize I'm holding my breath, waiting for Alice to get up and follow her. But she doesn't. She stays where she is. She sits alone with her head bent. A few minutes later, my neck stiff, I lower the binoculars. Alice hasn't moved.

"Claire," he says, "maybe you should talk to someone."

"Why can't I talk to you?" I say.

"I mean someone professional. Someone who might be able to help you sort things out. You seem so unhappy."

I stare out the window, into the blackness.

"OK," he says, "talk to *me.*"

I turn to face him.

"*Talk* to me," he says, standing up. "Talk to me," he says, coming toward me, coming closer until there is almost no space between us. "Talk to me," he says, wrapping his arms around me and holding me close.

But now that we are like this—now that I am almost literally surrounded by him—I can't think of anything that I want to say.

"Talk to me," he says.

"Don't move," I say.

Here I am again, on Loma Vista. I'm parked right in front of the
house, watching the rain run down the car windows. I'm supposed
to be buying myself a new dress—Thomas's idea—but I don't really
want one.

I think Alice is in there alone. Either that or no one's home; I saw
Carol leave about half an hour ago.

Go all out, Thomas said. Get something gorgeous. Surprise me.
This would surprise him: this waiting, this watching. But he'll never
know and what disturbs me is, he might not want to.

A light goes on in the living room and there's Alice, looking out
the window. Is she looking at me? I turn away and stare straight
ahead. I count to fifty, very slowly. When I'm done, I look back and
she's still there. She raises her hand and waves at me; my heart is
pounding. A moment later she opens the front door and comes
down the walk, a little red umbrella held open over her head. When
she gets to the car she comes around and I roll down my window.

"Can I help?" she says.

"Help?"

"Would you like to use my phone?"

"Oh," I say. "I hadn't thought of that."

"Come on in," she says. "You must be freezing."

I get out of the car and follow her up the walk, my legs like rubber.
When we get inside, she turns around and looks at me, and her face
is much younger than I ever imagined. There are wrinkles around
her wide-set green eyes, but otherwise her skin is smooth. "I saw you
sitting there—oh, it must have been a good hour ago," she says.
"When I looked again just now I couldn't believe you were still
there. Car trouble? The phone's through here." She leads me through

the living room to the kitchen. "I'm Alice Mehring, by the way," she says, putting out her hand.

"Thank you," I say, and shake it. She gives me a funny look. "Oh," I say. "I'm Claire, Claire . . . Thomas."

She looks me over and I think, Now she's going to realize she's let a perfect stranger into her house and she's going to get scared. But she says, "You *are* cold, aren't you? Would you like some tea?"

I open my mouth to answer, to say that there's nothing wrong with my car and I don't need the phone and I'd better leave; but nothing comes out.

"Is that a yes or a no," she says, laughing. She opens a cupboard. "We've got English Breakfast, which is what I drink, plus about ten kinds of herbal tea my daughter tells me to buy. I don't think she's ever actually tried any of them, but every now and then some new flavor pops up on my grocery list." She smiles at me. "What'll it be?"

"English Breakfast, I guess," I say. "It's so nice of you."

"It's nothing. Do you need a phone book?" She opens a drawer. "Help yourself."

I take the phone book and sit at the kitchen table. I watch her fill a kettle with water and set it on the stove.

I can't call home; what would I say to Thomas?

"Do you need a jump?" she says. "I could call my son-in-law, I'm sure he's got cables."

I look up at her. "There's nothing wrong with my car," I say. To my dismay, tears swim in front of my eyes.

She puts a hand to her throat and takes a step backward. "No?"

I shake my head. "I was just sitting there because I, uh—" I shrug my shoulders. My eyes are burning. Tears begin to trail down my cheeks.

"Are you OK?"

I nod my head, but I can't speak.

"Are you sure? Can I—is there anything I can do?" She takes a step toward me, then another, and when she reaches my side she touches my shoulder lightly. "Can I call someone?"

"I'm sorry," I say, standing up. "This is terrible."

"Please don't worry," she says. "Here—why don't you sit down."

I don't sit, but I don't move, either. It's all I can do to keep the tears back. If I really started, I wouldn't be able to stop.

A shrill whistle pierces through the kitchen and I gasp.

"The water," she says. "I got this ridiculous new kettle." She moves away from me to the stove. "Claire," she says. "Have a cup of tea. Sit down again and have a cup of tea."

I sit, and a few minutes later, when the tea is in front of me and she is sitting across the table, I begin to feel calmer. I take a sip and the tea is nice and strong. I reach into my purse for a Kleenex, wipe my eyes, and blow my nose. "I'm really sorry," I say.

"It's OK," she says. "Really."

There's a copy of *Gourmet* on the table and she reaches for it, then begins flipping through the pages. "Do you like to cook?" she says. "I was going to try this recipe, but I don't know, it might be too hard." She turns the magazine to face me and there's a big, two-page picture of a pastry fish on a silver platter. The fish is beautifully detailed; there are even delicate pastry fins. It's golden brown, like a fragrant loaf of bread just out of the oven. "It's called Coulibiac of Salmon," she says. "What do you think?"

I look into her steady green eyes. I think, How do you do it? My God, how do you do it? But I tell her that it looks delicious. "I think you should try it," I say.

It's dark and raining harder when I get home, and our house, light pouring out the big windows, looks warm and inviting. "Thomas," I call as I open the door. "I'm back."

"We're in here," comes his voice from the study.

I head in that direction, but stop for a moment at the hall mirror. We bought it in a musty old junk store in Florence, just two days before we were due to fly back to the States and get married. It's a big, unwieldy thing, with a heavy ornate gold frame; when I first saw it leaning against the wall, I was drawn to it without quite knowing whether I thought it was ugly or beautiful. The man who ran the shop was at my side in a second. "Signora," he said. "Bello, no? You have a very good taste, no? This is very old, very antique. Of the 18th century." Thomas came over to see what was going on, and the man said, "Your lady love she has a good taste. You want to make her happy I give you for three hundred thousand lire, very good price."

"Oh," I said, "that's too much."

"I kind of like it," Thomas said. He moved closer to the mirror and bent over to examine the finish. "It's in pretty good shape," he said. "It's just a little dusty."

"It's a treasure," the man said, pulling a rag from his pocket and wiping the frame off. "Two hundred eighty thousand lire, I'm giving it to you, you understand? A gift."

Thomas grasped the sides of the mirror and tried to lift it. "It weighs a ton," he said. "We'd have to ship it."

"It gives a beautiful picture," the man said. "Look at this." He leaned over and with a grunt lifted the mirror up so that our faces were reflected in it together. "A beautiful picture," he said again.

We looked at ourselves for a moment, and I whispered, "Shall we get out of here?"

But Thomas kept looking, until I was afraid the man would drop the mirror. "Two hundred fifty thousand lire," came the man's voice. "And I ship it for you free."

"OK," Thomas said, "sold." And when I turned to him in surprise, he shrugged and smiled. "You like it, don't you?" he said. He pointed at our reflections. "Don't you want to see what happens to the beautiful picture?"

Looking at the mirror now, it occurs to me that that was barely half a year ago: I haven't even given the picture time to change.

"Claire?" Thomas calls.

I take my comb from my purse and run it through my hair. "Coming," I call back.

When I reach the study doorway I stop, and there they are—
Thomas sitting at his desk; Jenny on the rug behind his chair, three
or four stuffed animals grouped around her. "Hi," I say.

He looks up at me and smiles, then swivels his chair around and
picks Jenny up. He stands her on his thighs so that they're both facing me, their heads together. "Who's that?" he says, his mouth close
to her ear. "Who's that?"

Three of the plates from their wedding china were chipped. Their narrow West Village backyard, a tangle of old bricks and weeds when they moved in, was full of flowers. They'd been married for five years and they wanted to have a baby, but it wasn't working.

"Sometimes it's just not meant to be," said Julia's doctor.

But they kept trying. They rushed home at lunch; they'd heard something about daytime body temperatures. They tried a variety of positions; they'd heard something about angle of projection. They went back to the doctor.

"Don't think in terms of fault," he said. "It could be any number of things."

There was a possibility of finding out what was wrong, though, so they had to try. They brought home glass tubes with little cork stoppers; they purchased a new thermometer, a plastic one with a tiny telephone cord attached to a box with a digital read-out; they set up a program on Henry's home computer to keep track of all the variables. Julia thought the program should be called simply "Baby," but Henry persuaded her to go along with his idea, "Conception Conundrum."

Julia was past her prime, reproductively speaking; they already knew that. The news was that Henry's sperm count was very low.

"Oh, well," Julia said. "We tried."

But walking through Central Park, or standing on a street corner waiting for a traffic light to change, Henry would see her stealing looks into other people's baby carriages and strollers: at tiny newborns in white crocheted jackets, at stout overall-clad toddlers with blond curls. Her lips slightly parted, she would bring her narrow fingers to her mouth, as if, Henry thought uneasily, to keep herself from crying out.

They stopped talking about it. Instead—*instead*, Henry marvelled, as if there could be a replacement—instead, they toyed with the idea of going to Spain in October, of a new kitchen, of a time-share condo somewhere near the water.

Then Julia's sister, Mindy, called from Seattle. She said that Henry should get on the extension. "I know you guys are going to want to say no," she said, "but just listen." Her babysitter was pregnant and it was going to ruin the poor girl's life unless a suitable solution could be found. She was Catholic, so forget an abortion, and in any case it was too late—she was already five months. She'd kept it a secret from everyone until Mindy had come upon her crying in the kitchen just the night before. Out it had all come: the father was hopeless, some kid from another school, and Mindy thought the girl's parents would ultimately forgive her—the same thing had happened to her older sister—but she couldn't live under their roof while it was going on.

"Mindy," Julia said.

"Just wait," Mindy said. "Don't be so quick." The girl wanted to find a good couple, a couple who couldn't have children of their own, to adopt the baby from her. She wouldn't ever want to see it, once she'd made sure of them. She was only sixteen, she wasn't ready for anything like the responsibility; and besides, Mindy said, she was very bright, she deserved a chance.

"I'm getting off now," Henry said. He waited, but neither Julia nor Mindy said anything, so he hung up. He went into his study, sat on the couch, and stared at the blank screen of the television.

He looked up when he heard Julia. She stopped in the doorway.

"God," he said.

"I know," she said.

"Mindy wants her to come live with us? Until the baby's born? Then she'd leave and it would stay?"

"And we'd adopt it," Julia said.

"That's not even legal."

"Actually it is. You know Mindy—she made sure of that. It's called open adoption."

He looked back at the television set. He could see his head reflected on the screen, a dark shape in the dark grey square. He turned back to Julia; she was leaning against the frame of the door, playing with a button on her sweater.

"You're not tempted, are you?" he said.

She shook her head, then came and sat on the couch, leaving a full foot between them. They sat still for a few minutes, not talking. Then she reached over and touched his shoulder. "One good thing would be that she lives all the way across the country," she said. "We wouldn't have to worry about running into her at the A & P."

Sylvie arrived on the first of September. She was six months pregnant, but she was a big girl, the baby aside. Henry was a big man—six foot two and on the soft side of two hundred pounds—and he kept looking at her, amazed by her shoulders, her wrists. She had long, unruly hair the color of pumpkin pie, and milky skin. Standing next to Julia in the kitchen before dinner, she made Julia—sleek, raven-haired Julia—look unreal somehow.

At the table Sylvie smiled a lot and politely answered their questions. Henry felt impatient, until he realized why: he was waiting for her to talk about the baby. Not about how it felt, being pregnant; those were the things they'd never know. And they'd already gone over all the details—her maternity clothing allowance, their religious and financial lives. He wanted—what? For her to say, "This is strange, but I think it will work out." He looked across the table at Julia. She looked the way she looked just before they fought.

For dessert she had made zabaglione, to serve with fresh berries. ("As if I wanted to impress her," she'd said to Henry as they left for the airport; "I know," he'd said, "I thought about having the car waxed.") After the first bite, Sylvie put her spoon down.

"It's zabaglione," Julia said. "Maybe it's an acquired taste."

"No, it's good," Sylvie said. "It's just—is there some kind of liquor in it?"

Henry and Julia exchanged a look. "Marsala," Julia said.

"It's a kind of wine," Henry said. "Although you wouldn't really want to drink it like wine."

Sylvie nodded but didn't eat anymore.

"Maybe you don't like wine yet," he said.

"Oh, I like it," she said. "But in my condition—"

"Oh, God," Julia said, "I wasn't thinking. Is it really true that you can't have *any* alcohol?"

"That's ridiculous," Henry said. "I'm sure my mother didn't give up her vodka martinis for me, and I turned out OK." He looked into his dessert bowl and very carefully maneuvered exactly one raspberry onto his spoon. "More or less."

"Actually," Sylvie said, "there really is a link between low birth weights and alcohol intake during pregnancy."

"You're right to be careful," Julia said. "Better safe than sorry."

"True," said Henry. "Although I don't think a little zabaglione could hurt anyone."

When they finished eating, Sylvie stood up and began clearing the table.

"Please don't," Julia said.

"You're a guest," Henry said.

Sylvie ran her fingers through her hair, pulling it from her face. "There's no such thing as a four-month guest," she said. "Anyway, I'm used to it—it's my job at home."

"You've had a long day," Julia said. "Tomorrow we'll figure out how you can help."

"OK," Sylvie said, but she didn't move, and Henry found himself staring at the table to avoid looking at her. He wished Julia would get her to go upstairs.

"Do you remember where your room is?" Julia said.

"Oh, yes. It's just, well, I wanted to thank you for having me."

"Of course," Julia said. "It's we who should thank you."

Henry stayed where he was while Julia came and went, carrying plates and glasses. When she'd finished in the kitchen, she turned off the light, and the whole downstairs, except for the dining room, was dark. She came and stood behind him, leaning down and putting her arms around his neck until their heads were close. He opened his mouth to say something, he hadn't decided what. "Don't," she said.

"How about going out for dinner tonight?" Henry said. "Just the two of us." He was at his office, talking to Julia at her office. They talked more these days, but about less. They talked about whether there was enough milk at home; they tried to think of movies Sylvie might like for the VCR. She had been with them for nearly three weeks.

"Henry," Julia said. "Remember Sylvie?"

"Just an idea."

"I'll make you something special tonight," she said. "What would you like?"

He twisted the phone cord around his finger. "Do you think she's bored?"

"Lonely, maybe," Julia said. "Not bored."

"She barely leaves the house, except to go swimming."

"She's busy."

"What, watching TV?"

"Growing the baby."

"If it were you, you'd be working nine to six on top of that."

"But it's not me."

There was nothing he could say to that. He told her someone was standing at his door, and he hung up. Five minutes later he called her back.

"I do feel bad," he said.

"Honey, we don't know it was you—it could have been me. I'm thirty-six, after all."

A tiny circle of pain moved into his chest, like a stitch in his side when he was walking fast. "I meant I feel bad for Sylvie."

Julia was silent.

"Jule?" He saw her at her desk, fingering the framed picture of him that she kept there. She'd taken it just a few weeks after they met at a wedding; she'd called him on a Sunday morning and suggested a walk. It was autumn, and she was wearing caramel-colored leather gloves and carrying her camera on a strap over her shoulder. She took his arm, and he had a barely perceptible feeling that she thought he was someone different from who he actually was: someone who knew how to have a woman on his arm. In the picture his expression, she always says, is one of ill-concealed boredom; she says it's part of why she fell in love with him—that no one else ever permitted himself to look bored in her presence. He'd actually felt uneasy, and now, waiting for her to speak, he wondered whether, as she looked at the picture, she was finally seeing some truth about him that had eluded her before—that he was cruel, stupid. "Julia?" he said.

"She's not unhappy," Julia said. "I can tell."

"Can you? How?"

"I call her sometimes."

"During the day? What do you talk about?"

She seemed to hesitate. "I don't know," she said. "I guess she tells me what's going on."

"Like whether the mail's come?"

She laughed. "Like whether the baby's moving. I felt it kick the other morning, after you'd left for work—it was amazing. You should ask her if you can feel it sometime; I'm sure she wouldn't mind."

"Listen," Henry said. "There's someone on the other line—I'll see you at home."

Henry decided to buy a book—something to give him some hard information, to let him know what to expect. At the store there were eight or ten shelves devoted entirely to pregnancy. There were books on having a glamorous pregnancy, there were books on having a low-stress pregnancy. There was even a book called *Pregnant Fathers*. Finally he settled on one whose cover appealed to him; it was a picture of a pregnant woman and a man, and they weren't standing in a field of daisies or staring blissfully into each other's eyes.

At home, behind the closed door of his study, he sat in the green glow of his computer and erased the contents of "Conception Conundrum." He looked at the title for a moment, then changed it to "Baby." He made a calendar and, copying from the book, began to type in what was supposed to happen when. During the trimester that had just ended, the second, the baby's eyes had opened and it had developed hair on its skin—lanugo, it was called. The book went on to describe the changes the mother would experience in the fifth and sixth months: indigestion and frequent urination, varicose veins and stretch marks. He pictured a big white belly, punctuated by small angry red lines, and he tried to see Sylvie's face above it. But to imagine her whole, pregnant, and naked made him too uncomfortable.

He went on to the next chapter, the third trimester. He flipped through it once, looking at the diagrams. A passage caught his eye. "During the last few weeks, your friends will begin to look at you with a critical eye, to determine whether your baby has 'lightened' or 'dropped.' 'Lightening' refers to the process by which the baby's head descends into the true pelvis, the position for delivery."

Henry stared at the screen of his computer. "Seventh Month," read the heading at the top of the column. He turned back to the beginning of the chapter. "Baby practices sucking," he typed. "May already suck its thumb."

They were walking up Madison, the three of them. They were on an outing. Henry was holding their elbows; it was up to him to steer them both through the crowd of shoppers. People were nudging each other and laughing at him. A teenager on a skateboard was mad at him for some reason; he kept racing toward them until he was only a foot away, then he'd wheel back up the sidewalk and do it again. The Don't Walk sign at the cross street began to flash, and Henry had to get them across before it was too late, but suddenly Julia wasn't there. He turned around, letting go of Sylvie's elbow, and scanned the crowd. Finally he spotted Julia, way down the block in front of a store window. He turned back, certain that Sylvie would have disappeared, but she had moved against the building, and she nodded at him calmly. He sprinted to Julia—he wanted to tell her to hurry—but she was leaning close to the window, hands on her knees, and when she saw him she straightened and put her fingers over his lips, then pointed at the window, where there was a pair of women's red crocodile loafers on display. "Perfect for the baby," she said.

He jerked awake. Relieved, he reached for Julia, but she wasn't there. He got out of bed and headed down the stairs. The kitchen light shone, throwing a band of white across the dark wood floor of the hallway.

He heard Julia saying, "Try not to, honey." Then a sniff. He stopped on the bottom step.

"It won't be the same after this," Sylvie said through sobs. "He'll go back to McCluskey's garage and those guys."

"How can you be sure? I'm sure he misses you, too."

"Then why doesn't he write? He *promised*."

"He's probably confused," Julia said. "This is hard on him, too, don't you suppose?"

"I guess." Sylvie sniffed again, then blew her nose.

Henry moved into the doorway. "He's probably afraid you'll be different," Julia said; she was facing him but she hadn't seen him yet.

"I will be," Sylvie said.

Julia shut her eyes, and her face seemed to close down in pain. Henry took a quick step back, out of the doorway. He didn't know what he'd do if she cried. He'd seen her cry only once before, when his father died. They got the news over the phone, from Henry's brother, and while Julia stood at the kitchen sink with her face in her hands, Henry stood beside her, afraid to touch her for fear that she would look up and see that his eyes were dry, and, without saying a word, reproach him somehow. She surprised him, though: after several minutes, without warning, she straightened up, wiped her face with the back of her hands, blew her nose, drank a glass of water, put her hand on his shoulder for a moment—and then turned back to the stove and finished sautéing the chicken breasts they were having for dinner.

Now Henry heard the sound of a chair scraping back. Julia said, "I'm going to make you some decaffeinated tea," in an even, controlled voice, and he felt his body relax. Of course Julia wouldn't cry; it would make Sylvie feel worse, and that was one of Julia's talents: never making anyone feel worse, or even bad. If Julia were pregnant, he wouldn't find her crying in the kitchen at three a.m. Although who could say? As Henry headed back up the stairs, he realized that he'd never actually imagined Julia pregnant, her face blotchy, her hipbones lost to flesh; she'd have hated wearing clothes like the big denim jumper Sylvie seemed to wear every other day. At least she wasn't going to have to endure all of that; he hoped she could see it that way, too.

Julia leaned against the door, a three-quarters turn away from him. They were in a taxi on their way home from a party. It had gotten awkward, seeing their friends: walking into their hosts' bedroom with Julia's coat at the beginning of the evening, Henry had felt a shadow behind him and had not even turned around—the sense of an extra presence in his life had become that familiar. But someone really was there, it turned out: Mona, his hostess, dressed in white clothing that looked like paper, her whole body narrowed into an expression of solicitude. He'd greeted her perhaps too exuberantly, and now, in the cab, he imagined the conversation about them that was taking place back at the party—her concerned report of his false cheer. He thought of telling Julia about meeting Mona in the bedroom but realized he couldn't: he might say too much.

"She asked me if we'd picked names yet," Julia said, turning to face him.

"Right," Henry said. "It's not that she wants to *pressure* us or *pry,* it's just, well, don't we want to *talk* about it?"

"What are you talking about, Henry? She's not like that."

"Are you kidding? You should have heard her in the bedroom when I was getting rid of your coat."

"No, no, no, not Mona. *Sylvie* asked me."

"Oh, sorry," Henry said. He licked his lips. "What did you say?"

"That we hadn't, of course. We haven't."

"I guess we should start thinking."

"I've been thinking. Haven't you?"

"I guess not. Not about that, anyway."

She sighed and looked out the window. "What, then?" she said. "What?"

"What have you been thinking about?"

He tried to focus on something outside the cab, but his eyes kept returning to the back of her head; part of her hair was caught in her collar, and he wanted to reach a finger in and flip it out.

She faced him. "I mean it," she said. "Are you in on this?"

What if he said no? What then? But he *was.* It was all just so strange. "Yes," he said.

"Are you sure?"

"Sweetie," he said, touching her leg.

After a moment, she settled back into the seat. He put his arm around her shoulders and she leaned her head into his neck and he reached his other hand up and touched her hair—but there, there it was again: the tightness in his chest.

Henry had spent the whole day at the office, even though it was a Saturday, and as he walked the last few blocks home he thought how nice it would be if Julia had a fire going. He'd forgotten his gloves and his fingers were numb; it felt more like February than the beginning of November.

"Hello," he called as he opened the front door. None of the down-stairs lights were on. He turned on the hall light, put down his brief-case, and hung up his coat. He moved through the living room and dining room, turning on lights. "Hello?" he called at the bottom of the stairs.

"We're up here," Julia called back.

He went into the kitchen and looked through the mail. The news-paper was still on the table and he glanced through it, although he'd read it before leaving the house that morning. He made himself a drink and climbed the stairs.

The light in his and Julia's bedroom was on, and he went in. Sylvie was sitting at Julia's dressing table, and Julia was standing over her, at work on Sylvie's mouth with one of her pencils. The table was lit-tered with small bottles and jars. Julia had Sylvie's chin in her hand, and Sylvie was looking up at her with an expression of wonder and admiration.

"Hi," he said.

They both looked around at him, and Sylvie blushed. "Hi," Julia said. "Just a sec." She tilted Sylvie's face up and finished outlining her lips, then she turned to Henry. "When you're pregnant," she said, "a little lift on a grey day can make all the difference." She turned back to Sylvie. "Here's the thing to remember about makeup: the less you want to wear it, the more you should."

Henry stood still, not knowing what to do.

"You look gorgeous," Julia said, taking a step backward to look at Sylvie. "Like one of those models wearing a flowing linen dress at some garden party."

Sylvie pulled her jumper away from her belly. "The only problem is that the dress flows out instead of down."

Julia laughed and picked up her brush. "I just want to try some-thing with your hair."

Henry picked up a magazine from his bedside table, held it for a moment, then set it down again.

Julia turned and smiled at him. "I'll be down in a few minutes," she said.

Julia had taken Sylvie shopping for something to wear at Thanksgiving. Henry was sitting at his computer, staring at the calendar. The baby's head was now in proportion to its body, and it had begun to shed its hair. Soon it would start to practice breathing, which would cause it to hiccup. He wondered what that would feel like to Sylvie. Like kicking? Julia had told him that the baby kicked a lot at night, keeping Sylvie awake, and he'd been about to explain to her that most doctors thought it wasn't so much the baby kicking more as it was the mother being more aware. He'd stopped himself just in time; he hadn't told her about the book.

He closed the file, ejected his disc, and left the study to go upstairs. Sylvie's door was closed, and it was with the consciousness that he was trespassing that he opened it and went in. He was expecting a mess, but the room was so still and neat that it looked uninhabited. Where was the tangle of laundry, where the sloppy bed? He thought of Sylvie at the dinner table, her breasts resting on her rounded belly. He thought of her in the easy chair in front of the TV, her hands crossed on her stomach. She always looked neat, in her huge dresses. It was, he realized guiltily, the mere fact of her pregnancy that made him think of her as slovenly.

He walked around her bed. The only things on her night table were a small lamp and a clock. He pulled open the drawer. It was empty except for a plain white envelope. He picked it up and held it for a moment, then untucked the flap. Inside were several photographs. He took them out and flipped through them, just glancing until he came to a picture of Sylvie sitting on the lap of a skinny teenaged boy.

They were both in cut-offs. The boy wore no shirt and his chest was pale and hairless. He looked defenseless, sitting there with his hand on Sylvie's bare thigh, staring straight ahead. Henry realized he had been imagining someone big, a football player with a chipped tooth. Someone whose child would grow up tall, like he was. But this boy was the father. My child's father, Henry thought.

Julia had flown to Milwaukee on business, so Henry was taking the morning off to take Sylvie to the doctor. She'd said she would go alone, but Julia had made him promise. "The doctor makes her nervous," she'd said. "You don't mind, do you?"

It was, he told himself, the least he could do. He wondered whether it was also the most. Sitting next to Sylvie in Julia's doctor's very feminine waiting room, he wondered what she thought of him. Across the room there was a man dressed almost exactly as he was—grey suit, blue shirt, striped tie—and Henry thought he was probably no clearer to her than that man was.

He turned to her. "How are you feeling?" he said.

"Fine, thanks."

"I mean, I was wondering how you were feeling these days. In general." According to the book, the last few weeks were very hard.

"OK," she said, smiling at him. "Fine."

"Good," he said. He continued to look at her, until he realized he wasn't going to think of anything else to say. Finally the nurse came for her and he sank back into his chair.

"Your first?" The man across the room was staring at him intently. They were alone.

"Yes," Henry said.

The man nodded. "Your wife seems so calm, is why I asked. My wife is pretty nervous. She's got four more weeks and she's already got the little suitcase packed." He laughed, his eyes still on Henry. "Hell," he said, "I'm nervous." He paged through a magazine, threw it back onto the table. "In fact," he said, leaning forward conspiratorially, "I'm scared to death." He grinned, as if challenging Henry to better him.

"It'll be OK," Henry said. He lifted his briefcase onto his lap and popped open the clasps. Sifting through papers, his head ducked low, he was afraid that the man would still be there when Sylvie came out. But after a few minutes the man's wife appeared and they left together, holding hands.

Whatever was happening, it was taking forever. Henry did a little work, scanned an article in *Parents* magazine about working mothers who wanted to breastfeed. The waiting room filled: two women, three, four, five—all hugely pregnant. He was the only man. He used the phone on the table beside him to call his office for messages. He closed his eyes for a little catnap. Suddenly his leg cramped, a quick, painful knot in his thigh. He shot out of his chair to shake it out, and all the women looked up at him at once, as if they had been just waiting for him to disturb the peace.

Sitting down again, he was afraid he might start laughing. He thought of Julia, saw her walking through an anonymous airport, so elegant, so composed; he waited for the ache of missing her to fill him. Then he remembered sitting with her in this room—how many times?—holding her cold hand. First the nervous hope, then the clutching fear, then the little pellet of shame he'd had to swallow and try to forget. He closed his eyes and felt the sag in his cheeks and mouth.

The forecast was for snow, a white Thanksgiving, but in the night the air had warmed, and Henry, waking as Julia got out of bed, heard the steady slide of a rain that would continue for hours. He rolled onto her side of the bed, gathered her pillow into his arms, and drifted toward sleep. He heard her come out of the bathroom, waited for her to move in next to him, instead felt her skirt the bed. He got up to shower.

In the kitchen he found her scraping potatoes at the sink, wrapped in his old plaid bathrobe. There was the familiar aroma of coffee and, just below that, the fat, uncooked smell of the turkey beginning to roast.

"It's raining," Henry said. "Reminds me of my childhood, my mother in the kitchen baking pies, the smell of cinnamon in the air."

She smiled and held her hand out for him; he kissed her. "Your mother never baked a pie in her life," she said.

He laughed. "Did I ever tell you about the Thanksgiving she had catered by the local Chinese restaurant? This was in the days of chop suey and chow mein, mind you."

"Come on," Julia said. "I'm sure that's only half the story. You were probably begging for Chinese food every other day that year and she was trying to please you."

"Apple pie would have pleased me."

She took his face in her hands. "Poor big baby," she crooned. She slapped him lightly.

"Are we having apple pie?"

"Of course. Sylvie and I made it yesterday afternoon, before you got home. She has a recipe where you put a little cider in the crust."

"I like your crust," he said.

"Henry," she said, "it was a tablespoon."

He turned away, got a mug from the cabinet and filled it with coffee. He sat at the table. Julia was still looking at him.

"We should make sure she gets a chance to call home today," he said.

She nodded. "After we eat."

"How can I help?" he asked. "Set the table?"

She bit her lip. "I told Sylvie she could. She insisted on doing something and I didn't think she should be on her feet in this hot kitchen all morning."

"Fine," he said. "I'll lay a fire."

The fireplace was in his study. He took his coffee with him. When he emerged nearly two hours later the rest of the house seemed to be humming with preparations. In the dining room, white linen and silver covered the table; looking more closely, he saw that Sylvie had folded the napkins into elaborate pockets and tucked the forks inside them. He wondered whether Julia had been tempted to ask her to do it over.

The turkey smelled like turkey now. Sylvie was sitting at the kitchen table, arranging broccoli in a dish. She had to reach way across her belly. She looked up and smiled at him, her face a soft pink from the steam of the kitchen. She stopped working. "I've got this obstacle here," she said.

"You shouldn't be doing that. It's awfully warm in here, isn't it?"

"It's OK. I promised Julia I'd sit." She picked up a piece of broccoli, dropped it back and held her stomach. "Whoa," she said, "he's full of beans today."

"Kicking," Henry said. "Does it bother you a lot?"

She smiled. "Actually, it feels great." She patted her stomach. "Want to?"

"I'll take your word," he said, blushing and turning away; it was like refusing to look at someone's family pictures. He took his empty coffee cup to the sink, then he turned around. "He?"

Sylvie's face filled with color. "Oops," she said. "Sorry."

"No, don't apologize," he said. "You think it's a boy?"

She grinned. "I can just see you teaching him to catch." Lowering her voice, she said, "OK, Hank, down thirty and out five."

He looked at her curiously; what else had she imagined? He didn't know how to respond. "I don't think it would be Hank," he said, finally. He glanced at his watch. "Where's Julia?"

The guests arrived shortly after one: just two other couples. Henry fixed drinks, and they ate Julia's soup in the study to be near the fire. It was the first time they'd had company since Sylvie's arrival, and he was relieved that she seemed to be at ease. She told a funny story about the nuns when she was a little girl, and Julia roared with laughter, leaning so far back in the rocking chair where she sat that Henry thought she would fall. It was this, Henry thought, her obvious affection for Sylvie, that was making everyone relax.

At the table they all admired Sylvie's napkins, and although Henry was afraid it would embarrass her, she seemed pleased. She stood up and gave a little demonstration of how she'd folded the pockets, and then, encouraged, went on to show how to make a flower out of a napkin; a bird, a bow. What are her other talents, someone wanted to know. There was an awkward silence and Henry cringed at the condescension. Then Julia rushed in with "baking," and Sylvie, crimson but laughing, patted her stomach and stunned Henry by saying, "Nothing's as loving as something from the oven."

Everyone laughed, and the pie was served as evidence. Raising his wine glass, Henry toasted the crust with the cider in it, saying he'd always known he could count on Sylvie for the magic touch. At the other end of the table, Julia cupped her chin in her hand and smiled a smile of pure love at him, and it occurred to him that in a few weeks Sylvie would be gone and his life with Julia would close back in on itself. And he knew, too, that someday, in a month or a year or five, he would discover that he had begun to think of the child as *their* child; it would just take time.

As they were leaving, one of the guests, Ivy, whose three sisters had made her an aunt three times in the last year, asked Sylvie how much longer she had, and when Sylvie said "Two weeks," ushered her into the hallway where she made her stand sideways, against the wall.

"What are you doing?" Julia asked.

Without thinking Henry said, "She wants to see if the baby has lightened."

Julia stared at him.

"He means dropped," Ivy told her. "Same thing."

Still Julia didn't speak.

"The baby's head," Ivy said. "It's in position for delivery, I can tell." She wagged a finger at Julia. "You haven't done your homework."

Now Julia turned away from Henry, and he saw the edge of a huge, gaping silence, and he knew he could do nothing about it. Then someone began taking coats from the coat closet, cheeks were kissed, goodbyes said, and the door was opened onto the dark rain.

Julia went into the dining room and came back with her wine. She took a sip of it, her eyes on Henry. "Explain," she said.

Sylvie touched Julia's shoulder. "You remember—when the baby's ready to come out its head moves down into the pelvis." She smiled. "It presses on your bladder and you have to pee all the time again."

Julia swallowed the rest of her wine. She stared at Henry, her lips narrowed into a thin line, and for a moment he was afraid she was going to throw the wineglass at him. "What I want to know," she said, "is where you got that word."

He hesitated. "I'm not sure," he said. "I must have heard it somewhere."

Sylvie put her hand on her stomach.

Julia turned to her. "Are you all right?"

"I think so. Maybe I should sit down."

"All that rich food," Julia said. "Let's put you in front of the fire." She avoided looking at Henry; instead she guided Sylvie into the study.

He followed them. The fire had died down and he added a couple of logs, then stood watching until the blaze began to climb again.

Sylvie was in the easy chair, her eyes closed, one hand on her stomach. Julia sat on the chair's arm, stroking Sylvie's hair. "I'll do the dishes," Henry said. He didn't wait for a response.

There were plates and glasses and pots and pans all over the kitchen. He began stacking them next to the sink, then decided to take a quick walk first, just a minute or two to clear his head. He took his umbrella from the closet, made sure the door would lock when he closed it, and went outside. It was only then that he patted his pocket and realized he didn't have his keys. He was about to knock on the door but stopped himself—they weren't going anywhere.

Walking through the quiet streets of his neighborhood, he breathed in the cold, wet air until his lungs began to ache. He found himself thinking of the night when he proposed to Julia. At the time, they'd known each other for only seven months, but the idea had been in his head for the last five; he would lose and regain his nerve several times a week. At one point he even bought a diamond ring only to return it the next day, telling himself it was absurd to think that to change your life all you had to do was buy a piece of jewelry. On the evening when he decided to ask her, she made dinner for the two of them at her apartment, and while they were eating he felt so sick with apprehension that he barely spoke. Finally, while she was in the kitchen making coffee, he couldn't take it anymore. He went and stood in the doorway until she turned around, and he said—and he hated this, what an oaf—"Julia, I want you to get married." But she didn't laugh. He would always remember that—it had saved him. She didn't even giggle.

The rain was falling harder. In the distance, Henry could hear the occasional swish of a car driving through a puddle. He turned up his collar and headed back toward home. When he got there, he knocked at the door, but no one answered. He knocked again, harder. Finally he made his way around the side of the house to the study window.

Sylvie was still in the easy chair, but Julia was on the rug. She was leaning sideways against Sylvie's legs. Her shoulders were shaking. Henry took a step closer and one of the spokes of his umbrella tapped against the window, but they didn't even turn to look. Sylvie leaned over and put an arm around Julia's shoulder, but Julia pulled away. Her face was in her hands, and she was shaking her head. Then she looked up and placed her hands flat on Sylvie's belly, and her face filled with all the anguish of a desire never to be satisfied. And Henry watched as Sylvie said the words that he had never once said—I'm sorry, I'm so sorry.

"Name the quad cities," said Tillman.

It was the middle of the morning and we'd just crossed the Mississippi and entered Iowa. I tried to remember the highway signs we'd passed. "Moline," I said. "East Moline." I was stuck. "North Moline and South Moline?"

"I'm sorry," said Tillman. "You do not win the walnut dinette set. The correct answer is: Moline, Rock Island, Bettendorf, and Davenport."

"Rock Island sounds pretty."

"It's the armpit of the Mississippi. How about a sandwich?"

I laughed. "Don't you want to save them for lunch?"

"No," he said. "We'll stop for lunch in Iowa City."

I reached for the cooler, which was sharing the back seat with our suitcases, a gift-wrapped bottle of Scotch, and Tillman's gun. The Scotch was for Tillman's brother, Casey, whom we were going to visit. The gun was so Tillman—and I—could shoot some pheasants. "Or maybe some ducks," he'd said. "We'll see."

The trip had come about almost by accident. Tillman and I had been keeping company for only a few months, but one of the routines we had established was that on Sunday mornings when we woke up together we'd buy coffee to go from the local greasy spoon and walk out to look at the lake: I grew up forty minutes from the Pacific Ocean and went to college thirty minutes from the Atlantic, but Tillman was from the dead center of the country and Lake Michigan still thrilled him. One chilly October morning as we walked along the city streets Tillman sucked in his breath and put a hand to his chest as he let it out again. "It's a perfect fall day," he said. "Makes me feel like killin' animals." I laughed, but I had seen the gun and knew he liked to hunt. His hunting belonged in a category with former lovers and the most crushing adolescent humiliations: I didn't think we were ready for it yet. "You laugh now," he said. "Wait till you try it. You're a lady who could shoot, I'd put money down." I experienced the usual guilty pleasure his calling me a lady made me feel—it wasn't something I'd ever been called by anyone I hadn't irritated in some way. ("Lady, move your car" I had heard before I met Tillman, but not "You're a lady I could see having dinner with," which he said about five minutes after we met.) I said I probably *wasn't* a lady who could shoot but that we'd never know, would we—and here we were.

I handed Tillman an egg-salad sandwich and took an apple for myself. "Isn't this fun?" he said. "And the great thing is, we've still got about six hundred miles to go."

I moaned. "Maybe we should play a license plate game or something. Did you used to do that when you were little?"

"I was never little," Tillman said. "You know those little white booties babies wear? I had basketball shoes."

"Come on—when your family went on trips? We'd have races to see who could spell out the European capitals first."

"That assumes someone knows them," he said. "Anyway, we didn't go on trips."

A light rain had begun to fall and Tillman switched on the windshield wipers. I looked at him. There was something in the way he held himself, in the relationship of head, neck, and shoulders, that made me very happy. And he had such a winning way of driving a car: one hand on the wheel, the other in his lap, an alert look on his face but not too alert—he wasn't looking for trouble but he could handle it.

"So you're ready for me to meet your brother," I said.

He pressed his lips together in a sly smile. "Amy. It's hunting we're going to do. Pretend it's a coincidence my brother'll be there."

"OK," I said, nodding. "That's what I'll do." And in that way we continued to keep on hold any discussion of our, as my friends called it, feasibility.

An hour or so later we began to see exit signs for Iowa City. Tillman had spent eight years there, first as a student at the University of Iowa and then working in a bakery, baking muffins from four in the morning until noon. It was hard for me to reconcile that Tillman with the one I had been getting to know, who worked as a lab technician at Northwestern Hospital, but he insisted the two jobs weren't very different: he liked his hours better now was the main thing.

We ended up in a crowded little diner where our waitress was actually a waiter: a man with a shaved head wearing a flowered dress of the type someone's mother might have worn to a garden party in the fifties.

Tillman looked up at him and smiled. "Howdy."

"Two fried eggs, corned beef hash, and coffee?" said the man.

"Sounds good."

The man looked at me. "Sugar?"

"He takes it black."

"You've got to love her," he said, winking at Tillman.

"My sentiments exactly," said Tillman.

"I know how he *takes* it," the waiter said to me. "What would you like, dear?"

"Grilled cheese," I said.

"Still in the windy city?" the waiter asked Tillman.

Tillman nodded.

"How is it?"

"Windy," Tillman said. "Meet Amy. Amy, Pruney."

Pruney held out his hand—more as if he expected me to kiss it than to shake it. I slipped my hand into his and wagged it back and forth.

"Delighted," he said. He turned back to Tillman and held his dress out at the sides. "What do you think?"

"It's a nice one," Tillman said. He reached up and adjusted the neckline, which came down just low enough to expose Pruney's wiry grey chest hair. "I really think you need some pearls or something, though."

"Baby, baby, don't I know it and haven't I tried." Pruney leaned forward and lowered his voice. "There are jewelry police all over this joint. Don't think I haven't already been busted." He shook his head and hurried back to the kitchen.

"Somehow," I said, "this isn't how I pictured Iowa."

"This is just Iowa City," Tillman said. "The Greenwich Village of the Midwest. Or is it the Paris of the Midwest? Anyway, wait'll we get to Nebraska—it out Iowas Iowa."

I nodded and smiled, but I felt myself slipping into dreaminess. I was thinking about what Tillman had said: "My sentiments exactly." Well, I thought, love! We hadn't talked about that so far, hadn't mentioned it. It would've been Talking, which Tillman seemed to regard as superfluous at best, a weakness at worst. A few weeks before, we'd taken a drive into the country; standing on the edge of a field, Tillman did a perfect bird whistle that brought answering calls from several nearby trees. "That was mean," he said. "Getting their libidos going." "Maybe it was an unsexual call," I said. "Like, 'Hey, nice day,' or 'Who wants to fly south with me?'" Tillman shook his head, a smirk appearing in the corners of his mouth. "Nope," he said. "Birds have it made. Once they've mated, they get to stop talking."

"Tillman," I said now, leaning across the table to touch his arm. "Seriously—are you glad you moved to Chicago?"

He shrugged. "Sure. But I also think it's sort of beside the point to ask yourself that kind of question. I mean, you're there, right?"

"The unexamined life—"

"Tell me about it," he said. "You want to buy a microscope cheap?"

Our lunches arrived a few minutes later and we ate quickly, without talking—it was the kind of food you have to face down in a hurry if you're going to manage it at all. I finished first and pushed the wilted pickle chips around on my plate while Tillman mopped up his hash with a piece of toast.

As we were leaving the diner Tillman slung his arm over my shoulders. "I can't believe I'm going hunting in Nebraska," I said happily.

"Why not Nebraska?"

"Ha ha," I said. "The emphasis in that sentence was on hunting. When I was little I went to this day camp where one of the activities was riflery, and my parents were so freaked out they had a meeting with the camp director to make sure I wouldn't have to do it. They wouldn't even let me watch. I had double sessions of lanyard-making while everyone else learned how to shoot."

Tillman laughed. "Don't worry—you'll get something."

"That's not really the point," I said. We had reached the car and I turned to face him. "It's the moral question."

"Worse comes to worse," he said, "we'll let you shoot Patsy."

Tillman, I thought. "Patsy?"

"Casey's dog."

"That's disgusting. That's terrible."

"I was joking." He unlocked the car door and held it open for me. "Patsy's Casey's girlfriend. We wouldn't let you shoot a dog."

The interstate was a straight shot across Iowa. I followed our progress on the map for a while, but it was depressing ticking off the little towns—eighteen miles, twenty-seven miles, forty-two miles and we stopped for gas. I offered to drive but Tillman said I might make a wrong turn.

We got back on the highway and I stared out the window. "This is my first time in Iowa," I said. "Where's the corn?"

It was the kind of question I was always asking him, one we both recognized as a little obvious, a little dumb. I couldn't help myself: he was an encyclopedia of exotic knowledge—what the bark of an elm tree looked like, how to tie a knot that would hold when a square knot wouldn't, the names of specific nails and bolts and screwdrivers—and I loved to hear him speak those slightly foreign languages. Or was it more than that? I was pretty sure I knew where the corn was: right there, everywhere, bearing little resemblance to corn as I knew it but corn nonetheless. Disturbingly, I realized that I enjoyed this appearing a little dumb: there was something protective about the boundaries of Tillman's knowledge surrounding me, making a little house for both of us to live in.

"Corn grows seasonally, Amy," Tillman said with a grin. "See the leafy brown stuff in that field?"

Somewhere west of Des Moines, out of desperation, I decided to attempt a nap. I reminded myself and Tillman that success was unlikely—I was a restless sleeper at best, and Tillman was the pea to my princess.

Suddenly it was dark. "Wait," I said. "I'm sure I had my mail forwarded. What?"

"Are you awake?" said Tillman.

I sat up quickly.

"You're cute when you sleep," he said. "Your mouth falls open and there's this little bit of drool on your chin."

I swiped at my face. "Liar."

"It's true," he said. "And you talked. Just now you said something about your mail."

My dream dashed in front of me and was gone. Then I caught a piece of it. "I was moving. Weird—to Nebraska."

"You're there," said Tillman. "Although we've still got a ways to go. Do you want to: A, stop for dinner; B, stop for the night; or C, press on?

I peered out the window but it was completely black—not a light in sight. We could have been anywhere. "Press on?"

"Good idea."

I leaned over the seat for the cooler. We each had half of the remaining sandwich, then took turns taking bites from an apple.

"Amy Levin," he said. "Tillman Crane and Amy Levin on Interstate 80."

"Getting philosophical, are you?"

He reached over and laced his fingers through mine.

"Maybe we should tell people my name is Amy Smith or Amy Johnson or something."

"You really are nervous about this, aren't you?" He pulled his fingers away, then put his hand on top of mine and curled it into a fist; he held my hand captive under his, as if it were a tiny animal that might dart away.

"I don't know," I said. "It's just—families. God, isn't it hard enough without having to contend with someone's family? If we were going to California I'd be nervous, too. I'd probably be more nervous."

He laughed. "You have a lot of faith in me, I see."

"That's not how I meant it," I said. In fact, I'd spent a good deal of time imagining just such a meeting: the two of us sitting side by side in my parents' living room, a convivial discussion of something other than the sorry state of the nation, during which my father would not raise his voice. I'd present Tillman to them as a kind of gift *qua* challenge: Look here, it would say, his parents didn't march on Washington or wear sunglasses for three days when Martin Luther King was shot. *And he hunts.* But I was afraid that, once I was back at home, some part of me would be in their camp with them, looking for the bright side.

Tillman let go of my hand, returning his to the wheel. "It's just my brother," he said. "You have nothing to be nervous about."

"I know," I said. "I guess I'm just nervous that I'll be nervous."

"Amy, Amy, Amy," he said. "Where did I find you?"

"At a boring party."

We were silent for a while. Then Tillman said, "I don't think it's so hard. Am I missing something? I thought we were having fun."

"Fun?" I said. "Fun? Is that the point?" I pulled my feet up onto the seat and wrapped my arms around my knees. "I've often wondered."

Tillman's parents had died four years earlier, when Tillman was twenty-seven, within four months of each other. He was flip with me about it at first, saying his mother had died of boredom causing his father to die of anger. Finally, in a bar one night, I told him that I thought it was strange he hadn't told me what really happened. I said it quietly, eyes downcast—I didn't want him to miss that he'd hurt me by not telling me. "You want the gory details, do you?" he said, and I blushed; but he didn't give me a chance to respond. He said in a rush that his mother had had a surprising, fatal stroke when she was sixty-one, and that after that his father just gave up on life. "Packed it in," he said. "Threw in the towel." I asked him what he meant and he took a sip of beer and gave me a look of such intense melancholy that I was certain I'd made a terrible blunder, one he could never forgive. In the moment before he spoke again I wanted to take it all back, to be someone other than myself—not just someone who could stop herself from prying, but someone who wouldn't even *want* to know.

"He sold the hardware store," Tillman said, holding out his thumb so he could enumerate his points, "where, incidentally, my brother worked." He pointed his index finger. "He auctioned off every piece of furniture in the house with the exception of one chair and one table and the fucking TV." He added his middle finger. "He gave away all of my mother's cooking stuff—to a little hog pit of a restaurant that has since gone out of business." His fourth finger. "He burned her clothing"—at this he raised his eyebrows and gave me a brief, horrible smile—"and then he sat around in his bathrobe, watched TV, and ate nothing but cold cereal and canned vegetables for three and a half months." Tillman picked up his beer and drained it.

"And?" I said reflexively.

"And he died. He died. He died."

"I'm so sorry," I said lamely. "That's awful."

Tillman picked up his empty glass and began tapping it on the table. "True love," he said, shaking his head. "Can you beat it?" Abruptly he stopped tapping the glass and stood up. "Let's go," he said. "This place is a pit."

Since then we'd talked little of his family, and because of that I'd told him little of mine. I did know a few things about his brother: that he lived in an apartment over a shoe store; that he didn't have a regular job but earned his living working for farmers in the spring and summer and being a handyman and sometimes a mechanic in the fall and winter; that he'd been married and had a seven-year-old daughter who lived with his ex-wife up in Rapid City, South Dakota. After lunch I'd learned that he had a girlfriend named Patsy, although about that Tillman could have been kidding. Did he have a dog? I wasn't sure, but I thought he might.

When we got to Barneyville it was nearly eleven; we'd been driving for days, weeks. "The strip," said Tillman, waving his hand at the car lots and fast food places we passed. These gave way to the kind of main street I'd been expecting—a row of small, sad businesses with names like Fin and Fur Pet Store and Dew Drop Inn. At the corner where we turned there was a bridal shop in whose window four or five mannequins with teased-looking plastic hair modeled bridesmaids' gowns in unnatural shades of violet and pink. There was no bride.

Half a block down the street Tillman pulled into a narrow alley and drove back to a little clearing where a toy-like dirty blue pick-up truck was parked. "Well, he's here," he said. "That's a good sign."

We got out of the car and unloaded our stuff, moving slowly because of the stiffness in our muscles. When everything was lying on the gravel Tillman took a few steps backward, leaned his head back, and yelled, "CA-SEY!"

A moment later someone was thundering down a long flight of stairs, and the back door opened. Out came Casey—a slightly older, slightly stocky Tillman. He had the same unruly light brown hair, the same droopy mustache; he was even dressed just like Tillman, in old jeans and a flannel shirt with the sleeves rolled up to reveal the forearms of a nubby white long-underwear undershirt. The resemblance was remarkable, but it didn't surprise me as much as the fact that he wasn't sixty-five years old and wearing a bathrobe; I'd been expecting Tillman's father.

"How do," he said to Tillman, and they shook hands.

"Not too bad." Tillman was grinning broadly—a bigger smile than I'd ever seen on him. "This is Amy."

Casey held out his hand and we shook. "Hi," I said and smiled at him; he didn't quite meet my eye. "It's nice to meet you."

Casey picked up our suitcases. "You see that Carson's is all closed up?" he said to Tillman. "Stupid son of a bitch."

"I saw."

Tillman grabbed the gun and the cooler, leaving me the Scotch. It was my gift to Casey, and I was regretting a little my choice of Cardhu, in which my father indulged himself once or twice a week. (It had been his suggestion; I'd thought it better than my mother's, "a nice basket of jams and mustards.") I was regretting even more the green and white striped paper and the blue ribbon with which I'd adorned the bottle. As I followed Tillman up the stairs I briefly considered stripping off the giftwrap, but I couldn't think of anywhere to put it.

We entered the apartment through the kitchen. A big black dog came bounding toward us, jumping up on Tillman and licking his face.

"What a beautiful dog," I said in my stupidest girl-voice.

"Perry!" Casey said, and the dog sat.

"Good boy," Tillman crooned, scratching the dog behind the ears. "Good, good boy."

Casey led us into a very small room off the kitchen—the floor was covered almost entirely by a double-bed mattress, made up with brightly flowered sheets and a pea-green blanket. "Great, Case," Tillman said. "Perfect. Thanks."

"Thank Patsy," Casey said. "It's all her mother's stuff." He set down our bags and edged by me to get back into the kitchen. "Want a beer or something?"

Tillman smiled at me and touched my hip as he followed Casey. "Great," he said. "Perfect. Thanks."

I left the Scotch on the mattress and stood in the doorway. Casey got two beers out of the refrigerator. He opened them both and handed a bottle to Tillman. Tillman turned to me. "Aim?" he said, not something he'd ever called me before.

"I'd love one."

Casey set his beer on the stovetop. "Sorry," he said to the floor. "Excuse my manners." He got another beer out of the refrigerator, but rather than handing it to me he set it down and opened a cabinet for a glass.

"Oh, that's OK, Casey," I said. "I don't mind the bottle."

He shrugged, closed the cabinet, and handed me the beer. "Suit yourself," he said.

We stood there sipping. Perry circled me and I reached a cautious hand out to pet him. Finally Tillman said maybe we could go sit down and Casey pushed off from where he'd been leaning and led us into the other room. It evidently doubled as his bedroom and living room: in addition to a few easy chairs grouped in front of a TV, in the corner there was a platform bed on legs about five feet tall. Underneath the bed were a primitive-looking bureau and, hanging from a pole which ran from one leg to another, four or five hangers for clothes.

Tillman crossed the room and bent to look at the arrangement. "Pretty nice," he said, turning back to look at Casey. "Been a busy beaver, hey?"

Casey smiled. "Look at this." He went over to the bed and fiddled with something on the underside of the platform, then swung a small ladder down. "Magnets," he said proudly.

Tillman motioned me over. "See how he's got this rigged up?" He demonstrated how the ladder swung up to rest against the platform when it wasn't in use, then swung back down so Casey could climb into bed.

"I didn't know you did carpentry," I said to Casey.

"I just fool around with it." He sighed and ran his hand through his hair.

"Shall we have a seat?" said Tillman.

There were exactly three chairs, and it occurred to me to wonder what we'd do if Patsy came over while we were there; on the whole, seating difficulties aside, I hoped she would. I went over and sat in the far chair, a worn-out crushed-velvet recliner. Tillman and Casey exchanged a glance. "Oh, I'm sorry, Casey," I said. "Is this where you usually sit?"

He snorted.

"That's the death chair," said Tillman with an uncomfortable smile. "That's where he never sits."

At six the next morning I allowed myself to get out of bed and tiptoe through the kitchen to the bathroom. I'd been lying wide awake almost the whole night, wondering how I had come to be where I was; I couldn't have felt more at odds if I'd been lying in a hut in the middle of the Australian Outback with no one for company but the strange man who'd picked me up hitchhiking late that afternoon. After fifteen or twenty minutes in the death chair I had pleaded fatigue, and when Tillman came to bed an hour or so later he gave me a vacant smile and was snoring inside two minutes.

Snapping on the light in the bathroom, I realized that I'd failed, the night before, to notice that it had a window. I pulled aside the lime-green gingham curtain (thank Patsy?) and looked out. It had snowed during the night, just a dusting, and across the whitened rooftops I could see a lone traffic signal, its red light pulsing on and off. As I watched, a tow truck made its way down the street and disappeared.

I sat on the closed seat of the toilet and picked up a warped copy of *Popular Mechanics* that lay on the nearby radiator. It opened automatically to an envelope addressed, in a child's hand, to Casey.

The postmark was Rapid City, SD. I slid open the envelope and pulled out a folded sheet of stationery. The paper was lined, with a row of strawberries along the top. "Dear Daddy," it read in painfully neat, rounded cursive. "How are you. I am fine. We are writting letters today in school today. Did you get your truck fixed? I hope you got it fixed. Tomorrow I am going to sleep at Julie's. Yours truley, Tina M. Crane."

I put the letter back in the envelope, the envelope back in the magazine, and the magazine back on the radiator. I used the toilet and washed my face, then tiptoed back through the kitchen to our room and slipped under the covers.

Tillman rolled over and put his arm around me. "What time is it?" he mumbled.

"Six fifteen."

He turned away from me, groaning. "A person needs to sleep," he said. Then he reached back, groped for my hand, and pulled my arm around his waist.

"Coffee," Tillman said. "I must have coffee. And food."

We were waiting by the truck while Casey took Perry for a quick walk. I was torn between wanting to look and wanting to avoid looking at the grey canvas vest Tillman wore under his jacket—there were little loops all over the front of it and I'd watched in a kind of strange fascination as he'd slipped his bullets into them. "Shells," he'd corrected me. He'd given me some long underwear to put on under my jeans, and an extra sweater to wear under my jacket, and I felt stuffed into my clothes like a little sausage bulging out of its casing. Already my feet were cold.

Casey and Perry appeared at the mouth of the alley. "What say we stop at Burger King?" Casey called.

Tillman waited for Casey to reach us. "Great minds think alike," he said. "Amy was just saying how hungry she was." He elbowed me. "Right, Aim?"

"Patsy'll be on," Casey said. "Did I tell you she made manager?"

"No," Tillman said. "I don't believe you did."

Casey nodded. "That's pretty good money, you know."

"And such a nice place to work," said Tillman.

Casey didn't reply. After a moment he walked over to look at Tillman's car. "How's it running?" he asked.

"Pretty good," Tillman said. He took a step closer to Casey. "It's not a bad little car."

Casey circled it, bending over here and there for a closer look. He turned to Tillman. "You end up getting a new starter?"

"Forty bucks."

Casey shook his head. "Should've got it here."

"I live in Chicago," Tillman said. "What am I supposed to do, drive fifteen hours to save ten dollars?"

Casey shrugged. "It's your car." He walked back over to the truck and let the gate down so Perry could jump in, then he opened the door and pulled a long-armed plastic brush from behind the driver's seat. He swept the snow from the windshield and climbed in. After a moment he leaned over and flipped up the lock on the passenger side.

Tillman gave me an awkward smile, then went over and held open the door.

We drove back out to the strip, where Burger King was situated between a Mini-mart and a car wash. Casey led us to a cash register manned by a teenaged girl with permed blond hair who giggled and blushed when she saw him.

"Kelly belly," he said. "What's good today?"

She shrugged her shoulders and giggled some more.

He leaned against the counter and pulled his wallet out of his back pocket. "I'll have the usual, Kelly," he said. "Put whatever these two want on my check." He took a ten from his wallet and handed it to her, then ducked under the counter and went back to the kitchen.

Tillman and I ordered, and when our food was ready we took our tray to a table near the window. Tillman handed me my coffee and unwrapped his egg thing. "Should we wait for Casey?" I said.

"This is Burger King, Aim."

"Aim?"

He grinned at me and bit into his breakfast.

"I don't think Casey likes me," I said. I stirred cream into my coffee and looked up at Tillman.

"He's just shy," he said. "Don't take it personally."

"It's hard not to."

"Well, do you like him?"

I blushed. "I guess I don't really feel I know him yet."

"Well, ditto, I'm sure."

I took a sip of coffee. "Is Patsy going hunting with us?"

"Here they come," Tillman said. "Let's ask her."

Patsy was a tiny, doll-like woman about my age—twenty-six or twenty-seven. Her coppery hair was held back in a girlish pony tail.

"I hear you're from California," she said to me once Tillman had introduced us. "Casey and I almost went to San Francisco last summer, didn't we, honey? We were going to drive out and stop in Reno to try the slot machines, but the truck wasn't working." She turned to look at Casey. "Right, honey?"

Casey had unwrapped one of three hamburgers on his tray, and had just, with his first bite, bitten off nearly half of it. He nodded.

"Nice breakfast," Tillman said.

"I know," said Patsy. "Can you believe it? Every morning it's three hamburgers and a strawberry shake. Least when I'm working —technically you're not supposed to offer burgers till breakfast is over. Tell them what you have when I'm not working, Casey." She leaned forward. "Burritos. From across the street. He's ruining the lining of his stomach."

Casey was impassive while Patsy spoke. He finished the first burger and began working on the milk shake. He appeared to be formulating a response, and I found myself fearing a little for Patsy. But when he finally looked up he just smiled at her and said, "I like burritos."

Tillman laughed. "'I like burritos,'" he said. "Spoken by a man who knows his own mind."

Casey unwrapped his second hamburger.

"Did Casey tell you what happened to Tina?" Patsy asked Tillman. "This girl in her class— her daddy works out at the Air Force base up there and they went out and had a tour one day. Tina got to climb into a B-1 bomber."

"She didn't get in it," Casey said. "They climbed up the stairs and looked in, they didn't *get* in. You think they'd let kids in one of those?"

"You're wrong, Casey. She told me herself. She sat in the driver's seat."

Casey turned to Tillman and tapped the side of his head. "In her dreams."

"Your own daughter told me."

Tillman touched my leg under the table and cleared his throat. "How's Tina doing?" he said. "Is she coming down for Thanksgiving?"

Casey shook his head. "Her mother says after Christmas." He wiped his mouth with a paper napkin. "She's getting married."

"Really?" Tillman said. "Teri?"

"She's just dumb enough to try it twice."

"Casey, you don't mean that," Patsy said. "What kind of thing is that to say in front of your own girlfriend? Honestly." She smiled and shook her head. "Sometimes I can't believe you." She took the shake out of his hand and sipped from the straw.

"We're going to take Amy hunting," Tillman said to Patsy. "What time do you get off? Want to come?"

Patsy shook her head emphatically. "This girl doesn't hunt. Casey got me out there one day last year? I just about froze my butt off."

"Perry was limping so I took her to scare the birds out of the cover," Casey said.

"But I scared them away," Patsy said with a laugh. "You have to be quiet," she warned me.

"What makes you think Amy's never hunted before?" Tillman said. He hit me under the table. "She happens to be a really good shot."

Patsy blushed. "Are you? I'm sorry. I guess they must have good hunting out in California."

"He's kidding," I said. "I've never even held a gun." I could feel Casey look at me and I turned to Tillman. "Maybe I should hang out with Patsy while you two go."

"I'm going over to my mom's," Patsy said. "Soon as I get off work. You could watch the shows with us."

Tillman put his hand around the back of my neck. "Don't tell me you came all the way to Nebraska to chicken out," he said. "Don't break my heart."

The snow had started up again, and we slid a little as we left the parking lot. The guns were on a rack inside the back window of the cab, and I began to feel nervous knowing they were there, just inches from my head.

When we were nearly out of town Tillman said, "Go by the house," and Casey turned onto a side street. He slowed down in front of a two-story white aluminum-sided house with a big screened-in front porch. A driveway led back to an open garage in which I could just make out a motorcycle.

"Well," Tillman said. "Here's where we grew up."

I nodded.

He pointed at the upstairs. "That was my room. That was Casey's. Our parents' was in back. We used to climb out our windows onto the roof of the porch and then jump down from there. Two or three in the morning, we'd walk into town and meet our girlfriends behind the high school."

"Oh, you did, did you?" I said. "Is this the truth, Casey? Were you guys juvenile delinquents?"

He smiled. "I wasn't—I went along to make sure Tillman didn't get into trouble."

"Oh, right," Tillman said, laughing. "Who went to third with Mary Beth Rivers in Hurleys' basement?"

Casey blushed crimson. He hit the accelerator and we spun down the block. We came to a stop sign and he braked and said to Tillman, "Should I tell her about you and that Lori girl?"

"Be my guest," Tillman said. "That Lori girl—oh, you mean Lorraine Miggle?" He turned to me. "Miggle. Can you imagine?" He looked at Casey. "What happened with her? I can't quite remember."

Casey shook his head. "Forget it."

"Oh, come on, Casey," I said. "Tell me. I'm all ears."

"He's too embarrassed," Tillman said. "You're a girl."

We started off again and a few minutes later we were out of town. We drove for miles, past snow dusted fields and small, nearly-collapsed farmhouses. The only sounds were the hum of the engine and the flapflap of Casey's windshield wipers brushing aside the wet snowflakes.

Tillman nudged me. "See there?" He pointed out the window at a little blue house. "Casey's ex-wife's folks'."

I turned to Casey. "How long have you and Teri been apart?"

He ran his hand through his hair. "Two and a half, three years."

"That must have been hard."

"Well," he said. "Her dad still lets me hunt his land."

"What a consolation," Tillman said, and they both laughed.

I began to feel concerned about the cold. I had gloves in my pocket but they were purple leather, not quite hunting gloves if such things existed. And then there was hunting—hunting! What kind of love-trance had brought me here? I tossed around in my mind the idea of waiting in the truck, but it wasn't really a possibility.

We turned onto an unpaved road, and Casey stopped in front of a wide gate. Tillman climbed out of the truck and held the gate open while Casey drove through, then re-fastened it and got back in. We drove another mile or so and Casey slowed down. He looked out at the field to our left, a city block of drooping mud-colored cornstalks. "Lot of pheasant here last week," he said.

"Looks good," said Tillman.

Casey cut the engine and Tillman put his hand on my leg. "Ready?" he said.

He got out and helped me down; almost immediately my hair was covered with snow. I brushed it off, then wiped my wet hand on my jeans.

"Don't you have a hat?" he said.

He had somehow managed to produce a coffee-colored cap, and he put it on. I turned and saw that Casey wore a nearly identical one.

"She doesn't have a hat," Tillman said, a trace of irritation in his voice. "Here, you'd better wear mine."

He took it off and held it out for me to take, but there was something about it: it was one of those Sherlock Holmes hats—with ear flaps that met and buttoned at the crown, and a stiff little bill—but made of flannel-lined canvas, a hat for a Sherlock Holmes who'd wandered far from Baker Street.

"I'll be OK," I said.

"Amy, come on," he said. "It's my fault, I should have told you to bring a hat."

I was wearing a scarf around my neck and I took it off and put it over my head, tying it under my chin. "OK?" I said. "My babushka look."

"Very fetching."

Casey went around to the back of the truck and lowered the gate, and Perry bounded onto the ground and started jumping around, nudging at Tillman and Casey as they reached into the cab for their guns.

"He's so eager," I said.

Tillman looked over at me and leaned his gun against the truck. "Unlike you?"

"It just sort of hit me what we're going to do."

"What?" he said. "We're going to have fun. Come on—a nice, bracing walk? You'll like it."

"Hey," Casey said.

We looked up as three or four birds rose from the cornfield and soared away.

"See there, Amy?" Tillman turned back to the truck. He took a couple of the shells—their cheerful, bright yellow casings suddenly seeming to me a lie against their function—and clicked them into his gun.

"Were those pheasants?" I asked.

"Yep."

"How could you tell?"

"Didn't you see the tags hanging off their feet?"

"Tail feathers," Casey said. I looked up and he seemed to be watching me—benignly, almost sadly. "Pheasants have long tail feathers. You can tell by the shape, too, and if you're close enough, the coloring. You never seen one before?"

I shook my head.

"They're real pretty. Colorful." He glanced at Tillman. "You'll see."

"If I get that close," I said.

Again Casey looked at Tillman but this time Tillman didn't meet his eye, and Casey pressed his lips together and shook his head. He leaned his gun against the truck and bent to tighten his boot laces.

"Here's what let's do," Tillman said. "I'll go across here, then Amy about twenty feet beyond me, then you."

Casey straightened up and adjusted his cap.

"OK?" Tillman said.

Casey picked up his gun. He walked away from us, down the road, Perry trotting alongside.

"Is he mad?" I said.

Tillman rolled his eyes. "He's not mad, he's crazy." He picked up his gun. "He's fucked."

"Tillman."

"Do you want to do this or not? My brother is my brother—there's no telling what his problem is."

I tightened the scarf, tucking the ends into my jacket. "Just tell me what to do. Just point me in the right direction."

"Hey." He put his gun down and pressed his lips to my forehead, then to my mouth. "This is supposed to be fun, too," he said. "Right?"

I nodded.

"Do you want to do it?"

I nodded again.

He took up his gun, and with his free hand under my elbow he walked me a few paces down the road. "We'll check out this field first," he said. "When we get over there if you're ready you can give it a try." He stopped. "OK?"

"OK."

"See where Casey's standing? I'm going to stop here, and you're going to stand halfway between us. We'll keep pace with each other as we walk. Just go in a straight line, between the rows of corn."

I looked at the field. Now that we were closer I could see how high the weathered stalks of corn actually were. Tillman and Casey would both clear them by several inches, but they'd come up nearly to the top of my head. "The pheasants are in there?" I said.

"Here's hoping."

I started down the road toward Casey, but turned back. "Shouldn't I be wearing something brighter? My jacket's almost the same color as the corn."

Tillman gave me a big grin. "We're not going to shoot you," he said. "I promise."

"I'm sure you wouldn't *mean* to."

"How could we shoot you if we weren't aiming at you? Can you fly?"

I smiled at him. "Silly me."

I headed down the road again, stopping when I got halfway to Casey; he was standing there watching me, his gun held loosely at his side.

We started walking. The terrain between the rows of corn was rougher than I'd imagined, and the light snow on the ground made me cautious about falling. I sensed the two men at my sides, but the corn was too high and too thick for me to see them. I walked with my hands stuffed in my jacket pockets, my head bent against the snow, my shoulders hunched up—making myself as small as possible.

It was very quiet. I stopped walking for a moment and all I could hear was a soft rustling—the wind in the corn, maybe, or the sound of their pantlegs brushing together as they walked. I moved forward quickly to stay even with them. I stopped again and tried to listen more carefully. Were they ahead of me or behind me? What if I had somehow crossed into the wrong row and was off track? I felt moisture seeping through my shoes, and I started to walk again.

There was a sudden flapping, and to my right a shot blasted through the air. I froze as a second shot sounded from behind me. I clapped my hands over my face and stood still, my heart beating wildly. There wasn't a sound. I could feel my pulse everywhere—in my fingers, my toes, my neck. After a moment I carefully widened the spaces between my fingers, the way I did at scary movies when I wanted to see if the awful part was over, and saw again the dark stalks in front of me. I heard Perry bark once, and then there was a frantic rustling and Casey burst through the corn. He came to a standstill when he saw me.

I dropped my hands to my sides. He held the gun clamped under his elbow, the barrel resting easily in his outstretched hand.

"Was that you?" I said.

"The first one." He had a slightly stunned look on his face—as if the shot had surprised him, too. "You OK?"

"I think so. The noise just got me—somehow I didn't expect it to be so loud."

He dug into his pants pocket, pulled out a bandanna, and offered it to me.

I touched my nose. "Am I dripping?"

"You're, um—" He licked his lips. "You're crying." He ducked his head, looked up and studied me for a moment, then headed away from me, down the corn row. I touched my face: he was right.

I heard him whistle sharply and call Perry's name, then I heard Tillman's voice, although I couldn't hear what he was saying. I wiped my face on the bandanna and blew my nose. I stood there for a few minutes, waiting for Tillman to come for me; but he didn't, so I started toward the end of the field.

The two of them were standing on a narrow dirt road that separated our field from another one. "You're a good luck charm," Tillman exclaimed when he saw me. "Look—we're two for two."

He held out, by its feet, a big brown-and-black bird. There was a streak of blood on his pants, at the knee, and I took a step backward. Perry growled at me, and I turned and saw the other bird, lying at Casey's feet, its head twisted backward. They *were* colorful —marked with blue, green, white, even red. But I couldn't look. I turned back to the field and craned my neck, trying to spot the truck.

"Over there," Casey said. He pointed at a ninety-degree angle to where I'd been looking. I located the truck and stared at it.

From behind me Tillman put his hand on my shoulder. "Lose your bearings a little?"

I nodded but didn't look at him.

"Hey," he said quietly. "Talk to me."

"It's just that I don't want to look at the birds," I said carefully. "I'd turn around but I don't want to see them."

"No problem," he said. "Turn, look."

I turned and he was holding up his arms—look Ma, no hands. But the pheasant's feet protruded from a big pocket on the front of his jacket, and there was a new smear of blood on his pants.

"Give it to me," Casey said.

"What?"

Casey yanked the bird out of Tillman's pocket and stooped to pick up the other one. He held them together by their feet, their heads dangling near the ground. "Walk around by the road," he said, and he stepped back into the cornfield.

Tillman's hand flew to his mouth. "I'm sorry," he said, shaking his head. "I'm sorry. I'm so stupid. I didn't think it would bother you." His face had gone slack: he looked defeated.

"I'm fine," I said. "No harm done. I just may not eat poultry for a while."

He took off his cap and looked at it. "I didn't *think*," he said quietly. He whipped the cap against his leg a few times and I reached out a hand to stop him. He put the cap back on and started down the road.

I watched him walk and suddenly I was twenty yards back, watching me watch him: me, standing by a snowy cornfield in Nebraska, dressed in borrowed long underwear, watching a man in a silly hat—a man who'd just killed a bird—walk away from me. I started to laugh. Tillman turned around quickly—to see if I was crying, he said later—and I laughed harder. He stood there watching me and I tried to stop, but I couldn't: what a pair, I thought giddily, what an impossible pair. I heard myself snorting with laughter and I tried to think of something sad—Tillman's father, summoning death. But when I imagined him alone in that white house, sitting in the red velvet recliner in his bathrobe, eating string beans straight from the can, he seemed like nothing so much as a grumpy father in a sit-com on TV. The laughter contorted my mouth and I tried instead to conjure my own father, sitting at his desk with a betrayed look on his face, entirely unable to imagine why his daughter chose to participate in something he abhorred. But I didn't even have the knowledge of my parents' disapproval to sober me: I'd told them nothing about the true purpose of our trip. I put my fist to my mouth and gnawed at my knuckles.

"What's so funny?" Tillman said. He put his hands on his hips and began to smile. "Hey—what's so funny?"

Years later, we'd recall these younger selves with wistful fondness, like parents thinking back to when the babies were babies: Imagine thinking we could leave our pasts behind! Imagine thinking we couldn't! How smug we've become—toting up the early mistakes and self-deceptions, marveling at the sheer unlikely luck that brought us together and keeps us that way: as certain that a particular grace illuminates our lives as all the other happily married people in the world.

"You," I said to Tillman on that day in Nebraska. "Me."

Shortly before my mother's death I said an unforgivable thing to her.
I did not at the time know she was dying, although if I'd known
better how to look at her perhaps I'd have seen that something was
wrong. By how to look at her I mean, of course, into her: past the
brilliant costume to the very blue flame of her heart.

It was Christmastime, and I was visiting her at her little house in
Palo Alto—her bungalow, she liked to call it. Between us there were
years of difficult phone calls and excessive gift-giving, but also some
good hours together, some lovely, lovely hours. I was in her small
guest room, still dressed but stretched out on the bedspread, when
she knocked on my door and came in to say goodnight: a tall woman
of sixty-four, handsomely dressed in a kind of red and gold hostess
gown, her face recently tightened.

She sat on the edge of the bed. "Buddy," she said, "Christmas
Eve. We should have driven to see the lights or made mulled wine
or strung cranberries or something."

"We could each eat a candy cane before bed."

"I love it!" She clasped her hands together and laughed, a little
too hard. "You definitely have a touch."

"Or maybe I'm a little touched," I said, tapping my head.

"I'm touched," she said. "I'm touched that you're here, Buddy, I
am." She fiddled with her bracelet, twisted it around her wrist a few
times. "There aren't many men who'd fly three thousand miles to
see good old Mom for Christmas."

"Not so old," I said.

"No, but really, you probably had loads of parties and so on you
could have gone to." She looked at me questioningly, and I shrugged.
"Or you might've wanted to visit your father . . ."

They had been divorced twenty-two years earlier, at the end of my freshman year of college. For years he had been like a ghost in our house, but that last Christmas I'd gone home and found him living in the guest room, unable even to join us for meals. My younger sister, Ingrid, and I prevailed upon him to have Christmas dinner with us, and when my mother brought him the turkey to carve, he sawed off one leg and then carefully set the knife and fork on the platter, suggested that it was time I learned, and left the table. By the end of my sophomore year he had resigned from the university, had moved away from California altogether to chair the English department at a small college in central Illinois. I talked to him three or four times a year, saw him occasionally when business took him to New York. He never mentioned my mother to me. Seeing him was like seeing a distant uncle who I knew would always wish me well. "Grand to see you," he'd say.

"You know I'm happy to come here," I said to my mother.

She patted my knee. "I know."

I swung my legs around and sat upright. "If we wanted to do something Christmasy tonight we could call Ingrid," I said. "Say 'Have a merry' to her and Bruce."

My mother frowned; for years she and Ingrid had been on poor terms. ("Have you gotten through to Ingrid?" I'd asked her on the morning after the big earthquake out there; it had taken her hours to reach me. "Once," she said. "She was about six at the time.")

"I'm sure she'd like to hear from you," I said, although I wasn't.

My mother sighed. "It's just so tiring talking to her, don't you find? She's so literal-minded, she hasn't changed a bit."

"She has," I said. She's happy, I wanted to say, but didn't. "Maybe I'll call her myself."

"Oh, Buddy." My mother moved closer to me, and I smelled her perfume, the familiar spiciness of it. "I want us to be friends."

I smiled at her. "I'm friends. Aren't you?"

"Then why won't you *tell* me about yourself?" she cried. "Is there a special man in your life? Are you in love? Do you know, I could die happy if I knew you were in love."

"Sorry."

"Well, what about your friends?" She looked up at me. "At least tell me about your friends."

I leaned my head back and closed my eyes. "My friends are dead or dying." When I looked at her again her eyes had widened, and for a moment I anticipated understanding, maybe even wanted comfort.

"Oh, poor Buddy," she said. "I know how you feel. Mine are, too. Why, talking to Ruth and Mary Ann these days I have to invent illnesses to get any attention."

Should I, at that point, have told my mother what I'd seen at the bedsides of men I'd loved? Would it have been better that way for her? For me? For us?

Instead I said, "If your friends were as sick as mine you'd drop them in seconds." And whether or not this was true—and I'm inclined, with all the aching generosity of hindsight, to think that it was not—my mother rose without speaking and left the room.

My friends were dead or dying, although I still had Kevin. Have. Have.

"Why couldn't I have said I was in love?" I asked him after she'd died.

"Because you weren't?" he said. "I guess you could have made someone up. You could have told her about what's-his-name."

"Dean?" I groaned. "I figured out what it was about him—he said 'dint.' Instead of didn't."

Kevin laughed.

"Plus those cowboy boots."

"You've never been a big fan of tooled leather," Kevin said.

When my mother was alive Kevin had a name for me: Robert the Jumper. As in jumping through hoops. He said if my mother called and told me she was thirsty I'd get on the red-eye with a bottle of Evian. I told him if *his* mother called and said *she* was thirsty he'd

Federal Express her a bottle of Evian with rat poison in it. He laughed and said, "So why are we both gay if you love your mother and I hate mine?" He was in therapy, so he thought about things a lot. I told him it was all much more complicated than that. Or much simpler.

After my mother died Kevin teased me less, asked me how I was doing, let me tell him stories about her.

A story: When I was five or six my mother took it into her head that I was Ready for Culture. That, in fact, time was wasting. Saturday after Saturday she persuaded my father to stay behind with Ingrid, for whom culture could apparently wait, while she took me to San Francisco to see ballets, concerts, operas. We had lunch beforehand, in dark velvet restaurants where the waiters brought me glasses of ginger ale and saucers full of maraschino cherries while she drank her vodka martinis. People stared at us, and I was embarrassed because I understood that my mother had invented for us a glamorous hint of tragedy only barely survived: at her cue we spoke in hushed tones, and because she only poked at her food I didn't eat much of mine. We'd get to the opera house just before curtain time and quickly look over the program together, my mother saying something like, "We'll see how they do with the Schubert, Buddy—I have my doubts." I loved that "we'll"—being included in the practice of judgment—but I knew that this, too, was meant for whatever audience we had. By the end of the performance I invariably had a stomach ache from the candy I'd eaten at intermission—entire boxes of Junior Mints or nonpareils; we'd blink as the bright house lights came up, and my mother would rest her hand on the top of my head, or touch my shoulder. Then we went home, to my father at his desk in the study, to Ingrid quietly schooling her stuffed animals.

"You wanted your mother all to yourself," Kevin said. "Herself would say you hated sharing her, with your father or with Ingrid."

Herself was Dr. Gold, Kevin's shrink. I loved her only a little less

than he did; she was reported to have beautiful rugs. "Duh," I said.
Kevin laughed.

"Anyway, what about how she embarrassed me? I was mortified.
Mortified at six, you never really get over that."

Kevin said he didn't know. He said he'd ask Dr. Gold for me.

In the long fall to where we ended up—my mother alone in her little
house in Palo Alto; my father alone in Illinois, in a house I knew
only as a street address; me alone, mostly alone, in my apartment in
New York; among us only Ingrid attached to someone, happily and
privately in Medford, Oregon—in that long turning away from each
other there were swift lifetimes when I imagined us somehow re-
united in a determination to be easy and sweet together. Like TV,
but without the washed-out saccharine mother. I wanted *my* mother,
my father, Ingrid, me—but matched. Perhaps because I couldn't imagine how this could come about, I leapt into the future and saw us all
equally blue-haired—aged as unconvincingly as Elizabeth Taylor
and Rock Hudson in *Giant*—and surrounded by nameless children:
certainly not mine, probably not Ingrid's, but children who would
save us.

There were also times—single days—when we fell long distances,
turned so resolutely there could be no turning back.

Stanford, 1960. This is before the hippies, before the peace signs
painted on the asphalt of White Plaza, before the torchlight sit-ins,
the broken windows—years before my best friend's younger brother,
sixteen and a track star, is shot in the leg at an anti-war demonstration in front of the football stadium. He is seven now and a pest;
when, on weekend mornings, his brother and Ingrid and I ride over
to the campus, we pedal as fast as we can so he will be left behind.
He always finds us, though: the university is the farthest we're allowed
to venture from home, and our favorite, inevitable destination there
is a small courtyard in the center of which is an octagonal pool with

a classically inspired fountain. We like the size, the scale, the modesty of this courtyard; we spend hours here, playing Statues: swinging each other around and freezing in positions we think are sculptural. Like our parents—two professors and their wives—we respect tradition when it comes to art. At the entrance to the courtyard a pair of empty niches face each other across an arcade, and we think it's a shame there aren't statues in them. Nothing modern—our tastes run to small cherubs, or replicas of Pan, flute in hand.

A hot Sunday afternoon in early September. Tonight is the annual beginning-of-the-year English Department party, a chance for the faculty to get together and welcome whoever is new. My father dislikes large parties in general and these in particular because, unanchored by the hospitality and comfort of real hosts and real houses, they are usually even stiffer than other gatherings of too many people. This year, though, is different: he is Acting Head and as such has adopted the party with a kind of zeal we don't usually see in him. He has commandeered the common room of one of the older, nicer dorms—the parties are usually held in a shabby meeting room on the second floor of the department—and devised a system whereby everyone will be sure to mix: a parlor game called "Who Am I." On arrival, each guest will be given the name of a famous person, and a card with that person's initials to pin to his clothes, and everyone will go around asking questions like "Are you Cordelia's father?" to determine each other's identity. It'll be a kind of walking Botticelli, the trick being that all the famous people will be figures from literature. My mother thinks it's the stupidest thing she's ever heard of, and she is still telling my father so as they are getting ready to leave for the party.

"At least let me be who I want," she calls to him; she's in the bathroom with the door ajar.

My father shakes his head sadly, as if to lament to Ingrid and me our mother's unwillingness to play fair. "Can't do that," he calls back. "Anyway, I don't have the cards—I couldn't do it even if I wanted to." He looks at his watch and frowns: he has been ready for fifteen minutes.

Ingrid and I lie on our parents' bed, arguing, idly, over whether or not to go with them: I want to stay home and read, but Ingrid not only wants to go but insists on my going too—she says she'll have a terrible time if she's the only kid. Our going at all was a last-minute, subversive suggestion of my mother's.

"Who do you want to be?" I call to her.

"Lady Macbeth," my father says, loudly enough for her to hear.

She pokes her head out the door. She's holding a lipstick, has already painted her lower lip a deep red. "Ha ha," she says. "So who *has* the cards?"

"We should be there," my father says. "Dick Traeger."

My mother smiles. "Buddy," she says to me, "run outside and see if the Traegers' car is still there."

"I don't feel like it." A year ago I would have gone.

"Ingrid?"

Ingrid shakes her head.

"Oh, for God's sake, Ingrid!" My mother slams the bathroom door.

"Go see," I say, poking Ingrid. "I'll go to the party if you'll go see."

Ingrid makes a face and rolls off the bed—literally rolls until she's lying on the rug. My father looks at her lying there: his solemn, brown-haired daughter dressed today, as nearly every day this summer, in the navy blue shorts and white shirt that were her day-camp outfit the first two weeks in July. He looks at his watch again.

"Better hurry," I say, and Ingrid gets up and trudges out; a moment later I hear the front door close.

"Hi, Robert," my father says.

"Hi, Dad," I say.

Lately I've been having trouble putting my feelings about my family into some kind of order. I've always wanted, more than anything, for Ingrid to try harder to please our mother; so why do I now feel guilty for making her check on the Traegers' car? Perhaps because I know our mother won't really be pleased. Ingrid is nine, two years younger than I; she was born in 1951 and as an act of solidarity my mother named her for Ingrid Bergman, whose recent scandalous behavior she applauded, her theory being that if you didn't live by your heart there was no point in living at all. It is a continuing disappointment to my mother—an affront, really—that our Ingrid has no taste for theatrics of any kind. I have heard my mother use the word "stolid" about our Ingrid, use it with a kind of pleasure.

"Ta da," says my mother, coming out of the bathroom and striking a pose. She is wearing a new dress, a very fitted sleeveless yellow dress that will demand from everyone who sees her in it a moment of uninterrupted attention: it is the shortest dress I've ever seen. It's an acid yellow, a shade maybe one woman in a hundred can wear, and she is that one. With her black hair and summer tan she looks glamorous, even dangerous.

"You've got to be kidding," my father says.

"What?" She leans over and runs her hands up her leg, adjusting her stocking.

"OK," he says. "You've had your fun. Change into whatever you're really going to wear and let's go."

"This is it," she says.

"Part of it, anyway," he mutters.

She looks at me and smiles conspiratorially. I smile back; I think she looks great, although I wish she wouldn't play him like this.

"Helen," he says.

"For God's sake, Harry, it's just a shift."

"And you look pretty damned shifty" is all he can manage.

She laughs and turns to me. "If he were a woman you'd think he was jealous."

He grimaces. "I think 'envious' is the word you're after."

My mother shrugs. We hear the front door open and close, and a moment later Ingrid comes into the bedroom and announces that the Traegers' car is still there. She doesn't comment on, doesn't even seem to notice my mother's dress.

My mother goes to the telephone and begins to dial. My father, I notice, looks irritated.

"Dick?" my mother says into the receiver. "This is Helen—from next door?" An intimate smile curls her lips, and she turns to the wall. "I hear you have the name cards, for the party. Are there any blank ones left?" She laughs. "I knew I could count on you. N.D. Nicole Diver. See you soon." She hangs up the phone and turns to face us. "Well," she says, "you kids coming?"

"Nicole Diver?" my father says. "Nicole Diver? God, that's rich."

"Who's she?" I ask.

My mother smiles but doesn't answer me. She picks up her purse and drops her lipstick into it.

"Who's Nicole Diver?" I turn to my father. "Dad?"

"Oh," he says absently, "she's just one of Fitzgerald's beauties." He pats his pants pocket, and I hear the jingling of his keys.

The boredom of being a child ignored by a group of adults. Ingrid and I skulk around the hors d'oeuvres table, spearing Swedish meatballs with toothpicks, using our bare fingers to pluck from their red sauce several pigs-in-a-blanket each. We sit on straight-backed chairs against the wall, and while Ingrid plays with her hair, braiding one lock and then another, I study the grown-ups in an effort to place my parents on a scale of normalcy.

It takes no time at all to see that it was my mother's goal to set herself apart from the other wives. They wear full-skirted dresses of ordinary colors and modest lengths; but the difference reaches way beyond my mother's yellow dress. The other women talk to each other, but my mother talks only to men—to groups of them, four or five or six at a time. And she has a way of scanning the room while she talks—at first I think she's looking for us, but she keeps doing it long after I've had eye contact with her. I realize, in the way you can realize old, familiar knowledge, that she's looking around to see if people are looking at her: that she *wants* them to be. I start to feel tense for her—I'll feel tense for beautiful, hungry people all my life —and I force my attention to my father.

About him, I cannot be so clear. He's wearing a summer suit and a tie, like all of the men except for Dick Traeger, our neighbor, and one or two others, who wear dark, open-necked shirts under their jackets. I'm happy to see that he's having a good time: he's making the rounds, taking people drinks as if this place were his home. But something else about him: his cheerfulness seems to depend on a kind of wall he's built around my mother, to keep her from coming into his line of vision.

Ingrid hits my leg. "Let's go to the courtyard," she says. "This is stupid."

Reluctantly, I stand up and follow her out of the room. She hasn't unbraided her hair, and sticking up from her head are two tiny braids that aren't coming undone by themselves.

It's seven o'clock on a Sunday three weeks before the start of classes, and the campus is deserted. When we get to our courtyard we head for the empty niches and climb into them—Ingrid's favorite thing to do when we're here alone. We sit facing each other across the arcade.

"You should see your hair," I say.

Ingrid touches the top of her head and encounters the braids; she makes quick work of disassembling them. "Look at that man," she says.

I lean forward and look: sitting on the edge of the fountain is a thin man with stringy shoulder-length brown hair. "So—he's not bothering you."

"I think something's wrong with him."

I look again. He's hunched over unhappily, his elbows on his knees and his chin in his hands: his feet are bare. He looks up and sees us looking at him; instantly he stands and heads our way. "Great, Ingrid," I say.

He stops when he's just a few yards away. He looks from me to Ingrid, then back at me. "What are you guys doing?" he says. There appears to be something wrong with his teeth.

"Just sitting," Ingrid says.

"Our parents are just over there," I add, waving in the direction we came from.

"You look like statues," he says. "What're your names? Mine's Bug."

"Your name is Bug?" Ingrid says.

"I'll bet yours isn't any better."

"It's Ingrid."

"You win."

She smiles. "Bug must be your nickname."

He turns to me. "So what're you, mute?"

I shake my head.

"Oh, yeah," he says. "Your parents are just over there."

I look at Ingrid and try to send a signal: stop *talking* to him. But she either doesn't get it or ignores it. "They're at a cocktail party," she says.

"How chomming," Bug says. "Is there perchance food at this affair?"

"Why?" Ingrid says. "Are you hungry? We could get you some."

"No, we couldn't. We should be going, Ing." I mean to jump out of the niche, but somehow I don't move.

"Are you?" Ingrid says.

Bug reaches into his pocket and pulls out a stone. He studies it carefully, looking at both sides—it's almost as if he were memorizing it—then he puts it back. "I can't remember what it feels like not to be."

"Are you *starving?*" Ingrid asks him.

"Well, I guess the answer is compared to who?" He runs a hand through his greasy hair. "I'm not in danger of dying today."

"When was the last time you ate?" she says.

He looks at me, and I see that his face is truly gaunt. I decide that he's probably telling the truth, but still, I want us gone.

"Friday," he says. "I had some doughnuts."

"Today's Sunday," Ingrid says.

"What are you doing here?" I say. "Are you a student?" He laughs, and now I do jump down from my niche. "Ingrid," I say.

She ignores me. "How old are you?" she asks him.

"Ingrid, Ingrid—so many questions." He moves a little closer to her. "It's my turn. What's on your shirt?" He points at Ingrid's chest —at the breast pocket of her camp shirt, where I know it says "Pine Hill Camp" in navy embroidery.

"*Now*, Ingrid," I say. "We'll get in trouble."

"It's my camp shirt," she says. "I'm going to get you some food— stay right here, OK?"

She jumps down and Bug goes over and boosts himself into her place. "It's still warm," he says, and he gives us a queasy grey smile.

As soon as we're out of his sight we start running. "You're so stupid," I say to Ingrid, but then I look at her and see that she's begun to cry. "What?" I say. "What?"

"He's *starving*."

I try to pat her shoulder, but running seems more important.

Something has changed at the party. People are talking louder, and their gestures seem exaggerated. They're drunk, of course, but at eleven I think the difference is about something else: how grown-ups live in a world that's more real than ours, noisier and brighter.

I leave Ingrid in one of the chairs against the wall and look around for my parents. Right away I see my mother halfway across the room: the glint of her dress, and then her profile, smiling a smile born of tedium. I think it would be better to find my father, but something makes her turn, and when she sees me she says something to the people she's with and heads my way.

"Darling," she says, "you saved me from death by boredom.

Having fun?" She reaches over and does something to my collar, and I twist away.

"Where's Dad?"

"Oh, who knows. Off serenading some thirteen-year-old girl, no doubt." She looks at me, then pulls my head close and ruffles my hair. "Buddy, honestly. He was R. M.—Romeo Montague. It's a joke, sweetheart. I haven't seen him in hours, or at least half-hours."

"I don't know," I say. "We met this man outside and he says he's hungry. Ingrid wants to take him some food, but I don't know."

"Wait a second, slow down. What happened?"

I explain as well as I can, but as I speak the whole thing seems to lose significance; I know she's not going to understand.

"Well," she says when I'm done, "take him some meatballs if you want. God knows no one's bothering to eat."

"He was sort of—weird."

Ingrid arrives at my mother's side. She's more composed, but it's evident she's been crying.

"What is it, honey?" my mother says to her.

Ingrid shrugs, tears gathering again in her eyes.

"You kids had better just stay here." My mother reaches out to someone behind me, and Dick Traeger joins our group. "Dick," she says, her hand on his arm, "my kids met up with some character who wants our food. What do you think?"

Dick Traeger looks at us carefully. He has unbuttoned the second button of his shirt, and there's an unpleasant triangle of hair curling there. He turns to my mother. "Far be it from me to be an elitist. The more, the merrier."

"He was hungry," Ingrid says, and tears begin to spill down her face.

"According to Buddy," my mother says to Dick Traeger, "he was also 'weird.'"

"Weird," Dick Traeger says. "Do you mean different? The world is a wide and wonderful place, Buddy. We have to embrace difference."

"Don't tease him," my mother says.

"Who's teasing? I'm serious."

Ingrid sobs. "Will you come with us?"

My mother and Dick Traeger look at each other. "We'll all go," Dick Traeger says. "Safety in numbers, eh?"

"I don't want to go." I know I sound petulant, but I don't care. "Where's Dad?"

"What difference does it make?" my mother snaps. "Ingrid, go get one of those little plates and load it up. Let's go if we're going."

I catch a glimpse of my father leaving the room, and I hurry after him. "Dad," I call when I get to the exit; he's halfway down the hall to the men's room. "Dad."

He turns around. "Hello," he says, smiling genially at me. He comes back to where I've stopped. "Don't I know you?"

"Dad," I say. I feel myself starting to cry, and I turn away from him.

"What's wrong, Robert?" He puts his hand on my shoulder.

I explain what happened—better, this time. I watch my father's expression change, and even as I feel relieved that I've made someone understand I regret a little bringing him into it: telling both of them was a mistake.

Ingrid appears in the doorway, plate of food in hand, my mother and Dick Traeger just behind her. She's stopped crying: this is fun now. "Dad," she says. "Want to come?"

My mother and Dick Traeger exchange a glance.

"What are you doing, Helen?" my father says.

"There's some poor hungry wretch out there and my tender-hearted girl"—my mother reaches out and takes hold of Ingrid's shoulders, pulling her close—"wants to feed him."

"That hungry wretch scared your children," my father says. "You're not going anywhere." He steps forward and takes the plate from Ingrid. He doesn't seem to know what to do with it: after a moment he puts a meatball in his mouth and begins chewing angrily. "Have one," he says to me, his mouth still full.

"Don't be ridiculous, Harry," my mother says. "Of course he scared them. Hunger's scary. You think someone who hasn't eaten since Friday should be polite?"

Dick Traeger clears his throat. "It does seem too bad just to let him get away with it. I mean, I figured if we went too the kids wouldn't have to feel bad about letting him go hungry, and we could, I don't know, let the creep know that he can't just go around frightening our children."

"I'm stunned," my father says to my mother.

She brings a hand to her throat. "What?"

"Stunned," he says, "*stunned* that you would use your children like this."

"I don't know what you're talking about—Harry."

My father turns his back on us and walks a few paces away. He brings his hands up to his face, and I know what he's doing: pressing his fingertips to the bridge of his nose. I'm afraid he's going to yell, although this is something I've rarely known him to do. I'm preparing to be mortified, but when he finally turns he hands me the plate of food and says, "Well, go then. All of you. Go."

It's tough, it's tough to be a child and have to face a parent's infidelity. It's embarrassing: not just because you know it's about sex—appalling even when you think of them doing it with the person they're supposed to do it with—but also because it's wrong and weak and therefore childish. Your parent has come down to your level, and there isn't enough room there for both of you. Not to mention the vacuum left behind.

It's getting dark out when we leave the party, dark and a little cool. "Look, goosebumps," my mother says, holding out her bare arm for me to see. "There's a ghost walking over my grave."

We have arranged ourselves into an odd pairing: Ingrid and Dick Traeger, my mother and me. Ingrid and Dick Traeger are ahead of us, Dick Traeger now carrying the plate of food, his posture some-how grim. Ingrid doesn't seem to mind walking with him—as we followed them through the door I heard her ask him if he liked ten-nis. I can't imagine where she got this: not the question, but the poise.

I don't respond to my mother, and she glances at me and begins rubbing her hands up and down her arms. "Brrr," she says.

Still I don't speak.

"Ah declayuh," she says. "Ah don't know how y'all kin stayund it heuh. Mah Suthun blood just tuns to ahss in these pots."

This is my cue, her final plea. I look at my mother: she is shiver-ing, but what decides me is something in her eyes, a vague but defi-nite promise. "You Suthun gulls," I say. "Y'all are fragile."

My mother laughs and puts her arm around me. "Look," she whispers. She takes hold of an imaginary plate of food, sets her face in a grimace, and walks a few paces with her toes angled way to the sides. She's doing Dick Traeger, and she's got it just right: he is duck-footed.

I laugh. And, unforgivably, do Ingrid: plod, plod.

Then we round the final corner, and Bug is gone.

"Oh, no," Ingrid wails. She turns around and stamps her foot.

"He's gone," I say to my mother.

"He's *gone?*" Dick Traeger says.

My mother starts to giggle. She puts her hand over her mouth, and she laughs and laughs.

"It's not funny," Ingrid says. "It's not fair."

Dick Traeger steps over to a trash can and lets the plate of food fall from his hand. He faces my mother and crosses his arms over his chest. "You find it funny," he says.

She turns away from him, biting her lip. I can see she's biting it hard, hard enough for it to hurt, and I know what she's doing: try-ing to sober up. It's what I do in school to stop myself from laugh-ing—that, or I say to myself, over and over again, My grandfather's dead, my grandfather's dead, and although I never knew him, my mother's father, it works.

"Come on," I say to Ingrid. "Let's go see if it's still warm."

We leave them standing there and cross the arcade to the empty niche. It's not warm, but there's a stone in it, and I say, "Hey, what's this?"

"A rock," Ingrid says. "You stupid."

"I think he left it here for you." I pick it up and see that it's got some kind of writing on it. "It's got a message on it," I say.

"It does not."

It's too dark right here to read it, so I step into the courtyard, out into what's left of the daylight. The stone is about the size of a hamburger patty, bigger than it looked when Bug took it from his pocket; painted on it, in dark green letters I can barely make out, are the words "Please Turn Me Over." I turn the stone over. "Thank You," it says on the other side.

I turn around. Ingrid is leaning against the wall, pouting—apparently not really looking at me. I pretend to throw the stone toward the fountain, just in case she is looking, then I put it in my pocket. I decide that I'll wait and give it to her when we get home tonight. Or maybe tomorrow.

I go back under the arcade. "Let's go tell Dad," I say.

"Tell him what," she says, but she follows after me. We walk past my mother and Dick Traeger, both of whom now have their arms crossed over their chests, and I hear my mother say the word "mistake." We keep walking.

After my mother died Ingrid and I picked a weekend and met at the house in Palo Alto to sort through her things. Instead of having children Ingrid and Bruce had bought a Universal gym, and Ingrid was lean and hard, her hair blown dry so you could see the comb marks in it.

"You know what I was imagining driving down here?" she said.

"Big fights over china and silver, like I even care." She looked around our mother's living room, all blue and green silk—tasteful, you could have said, to a fault. She picked up a throw pillow, a little jade jewel. "What, for example, would I do with this?"

"Sit on it?" I said. "Listen, this isn't about apportioning, is it? Let's just make sure we know what's here and we'll sell it, OK?"

"Sure."

Her purse still hung from her shoulder. "Shall we have a seat?" I said.

She set the purse down and sat on the edge of the couch. I sat opposite her, my mother's wide glass coffee table between us. "Something to drink?" I said. "I picked up a few things on my way from the airport."

She smirked.

"Mr. Host," I said. "Sorry."

"Better you than me." Ingrid sat back and put her feet up. "Do you realize that until she got sick I hadn't been here since my wedding? All I can think about is standing right over there in that horrifying dress she made me buy and her making these little disappointed sounds like *I'd* picked it and she didn't really approve but she wasn't going to say anything. I can't tell you how close we came to blowing the whole thing off and just going to a justice of the peace."

"If we cantaloupe," I said, "lettuce marry, and we'll make a peach of a pear."

"Ha, ha," said Ingrid, but she smiled and seemed to relax a little.

Her wedding had been the killing blow for her and my mother: when Ingrid announced that she was going to marry, my mother's vision blurred past Bruce, who coached girls' soccer and softball at a junior high school, and past Ingrid, whom she could never clearly see, and focused instead on some kind of ur-wedding, for which, at the very least, special orchids would have to be grown. It was a beautiful, beautiful wedding, a huge, gorgeous straw on the back of a very weak camel.

"You know what was in the freezer?" I said.

"What?"

"A piece of your wedding cake."

Ingrid grinned. "I guess she forgot to put it under her pillow so she'd dream about the man she was going to marry."

"Maybe she was afraid she'd dream about the one she did marry."

"Poor guy," said Ingrid.

We started in the bedroom. Ingrid wanted a picture of the four of us on the beach when she and I were very young, and another of me at my college graduation, hair to my shoulders and a wide paisley tie. I said that I'd take my mother's bedside lamp. We stood at the dresser and looked uneasily at each other.

"I'm not really sure I feel up to her underwear," Ingrid said.

"Courage."

She pulled open the top drawer and her mouth fell open. "What?"

Inside were perhaps forty small boxes—china boxes, papier-mâché boxes, silver and straw and wood boxes. Most of them had been gifts from me, but seeing them all together was a shock: the collection seemed to amount to a kind of fetish. (But whose fetish? My mother's or mine? And *boxes*—what would Herself say?)

"Jesus," Ingrid said. She opened a box; inside was a pair of earrings. She opened another: the same. She began pulling the boxes out of the drawer and opening them: a pin, more earrings, a bracelet, tiny locks of our baby hair tied in blue and pink ribbons (and here Ingrid looked away from me, hurried on to the next box), more earrings, another bracelet. "Why didn't she just get a jewelry box?" she said.

I saw how she could think that, I really did. But I missed my mother so much at that moment that I felt breathless: how we'd have laughed together at the idea that one thing could ever have been as satisfying to her as forty things.

"Are you OK?" Ingrid said. "Do you want to take a break?"

"I'm fine."

"Sure?"

I nodded.

She opened a square leather box I'd bought for my mother in Florence. "What's this?"

In the box was a stiff, yellowing card, soft-cornered, on which were printed two letters: N. D.

"God." I took the card out of the box.

"What is it?"

I thought: If she doesn't remember, why dredge it up? Although, to be honest, I'm not sure whom I thought I was protecting. I put the card back and closed the box. "Actually," I said, "maybe we should take a break. I mean, we've been at it for what, fifteen minutes? I bought some cheese and crackers."

"Robert." She opened the box again. "Tell me."

You hated sharing her, I heard Kevin saying. *With your father or with Ingrid.* "Don't you remember that night?" I said. "The English Department party and that guy Bug?"

Ingrid blushed deeply. But: "No," she said.

"Well, then—it's too hard to explain."

She bit her lip. She took a long breath and sat on the bed. "You know what kills me?" she said after a while. "She really didn't give a shit what we knew or didn't know."

I thought that this was wrong, at least in my case. She wanted, needed me to know.

"You know?" Ingrid said. "I mean, do you think Dick Traeger was even the only one?"

I knew he wasn't: his distinction was that he was the first. "Probably not," I said. "In fact, she once had me help her choose what to wear to an assignation."

Once?

Ingrid rolled her eyes. "Assignation," she said. "That word makes it sound so romantic." She watched me for a little while, and then she reached into the drawer for another box.

It was romantic, Ingrid. It was. "What do you think, Buddy?" my mother says. "With the belt or without? With the earrings or no? This scarf?" It's a Saturday morning; Ingrid is out roller-skating, my father is at his office on the campus. I'm sitting on a stool in my parents' bathroom, watching my mother as she turns from side to side, admiring herself in the mirror. Her face is slightly flushed, intense, her mind racing ahead to the moment when he first sees her. We are pretending, both of us, that she's going to meet a woman friend for lunch, and we both know that we both know we're only pretending. My mother slips on her shoes and reaches for a bottle of perfume. She turns to face me. "Come and smell, Buddy," she says. "What do you think?"

Late on the night of my mother's yellow dress I heard my parents arguing in their bedroom, and even later I woke to find my mother in my room, standing at the window: I couldn't see her so much as feel that she was there. Somehow, without my even rolling over, she knew I had awakened, and she started to talk to me.

"I'm not going anywhere, Buddy," she said. "I wasn't meant to live this life, but that doesn't mean I'm going to leave it." She moved over to my desk, and I heard her pull out the chair and sit down. "Would you like to hear a secret?" she said. "My daddy would hate it if he knew I'd married your father."

I didn't say anything. I was beginning to be able to see, and I saw her pick up something from my desk and hold it to her face. Bug's stone. I was afraid she would ask me what it was, or turn on the light to see. I imagined her reading it aloud, whispering, "Please turn me over. Thank you." I knew it was something she would love —"That's just how I feel," she would say, laughing a little. "Can I have it, Buddy?" And I would give it to her.

She shifted in the chair. "I was just starting to date your father when Daddy got sick," she said. "I took the train from New York City to New Orleans, and Daddy himself met me at the station, weak as he was. First thing he said to me was 'How's your love life, Hellie?'—he was always asking me that. I told him I was dating a fellow from Columbia University. Daddy asked was he Jewish, and when I said no he said too bad he wasn't because it would've given him a reason to make me break it off. He said a university professor wasn't anybody a girl like me ought to marry. I told him I wasn't about to marry anyone, and he said to me, 'Hellie, the one to marry is the one who makes you burn.'" My mother laughed. "I was twenty-one years old," she said. "I thought that in all the world no father had ever said such a thing to his daughter. He said, 'There's never been a university professor who knew a thing about that.' And you know what? He was right."

She stood up. "I was twenty-one years old," she said again. "Your father and I gave off some heat together and I took it as a sign." She set the stone on my desk and came over to sit on the edge of my bed. In the dark her hand found my ear, and she stroked it. "I kind of had fun tonight in my new dress," she said. "Do you know what I mean?"

I nodded.

"He's nodding," she said. "Nodding off." She leaned over and kissed my forehead. "Don't worry about anything, Buddy," she whispered. "None of this has to do with children."

Ingrid took the two photographs, my mother's wedding ring, and, saying it might come in handy some day, a Pyrex casserole.

I took the lamp and the card that said N. D.

The rest we arranged to have sold along with the house, while my mother's voice whispered, *Buddy, the silver? The good linens? Buddy?*

The lamp I needed. The card I put in the bottom of a drawer, to come across years from now when I've forgotten about it again, like an old program that reminds you not just of the glittering lit-up stage, but of afterward, too: the dusty red-velvet seats and the sound of rain falling outside, rain that's been falling for a long time.

The stone I keep on my coffee table, as I have since I've had a coffee table, with the "Thank You" side up, which I suppose reveals something about me, I'm not sure what.

August 4th, and it's Papa Louie's birthday again! Up from San
Francisco, Berkeley, and Sacramento, down from Auburn and
Truckee, daughters and grandchildren and even a great-grand, nieces
and nephews and cousins, and friends, for Papa Louie has many
friends and admirers: they come to Placerville. They come to swim
in the pond, for hamburgers grilled by Uncle Don, Miriam's home-
made bread and butter pickles, and pears, pears, pears: Papa Louie
lives on a pear orchard and attributes his long, long lease on life to
the numerous pears he eats *every day*. A perfect pear is a beautiful
thing! The hipsters come up from L.A., and from Menlo Park come
Ellen and Matt and their sadness.

But at ten o'clock it's still quiet, not yet hot. Back from the first of his
three daily walks around the perimeter of his property, Papa Louie
lies on the bed in his study and addresses himself to a set of calculus
problems from a college textbook left at the house long ago by someone—who knows who. One of the acceptable things about losing
your memory, he thinks, is that you can solve the same problems
from the same book, over and over again. Find the slope of . . .

Miriam, the eldest of his three daughters, stands at the oven in the
kitchen, impatient for the last pear tart to brown. Up since six, she's
been, because the tarts *must be fresh:* this is her father's one desire.
Who wants a ninetieth birthday party? But by God, if you're going
to have one, at least give them a nice pear tart. Ten nice pear tarts!
Miriam sighs. Her sisters will arrive in an hour, wanting to help, and
she'd love to tell them: No, it's too late, I've done it all myself. The
day that happens! What she'll really say is: Nonsense, chickies, let's
relax and have an iced tea before the mobs get here.

She goes to the study door, hesitates a moment, and knocks.

NINETY

"Miriam?" her father says.

Who else? She doesn't exactly live with him, but she's in Sacramento, close enough. Yet she hesitates again—to be sixty-six and afraid of your father! "Yes, it's me, Dad," she says.

"Well, what is it?"

She opens the door. "Would you like a cold drink?"

"No," he says, glaring at her, "I wouldn't."

She nods and closes the door again. If only he would let her shave him! But this he reserves for the weekly visits of Pansy, her youngest sister. "Pansy has the stillest hands," he says. Pansy, who doesn't even care how he looks. "Oh, let him," she says—wander around in pajamas all day, eat with his hands, pass gas at the table.

Miriam goes back into the kitchen and checks on the tart: a little anemic-looking, but she takes it out anyway.

The San Francisco contingent is stuck on the Bay Bridge: a baseball game at the Oakland Coliseum has traffic backed up almost to the city. No one mentions it, but they're all thinking of the same thing: the earthquake, almost a year ago now. Who can bear to be stuck on the Bay Bridge *ever again?*

Louisa, Papa Louie's middle daughter, is in the back seat; although her daughter Lucy is thirty-six, she still likes to ride up front, and what reason can Louisa give to deny her? "Try the left lane, dear," Louisa says to her husband.

Keith puts the turn signal on and turns the wheel so the car is pointed, more or less, to the left.

"There," Louisa says.

Still they don't move. Louisa twists her rings around her finger and wonders how Miriam is getting along with the preparations. She wanted to go up last night, but somehow something prevented it, she can't think what right now—and then she remembers: Ellen. Ellen called just as she was going to suggest to Keith that they call Lucy and leave that very minute. She talked to Ellen for an hour, and by then it was too late. Poor Ellen! Louisa doesn't know what to do about her younger daughter.

She leans forward. "I hope Ellen will make an effort today," she says. She doesn't mean it like *that*, but Lucy turns around and gives her a reproachful look—as if Louisa weren't just broken up over it all! She only wants what's best for her daughter, her baby. "I mean for her own sake, Lucy," she says.

Lucy shrugs.

The cars in the far right lane have begun to move. "Oh, look," Louisa says. "Now they're moving."

Keith switches the turn signal and turns the wheel all the way to the right.

Uncle Don hefts a twenty-pound bag of charcoal into a wheelbarrow and pushes it to the stone barbeque twenty feet away: he's not so young anymore himself, although he's nothing like ninety. Papa Louie is Don's half-brother—half brother, half friend, that's what Louie always said!—and Don wouldn't dream of begrudging Louie or his girls an afternoon of barbeque duty. Anyway, the barbeque's close to the house, so he can get a cold beer whenever he feels like it. None of that keg stuff for Don! Miriam keeps a case of Bud in the second fridge for him; it's their secret.

Pansy sits in the back seat of the Jaguar her sons bought together last month. Two grown men sharing a car! But Jeremy and Stuart are like they were at five, bickering and in love.

Next to Pansy sits her grandson, Elias, Jeremy's child. Last night, when the boys arrived at her house in Berkeley, Pansy could hardly believe the change in Elias: four going on forty, the poor thing. Jeremy had him decked out in something absurd, and Stuart kept saying, "Ma, look at Elias's boots," and "Ma, wait'll you hear Elias on the piano." First thing out of the car in Placerville, Pansy's going to go in and lock the door on the piano room.

She looks across Elias's curly head—was his hair always so curly?—at Jeremy's girlfriend: Jane, or Jade as she seems to be called now. "Have you and Jeremy been enjoying the beach?" she says; in May Jeremy bought a house in Malibu.

Jade turns her lovely head and smiles at Pansy. She doesn't answer, but this isn't unusual; indeed, Pansy didn't expect an answer.

"Ma," Stuart says from the front seat, "wait'll you see Elias swimming!" He turns to look at his brother, and Jeremy shakes his head ever so slightly, a gesture meant only for Stuart.

"Do you like to swim, Elias?" Pansy says.

Elias looks up at her, his eyes so like the boys' when they were young: wide and brown and innocent.

"Answer Grandma," Jeremy says.

"Oh, no," Pansy says. "He doesn't have to."

Miriam is changing into her party dress—such as it is—when she hears the sound of the first car coming down the long driveway. She hasn't decided which pair of sandals to wear, and now she doesn't really have time to choose carefully. She puts on a pair with inch-high heels, an absurd thing to wear at the ranch but she thinks they flatter her legs, the only part of her still worth flattering. She hurries over to the mirror. A barrel with chorus girl legs, that's what Dad said the other day. She puts on lipstick and goes to the window to see who it is, Louisa or Pansy, but it's neither of them, and Miriam draws back to avoid being seen. She didn't recognize the people getting out of the car—Pansy's new neighbors, maybe, or friends of Louisa and Keith—and she allows herself to imagine that she can hide in here until one of her sisters arrives.

Lucy shifts in her seat, and her father pats her leg and then returns his hand to the steering wheel. Her mother, she thinks, has fallen asleep.

"Have we passed the Nut Tree yet?" she whispers.

"About twenty minutes ago," her father whispers back.

When Lucy and her sister were little, the drive up to Papa Louie's seemed endless, and they always begged to stop at the Nut Tree for treats—you could get delicious little miniature loaves of nut bread. Now here Lucy is, thirty-six years old and she's still being taken by her parents to see Papa Louie. For a moment she's so envious of her sister it feels like an engine racing in her. Ellen, married. Ellen never even wanted to get married! She wanted to be a nurse and go to Africa. *Lucy* wanted to get married—at eight she spent an entire summer making lists of the names of men she might marry. She had the wedding all planned: ten bridesmaids and a flower girl who was, somehow, her own eight-year-old self. Ellen was six, and she made lists of the names of the children she would bear.

It's like roads to Rome. All Lucy's thoughts these days lead her to this place: Ellen's grief, the baby stillborn at eight and a half months. Lucy's grief is that Ellen won't talk to her about it, will barely talk to her at all.

There are ten or twelve cars parked along the narrow drive down to Papa Louie's, and Jeremy slows the Jag down to a crawl: not a scratch on this baby is the motto. The house comes into view, and behind it, way in the distance, the mountains south of Tahoe. Jeremy loves it here, perhaps the one secret he has from his brother.

"I need a toot," Stuart says under his breath.

"Let me get Elias settled," Jeremy murmurs back.

He slows even more as they pass the twenty or thirty people already assembled on the terrace, then he eases the car around the back of the house and stops under the one anomalous peach tree. Pansy is out of the car before he's even cut the engine, saying something about Miriam.

"Let's go, troops," Jeremy says. "Party time."

He gets out of the car, leans into the back seat to help Elias out, and finds Jade staring at him blankly. "Babe?" he says.

She opens her door and unfolds her long, beautiful body, which is clad in something black and stretchy and minimal. She stands up, and to Jeremy it's like a command: adore me. He does. She is twelve years younger than he, twenty-three and utterly empty-headed, but it doesn't matter: it thrills him just to contemplate her arms.

"This is it, Babe," he says. He makes a grand sweep of his arm, encompassing the pear trees, the house, the pool, the gorgeous view across the hills to the mountains: the good fortune they all have to be here, and especially the good fortune he has to be with her.

"Toot time," Stuart says, patting the breast pocket of his Hawaiian shirt, and Jade turns toward him, smiling.

"Jeez," Jeremy says, "I think maybe Mom didn't hear that, you want to try again?" He looks, guiltily, at Elias—but what's toot to his son but the noise a train makes? "What do you say, champ?" Jeremy says.

"Thank you," Elias says.

"I love it," Stuart says. "Where's Ma? She's got to hear this kid."

But Pansy is in the house, in conference with Miriam. "Just go ask him," Miriam is saying. "He'll listen to you."

"Does it really matter, Mim?" Pansy sidesteps Miriam's gaze and goes to the refrigerator. She didn't know it until she stepped into the kitchen, but she's dying for some pear juice.

"On the door," Miriam says. "By the milk."

Pansy finds a bottle of clear, pale juice and pours some into a glass that's sitting on the counter.

"That was going to be for Dad's iced tea," Miriam says.

"Sorry," Pansy says. "I'll wash it, OK?"

"Could you just please go in and *ask* him?"

Pansy takes a sip of her drink. "Ask him what, hon?"

How, Miriam asks herself, can someone so vague get along living alone? Pansy's exactly like Dad, in fact. "To get dressed," she says. "Honestly, Pansy."

"All right," Pansy says. "But first I'm going to lock the piano room."

"Aw," Miriam says, "why? Remember last year after most everyone had gone, and Jeremy played the piano and we sang?" Miriam can't remember what the song was: something by a rock band, a song the kids knew. "Such a lovely place, such a lovely face"—that was part of it.

Pansy considers telling Miriam that she's worried about Elias, but decides not to. "Mom's teacups are in there," she says. "There were so many little kids last time, it just seems safer this way." She puts the empty juice glass in the sink. "What do you want him to wear?"

"Clothes!" Miriam says. "And see if you can shave him."

The *heat*. It's ninety-seven already, and climbing. Harvest starts Monday, and if you know what to look for you can just smell the pears: a hint of cinnamon in the orchard.

A couple dressed in silks and linens comes walking down the driveway. She's in high white heels and isn't having an easy time of it; the driveway's unpaved. This is their first time at this party, and to see the little groups standing around in shorts and sundresses, kids running barefoot, and Don in his greasy chef's apron loading briquets into the barbeque—it's nearly too much to bear.

"How cozy," she says. "Too bad we didn't rent a child to bring along, or a dog. Don't you think a dog would behoove us?"

He ignores her. He's thinking: stash the jacket and tie, roll up the sleeves, lose *her*. Then find the old man, right away, and say something cool and easy. "It's really a pleasure to meet you, sir." "I've been looking forward to this day for a long time, sir." He wipes the sweat from his forehead. He doesn't know a soul here, doesn't even know who sent him the invitation—probably someone who'd heard that his father had died.

"Oh," she says, "burgers, yum. I don't know when I last had a burger."

All those times his father wanted him to come along. All those times he said no. "Shut up," he says. "Just shut the hell up."

Right away Lucy sees Jeremy and Stuart and Jade, sitting with their
feet in the pool. She fills a plastic cup at the keg, and then, saying hi
to people, hello, nice to see you, she weaves through the crowd and
joins them.

"It's the hipsters," she says, kicking each of her cousins in the small
of the back. "How's the hippest place on earth?"

"Hip," Stuart says.

"The hippest," Jeremy says.

"Hi, Jane," Lucy says. "We met at Pansy's birthday, in April."

"Yes," Jade says. "I remember."

It shouldn't be legal, Lucy thinks, to look like that—at least not
when Lucy's around! "Nice to see you again," she says. "Nice of you
to put up with this character here." She means Jeremy: her *cousing*,
she thinks affectionately, remembering the long-ago term.

"It's Jade," Jade says.

Lucy looks at Stuart—he's rolling his eyes, meaning what? "Forgive
me," she says. "I was sure it was Jane."

"It was in April," Jeremy says. "Now it's Jade."

Lucy kicks off her shoes and sits next to him. She puts her feet in
the water, but she's no longer thinking about any of them, cousings
or their silly girlfriends. Here come Ellen and Matt.

What Matt sees is kids, everywhere, and he tightens his hold on Ellen's
arm. He doesn't remember there being nearly so many kids last
year, and in trying to recall last year in any kind of detail he comes
smack up against It: last year Ellen was pregnant, just—the news
was maybe a week old and they were giddy with it.

He glances at her: she's pale and thin, so thin. She was worried
about not being able to lose weight after the baby was born, but it's
been just four months and she's slender and tense as a stick.

"There's Don in his apron," Matt says, for something to say.

"Stop!" She shakes his hand off her arm.

"What?"

"I don't—want to be seen. I'm cutting through the trees, you can —I don't care what you do."

She leaves the driveway and begins to walk in an arc that will take her around the nearby two-acre plot of pear trees—the home trees, Papa Louie calls them—to the back of the house. Everyone, Matt knows, has seen them.

He follows her. "Wait," he says. "Ellen, wait, I'm right behind you."

Louisa knocks at her father's study door. "Papa Louie?" she says. "It's me, Louisa."

The door opens and there he is, like her sisters said: in boxers and his old seersucker robe. "Hi, Louie," he says.

"Hi, Louie." She goes in and kisses him. "Happy birthday—you're not getting older, you're getting worse."

"I've got a question for you, Louie," he says. "Come into my office." He walks her over to the bed—slowly, slowly—and they sit down on it, side by side.

"So?" she says. "Don't keep me waiting."

"I want you to tell me how I got here."

She picks up his hand and pats it, then laces her fingers through his. "It's like this," she says. "You and Mom were driving from Sacramento to South Lake Tahoe—you were going gambling. And you hit Placerville and she needed to pee, so you got off the road and you drove until you found her a good place to pee, and this was it, so you bought it and built a house here."

He nods. "And your mother?"

"She's dead, Louie. She died a while ago."

"That's right," he says. "That's right—I knew that."

She kisses his cheek. "There's some people out there who want to say hello," she says. "What about putting on some pants and we'll go out and try one of Don's burgers?"

"I don't like pants."

Louisa turns away from him; she doesn't want him to see her tears.

"I'll wear shorts," he says. "And my baseball cap."

Pansy and Miriam sit on the back steps, their four feet lined up like
soldiers. Pansy thinks of their mother: it wasn't ladylike to refer to
your *feet*—you could say "My foot hurts," or, better, "I have a sore
toe," but never "My feet hurt." Pansy's feet are still ladylike—7 1/2
AAA she wears, at sixty!—but Miriam's seem to be spreading; or
maybe it's just the spindly little sandals she has on.

"There's Ellen," Miriam says. "In the orchard, coming this way.
Don't say anything about the baby."

"I won't," Pansy says. How could Miriam even *think* she would?

They're both thinking: poor Ellen. What they really mean is:
poor Louisa. Louisa *suffers* over things.

"I don't see why she doesn't just go ahead and try again," Miriam
says. "Remember how she'd bring her dolls up and set them in the
dining room chairs? And Mom would make real tea for them? She
should have six babies."

"She loved her dolls," Pansy says. She remembers one time—she
was so embarrassed!—Stuart stole one of the dolls and ran down to
the pond and threw it in. Ellen cried and cried; in a way, Pansy
thinks, Ellen never did forgive him for that.

Now Ellen is before them, in shorts that *hang* off her. She looks
terrible. Behind her is Matt—handsome Matt, that's how Pansy's always thought of him. He's tall and shy, and you can tell just by
looking at him that he's miserable.

Miriam stands up. "Ellen, honey—how wonderful." She puts her
arms around her niece, who holds herself absolutely rigid, and
Miriam feels just as awkward as she did when her sisters' children
were small and submitted to her clumsy hugs.

"Is Mom inside?" Ellen says.

"She's in with Papa Louie, hon," Pansy says, and Ellen slips between them and enters the house.

"I wish you wouldn't call him that," Miriam says. Both her sisters do it, as if they were the kids. He's their *dad*.

But Pansy's watching Matt. Over by the path to the pond is an old swing set, and Elias has been standing near it for several minutes. Now Matt walks over there and says something to him. Pansy finds she's holding her breath waiting for Elias to get on the swing, for Matt to push him. But they just look at each other, and then Matt disappears around the side of the house.

It's two o'clock, and Don's ready to start cooking the burgers. No one seems interested, though—they're spread out around the pool, talking away, and a little while ago six or eight kids went racing down the path to the pond: he can hear them splashing. Pansy's Jeremy appears from the house, sniffling and looking around, something sneaky about him—but then he sees Don looking at him and he comes over and offers Don his hand.

"Going to cook some burgers, Uncle Don?" he says.

No, Don thinks, I'm just standing here because I like the heat. "That's the program," he says. "Time for the big feed." This strikes him as pretty damned funny, and he laughs.

"Want a hand?" Jeremy says. "I've flipped the odd burger in my time."

"No," Don says. "I don't begrudge it, not a bit. Your grandfather's been good to me."

"See over there?" Jeremy says, pointing at a skinny girl by the pool.

"The lady there?"

"I'm going to marry her," Jeremy says. "What do you think of that?"

Don laughs—what a mistake he's made! "Hell," he says, "I've been talking to you all this time and I thought you were the other one, I thought you were Jeremy. Ha! Identical twins, you boys fool me most every time I see you."

"I am Jeremy," Jeremy says. "And we're not identical, we're fraternal." He turns to leave, wondering why he was talking to Uncle Don in the first place: he and Lucy used to call him The Uncle Don Trap—they'd *hide* from him when they were little.

"But I thought you were already married," Don says.

"Ever hear of divorce?" Jeremy says. "It runs in the family, you know. Mom and Dad, my wife and me—I've got a kid and I'm doing everything I can to make sure he grows up and ruins someone's life, too." He stalks away.

Don turns back to the barbeque and begins slapping hamburger patties on it. They can eat 'em now, he thinks, or they can eat 'em cold.

Matt wants to find Lucy. He decides to check the pond, but on his way down the path he sees an unfamiliar woman sitting on a bench that rings a tall pine tree, and something about her makes him stop—maybe that she's incredibly dressed up, *over*dressed.

"Hi, there," Matt says.

She looks up and squints at him. "Hello. Do you know what time it is?" She's about thirty-five, he thinks, but looks about forty-five.

He checks his watch. "Two-fifteen."

"What do you think?" she says. "About two more hours?"

"I don't know," Matt says. "Two or three."

She opens her purse; it's small and white and—lizard? Ellen would know. She withdraws a pack of cigarettes and pulls one out. "Do you have a light?"

Matt pats his front pockets, although he knows he doesn't. "Sorry," he says. "Would you like—would you like me to get you a drink?"

She laughs. "No," she says. "I'm just fine." She pulls a lighter from her purse and lights her own cigarette.

"Well, bye," Matt says. "See you later."

The children have divided into three groups. The largest contains most of the boys and two or three girls; they've taken the opportunity to shed their parents and their clothes, and they're running in their swimsuits between the pond and the table up by the house, where the potato chips are. They send two emissaries at a time; as soon as one pair returns to the pond with a paper plate full of chips, the next sets off at a run, so they are almost never without provisions.

The second group is four or five girls who have their swimsuits on under their clothes but don't want to swim in the pond, because it's murky, or in the pool, because all the grown-ups are sitting or standing near it. They sit at the one picnic table, which is shaded by an umbrella, and talk about the counselors they had at camp this summer.

The last group isn't really a group at all: a few toddlers playing in the sandbox Papa Louie built long ago for Lucy, his first grandchild; two serious little boys who found a checkers game in the house and are lying on the living room rug, talking about the best openings; and Elias.

Elias has finally gathered the courage to lean against the swing. He's not quite tall enough to climb on it, but he thinks that sooner or later his dad will come along and lift him up. A while ago a man asked him if he was having fun, and he said yes, but the man didn't seem to care one way or the other—he stood there for a while and then walked away. Elias knows he's supposed to have fun—his mother told him he would have a blast.

Just when he's thinking of her, up walks his uncle Stuart, whom Elias knows she doesn't like—she said once that Stuart was a little devil on his dad's shoulder. Stuart is just as tall as his dad, though: Elias checked.

"Elias, my man," Stuart says. "Lunch time! What do you say to a burger?"

"OK," Elias says.

Stuart is wearing a shirt just like his dad's—just like Elias's, too, only bigger. It's a special kind of shirt that has to be dry-cleaned. Once Elias saw Stuart sitting at his dad's desk and he thought Stuart *was* his dad. He stood in the doorway and said, "Hi, Dad," and Stuart laughed—with him, his dad said later, not at him. Elias will never make that mistake again.

Louisa finds Ellen upstairs, in the bunk room. She's got the shades drawn; she's lying on one of the little iron beds.

"Can I bring you anything?" Louisa says. "Iced tea? A pear?"

Ellen smiles wanly, but she doesn't make the family joke: Oh, are there pears? "No, thanks," she says.

Louisa sits on the edge of the bed and pats her daughter's hip. "I was thinking about what you said on the phone last night, hon. About you and Matt maybe going away for six months or something? I think that's very smart, and Dad and I would be happy to help out. You could go somewhere exotic and wonderful."

Ellen rolls over so she's facing the wall. "What would be the point?"

"Well," Louisa says, "it might give you something else to think about."

Now Ellen doesn't say anything.

"You know?" Louisa strokes Ellen's hair, her pretty dark hair.

"I'd kind of like to be alone, Mom," Ellen says.

Louisa pulls her hand away and stands up. "OK," she says. "I'll be outside if you want me."

She closes the door behind her, but hesitates before starting down the narrow staircase. Last night Ellen was so open with her—Louisa felt that perhaps she had finally reached a turning point. Today it's as if they never even had that conversation. It's strange to Louisa— strange and sad—that the best talks she's ever had with either of her daughters have all been on the telephone.

Lucy's out on the raft in the middle of the pond, motioning for Matt to join her. He didn't bring his swimming trunks, but he thinks, Oh, who cares?, and he takes off his shoes and shirt and dives in. The water is warm and green, mucky: he's never understood why everyone swims here when there's a perfectly good pool up by the house.

He pulls himself onto the raft, but suddenly he feels shy; since Ellen lost the baby he and Lucy have taken to doing this, going off and talking, and he feels at once protective of and a little guilty about this new standing with his sister-in-law.

"Hey," Lucy says. "How are you?"

"Mezzo," he says. "Mezzo-soprano."

She smiles and scoots over so he can lie next to her. "Is it burger time yet up there?" she says. "I felt a hunger pang a while back."

"Any minute now."

"Ellen's inside?"

"Upstairs."

They lie quietly. The sun feels nice on Matt's back; he even likes the thick green smell of the water drying on his skin.

"Hey, did you see Elias up there?" Lucy says. "In that little Hawaiian shirt?"

"I didn't know they made them that small."

"They probably don't. Jeremy probably had it made—at considerable expense." She lowers her voice, although of course no one can hear them. "I have this horrible feeling that someone made him get a perm. His hair wasn't that curly at Pansy's birthday party."

"Really?" Matt says. "You're kidding."

"I wish."

"He doesn't really seem like the happiest kid in the world, does he?"

"No," Lucy says, "and you know what? I'm not sure Jeremy's the happiest man in the world, either."

"I'd trade him my mood for his car."

She laughs. "What a deal."

They're quiet again. The stillness of the day, the pond—it feels to Lucy like something breakable.

"She won't sleep with me," Matt says.

Lucy raises herself onto her elbows and looks at him.

"No," he says quickly, "I mean *sleep* sleep. She's started sleeping in the living room—except I don't think she really does. Last night I swear I heard her wandering around for hours."

"God," Lucy says. "*God.*"

"I know." Matt sits up and gazes across the pond: at the dock, at the pear trees behind it. He looks back at Lucy. "Did I tell you Dr. Berg suggested we try imaging?"

She raises her eyebrows.

"You know—that horseshit about picturing your unhappiness, giving it physical attributes so you can be the master of it? Well, I did it, and now I can't get the stupid thing out of my mind."

"What is it?"

"A solid block of ice—black ice, don't ask me. We've both got one, me and Ellen. Mine's sitting behind my lungs—just sitting there mostly, but every so often it bumps me with its sharp corners."

"And Ellen's?"

"Ellen's melted," Matt says. "It melted and now her whole body's full of cold grey water." He laughs a little and lies back again. "Heavy, huh?"

"It is," Lucy says. "It all is."

Jade is by herself—sitting in the sun, leaning against the pool house. A few feet from her several little girls sit in a circle on the grass, and Jade has been trying to decide which of them is most like her former self. She's giving up, though—they're all too poised and self-confident. When Jade was their age, seven or eight, she was gawky and shy, so gawky and shy that she only had one friend: Gretchen Spengler. The hours, the *years* she spent in thrall to Gretchen Spengler! Gretchen, who today is probably some dumpy little housewife in the Valley. It's not that Jade thinks *she's* so great, but she'd love to run into Gretchen one time—at Ma Maison or one of those places Jeremy always wants to go. If Stuart were along, too, it would be even better: Gretchen could think Jade was with both of them. She'd love to see Gretchen's round, freckled face just *fall*.

A shadow crosses over Jade, and she looks up: standing there is a man dressed in white linen pants and a pale yellow washed-silk shirt with terrible sweat stains in the pits. He hunches down next to her. "You look like you're thinking of something delicious and naughty," he says.

Jade gives him a medium smile—she's suddenly realized that if Gretchen *were* a dumpy little housewife in the Valley she wouldn't *be* at Ma Maison. She wishes this guy would leave so she could think of some other way.

"Are you one of Lou's grandchildren?" the man says.

"No," she says. "Are you?"

"That's great," he says, laughing. "Funny lady."

It was just a question, not really funny at all, but Jade's come to expect men to react strangely to what she says: it's because of how she looks.

"My old man worked with Lou," the man says. "For Lou, I should say. I'm really looking forward to meeting him, getting to know him a little. Have you seen him?"

"No," Jade says. "I think he's pretty old, though." She sees Stuart over by the keg of beer, and she points and says, "See that guy? He's one of the grandchildren."

The man stands up and runs his arm across his forehead—he's really *sweating*. Jade's so glad she doesn't sweat: she used to, but it was one of those mind over matter things and she doesn't anymore.

Louisa finds Pansy talking to a boy of eighteen or nineteen—he's someone's son, she can't remember whose. "Pansy," she says, "can I borrow you for a minute?"

Pansy follows her away from the crowd. "He'd like to be shaved before he comes out," Louisa says. "Do you mind?"

"Of course not," Pansy says—she would have done it before, but he said he wasn't ready. Why do Miriam and Louisa act as if she's stupid or mean?

"I just meant do you mind doing it *now*," Louisa says. "You were talking to that boy and I interrupted you." She glances over Pansy's shoulder and the boy's still there: longish hair and no shirt. He smiles and she smiles back at him. "Who is he, anyway?"

"I don't know," Pansy says. She shrugs her shoulders and holds up her hands as if to say *No idea*, and in a moment they're both laughing: laughing and laughing.

Miriam gets a cold Bud for Uncle Don and goes outside. The table with the burger fixings is mobbed, but she can see that her bread and butter pickles are going like racehorses—as usual!

Don spots her from across the yard and when she holds the can of beer up for him to see, he waves and smiles. "You're a mind reader, Mim," he says when she gets to him. He puts his arm around her and squeezes. "What a gal."

Wouldn't it be nice, Miriam thinks, if her father were so easy to please?

"What's Louie doing in there, anyways?" Don says. "Should I put one on for him yet?"

"It'll be about ten more minutes," she says. "Better wait. He likes them very rare."

"I know that," Don says. "Sheesh—I've done this before, you know."

"I know," Miriam says. "And I appreciate it."

Don stands a little straighter. "I don't begrudge it," he says. "Not a bit."

A man Jeremy doesn't know is shaking Stuart's hand—he walks away from Stuart just as Jeremy reaches him.

"Have you seen Papa Louie?" Stuart says.

Jeremy shakes his head. "Still in the house, I think. Why?"

"Guy wants to meet him."

"Good luck. I'm not even going to try to introduce Jade—I figure it would just go over his head."

"Or hers."

"Fuck you," Jeremy says. *"Fuck you."*

"Touchy, touchy. You yourself said she's not exactly brilliant."

"Go to hell."

Jeremy steps around Stuart and fills his cup at the keg. When he turns back Lucy has arrived, wet and smelling of the pond, and he doesn't know what to do but join them.

"How's the water?" Stuart asks her.

"Divine," she says, and she and Stuart laugh—it's what their grandmother always said about it, although no one ever knew her to get past the dock.

"Where's Ellen?" Jeremy asks Lucy. "How's she doing?"

"I think she's upstairs," Lucy says. "I'm going to go in in a minute and check on her."

Jeremy nods. "Hey, where's Elias?" he says to Stuart. "I thought you were getting him some lunch."

"He wanted to eat by the swing," Stuart says. "I actually just came over here for a beer—I was going to go back and sit with him."

"That's really not good enough," Jeremy says, and he turns and leaves the two of them standing there.

He heads around the house toward the swing set, not really worried but at the point where he could easily become worried. Elias is there, though, sitting on the ground with his half-eaten burger on a plate in front of him, and Jade is sitting with him—not talking, but *there.* Jeremy is very happy to see her. "Both of you together," he says. "Terrific."

He sits down with them, thinking that everything would be perfect if only he could silence the little part of himself that wishes Stuart were there, that's dying to turn to Stuart and say, very quietly: at least *she's nice.*

In the house Papa Louie is ready. Ready to be shaved! Ready to eat! Ready to schmooze a little! "I'll sit at the picnic table," he says. "I'll have a hamburger with lettuce and ketchup and a couple of those little pickle chips."

"That's right," Miriam says. "And we'll sit with you."

"No," he says, "I'll sit alone. I like to eat in peace."

The sisters exchange a three-way look. "Whatever you want," Louisa says. "You know everyone'll want to say hello."

"They can say hello after I eat," he says. "Well, miss, are you ready?"

Pansy moves a kitchen chair close to the sink, which she's filled with hot water. "Right here," she says.

He goes over to the chair and sits in it, heavily.

"Want to take your shirt off, Louie?" Louisa says.

"That's OK," Pansy says. "I won't get it wet. You'd better take off that cap, though, so I can see what I'm doing."

He takes his cap off and holds it in his lap. Miriam looks at it, an old Giants cap so dirty and worn she herself can't bear to touch it, and she surprises herself by thinking: Oh, let him.

Pansy dips her fingers in the sink to wet them, then wets his face. She shakes the can of shaving cream and sprays some into her hand, then she spreads it onto his face, little by little, gently, how he likes it.

She's about to start shaving him when the door opens and in comes Lucy, followed almost immediately by Jeremy and Elias. They all stop just inside the doorway.

"Who's that?" Papa Louie says; they're behind him.

Louisa motions for them to get where he can see them, and they do. To Lucy she points at the ceiling and raises her eyebrows, and Lucy nods.

"Hi, Papa Louie," Lucy says, just as Jeremy's saying, "Hey—Papa Louie."

"Who's that?" Papa Louie says again.

Lucy and Jeremy look at each other.

"Your grandchildren," Louisa says.

"Whom you love," Pansy says.

"I know who they are," he says. "I mean *that*." He raises a shaky finger and points at Elias.

"Why that's *my* grandchild," Pansy says. They all look at her, but it's too late when she finally realizes what she's supposed to say: whom *I* love. She feels herself getting teary, and she thinks that her sisters are right—she's stupid *and* mean.

"Who needs to pee," Jeremy says finally, and they're all so relieved they laugh.

"Well," Papa Louie says to Elias, "you've come to the right place, son."

"Listen," Jeremy says to his grandfather, "according to Stuart there's some guy out there who wants to meet you."

"Out of the question," Papa Louie says. "I don't want to meet anybody I don't already know."

"Dad," Miriam says.

"I SAID NO!"

Everyone is silent for a minute or two. Finally Jeremy shrugs. "Fine with me," he says. "I just thought I'd tell him." He puts his hand on Elias's shoulder, and Elias follows him out of the room. After a moment Lucy leaves, too—heading upstairs.

"Well," Miriam says uneasily. "Where were we?"

Pansy picks up the razor, but Papa Louie is getting to his feet—he pushes the chair away so roughly it nearly falls over. He turns and looks at her with something like rage. "No one," he says, "no one should ever tell anyone else *whom he loves!* I may love them, but that's *my business!*"

The sisters look at each other and begin, each just a little, to tremble. But then it just drains out of him. They can see it happening, and they all think: thank God.

"I'm sorry," Pansy says. She knows this is all her fault, but she can't stop herself: in a small, weepy voice she asks, "Do you love me?"

"Certainly," he says evenly. "You're my daughter."

Miriam and Louisa glance at each other. "And me?" Miriam says.

"Of course—you're my daughter."

"And Louisa?" Miriam says. "Do you love Louisa because—just because she's your daughter?"

Papa Louie wipes the shaving cream from his face with a kitchen towel, then puts on his cap. "No," he says thoughtfully. "No—I really love Louisa." He walks over to the door and opens it, and everyone outside stops talking and looks at him.

Her back against the wall, Ellen sits on the little iron bed in the bunk room and listens to Lucy's footsteps going down the stairs: she just sent Lucy away.

She doesn't want to talk to Lucy, to anyone.

She doesn't want to hear anyone tell her that she should try to get over it.

She wants to be by herself, so she can think about her baby.

Her baby. In her mind, despite what everyone said, she named her baby—an extravagant, absurd name. Elizabeth Caroline Natalie Louisa McGee. If the baby had lived she would have had a simple name, but Ellen believes that, dead, she needs more names, stronger and better ones. Elizabeth Caroline Natalie Louisa. When she first chose these names Ellen felt like her six-year-old self, who wanted four daughters to name Sandra, Andrea, Diana, and Cassandra. She liked the fat letters then, *a*'s and *d*'s and *n*'s. She wanted four fat babies with red hair, felt she was owed them. What she got was one skinny, shriveled baby with a blue face, but it didn't matter because she loved, *loves* her baby. She's crying again now, but that doesn't matter either—crying or not crying, it's all the same. Here's what she's learned: you can't cry forever. At first she was afraid she would, but it's not like that—you cry, stop crying, cry again, and each time it's a little different, a slightly different piece of you falling away. She cries and cries, and she's crying so hard now that at the sound of the first shout from outside she's not sure she heard anything. She stops herself and listens: another shout. After a minute or two there's another, and soon another. At the fifth shout Ellen's curiosity gets the better of her, and she goes to the window and pushes aside the shade.

Down in the yard, Papa Louie sits alone at the picnic table. Everyone is grouped around him, and one by one Miriam and Louisa and Pansy carry the pear tarts to him, a single burning birthday candle held at each center. One by one he blows them out, and each time everyone roars with approval. To Ellen it sounds like this: Ah! Ahh! Ahhh! There are so many people down there: she sees her father and Lucy, Jeremy and Stuart, Uncle Don in his apron. Matt. And children— Ellen sees lots and lots of children. Yet she looks.